An Inconvenie

by

Audrey Har

Published by Audrey Harrison

Copyright 2014 Audrey Harrison

This book was proof read by Joan Kelley. Read more about Joan at the end of this story but if you need her, you may reach her at oh1kelley@gmail.com

Dedication

This book is dedicated to a great character, Walter Reid.

I had the pleasure of working with Walter a few years ago at the National Trust. We acted as servants in the year 1913, and Walter was the butler. I have never come across a more talented butler and just had to use him in one of my books!

His humour, spontaneity and talent made the job of the other servants so much more fun. So, although my characters are fiction, Walter is based on Walter! I hope you feel I have done you justice, Walt.

Lots of love, Audrey.

Chapter 1

London, January 1816

"Kiss me, sir!" came the unexpected request as Stephen was pulled into the darkened room.

He started to chuckle, thinking it was some sort of joke set up by his friends. Slender arms wrapped around his neck and pulled his head downwards. The slim figure holding onto him pressed herself against his large frame.

"Please kiss me, hide me, please don't let them find me!" came an urgent whisper.

Whether it was the sound of real fear in the whispering voice, or the devil in him, Stephen bent down and kissed the lips being offered. He turned his back to the door and kicked it shut, enclosing them completely in darkness. They were hidden from the rest of the company. The noise of the party was deadened by the thick wood of the door, focusing his attention on the unexpected diversion.

He had not seen the lady accosting him, but he could tell by her voice he did not know her. He might not always remember the name of every lightskirt he had sought pleasure from, but voices and bodies he did remember. She had sounded young and slightly frightened, which was unusual in a household connected to his acquaintance, Baron Kersal. The 'ladies' who attended his house parties were usually a lot older in years and ways, so it was odd to hear the voice of someone younger than normal. Although they tried to hide it, the weariness of life could often be heard in the voices of the ladies who worked there. This voice sounded frightened, desperate maybe, but not world weary, not yet anyway.

He should have resisted the kiss; the fear in her voice would have given any decent man pause but, although he did wonder about her identity, the moment her lips touched his more firmly than the hesitant touch that had first been offered, he forgot all his musings. He had never been kissed by an innocent, but he knew immediately that she was. Her kiss was tentative, delicate and yet searching, as if she were desperate to make the kiss count. He found the

3

combination to be an unexpectedly heady mix and, for a few moments he was lost to the experience, something uncurling in his stomach and filling his body with warmth. He wondered at the sensation, and it was enough to bring him back to his senses.

He tried to pull back from her; he might be a devil, but he did not ruin young girls or put himself in the position of being forced into marriage. Dallying with innocents ran the risk of unwanted and unlooked for consequences. His thoughts made him pause and move away a little as if to release him from her hold, but his slight movement caused her to wrap her hands more firmly around his neck.

"Please," she whispered against his lips. "I need you. Only you."

He was lost. Never in his life had he been asked in such a heart wrenching way for anything. He had been persuaded, cajoled and even demanded of by one or two forward ladies but never with such desperate appeal and never for his help. Most of the ladies of his acquaintance wanted his money, jewels or, worse still, marriage, but they never wanted *him*. He returned the kiss, gently at first, guiding her inexperience. She moaned against his mouth, and he suppressed a smile; the old Halkyn charm could still work even in the dark. He continued to plunder her mouth, using his tongue to explore every part of her. As his kiss deepened, she leaned into him even more, using his body as support.

They both paused when the door opened, and the voice of Baron Kersal interrupted their kiss. "Someone's in here. Who is it?"

The girl inhaled sharply and tried to huddle into Stephen. She moved her hands from around his neck and tucked them in front of her, trying to make herself as small as possible. Stephen moved his hands slowly across her back in reassurance. "It's Halkyn; close the door!" he snapped, not even looking back.

"Who's with you?" the Baron demanded, "Let me see her."

Stephen turned further away from the door. "The lady is in a state of, let's just say, disarray. I don't think it's fair to put her on display for your lecherous pleasure, do you?"

4

The voice of another man was heard to mutter into the Baron's ear. "Halkyn, what the hell are you doing in the dark?" the Baron asked.

"What the bloody hell do you think, Kersal? Not all of us need light to have a good time; sometimes with the women you provide, light is a distinct disadvantage," Stephen retorted, holding the girl tightly. She tried to pull away at his words, but he was not going to let her show herself because of his throwaway retort. There was obviously something going on that was not quite right and, although he had an urge to know exactly what was happening, he was not about to put his new acquaintance into whatever situation she had tried to hide from.

Stephen's words had caused laughter to erupt behind Baron Kersal. The Baron told his associates to shut up and then turned back to Halkyn. "We are looking for my, err, niece: she shouldn't be in this part of the house; have you seen her?"

"Does it look like I've seen her?" Stephen said shortly. "Kersal, you are doing nothing to improve the ambience of this room. Unless you have a damn good reason to continue with this interruption, can I suggest you leave us alone? I haven't met your *niece,* but if she appears in here, I shall be sure to send her to you." Again, the body in his arms stiffened, but he leant down and started to kiss her, ignoring the men standing behind him. She did not respond immediately, but within a few moments, she seemed to forget about the men at the door and relaxed, leaning into him again.

Stephen heard the men mutter behind him, and the door was closed. It seemed his performance had convinced them. For a few moments he continued to enjoy the great deal of pleasure he was receiving from the stranger's kiss. He had never actually wanted to continue a kiss as much as he did this one, but eventually he pulled away slightly and leant his head against her forehead.

"I think we need to become acquainted more formally," he said, his voice husky.

"Will you send me to the Baron?" she asked in a frightened whisper.

Stephen paused before he responded. He probably should do; there was obviously something going on here that did not involve him, and he should extricate himself before he added further complications to the situation. There was something about this girl though, and he was sure she was a girl. He wanted to get some light into the room, but he did not want her to become more frightened and do something that would put her at risk. He could not shake the feeling she was in danger.

He moved his hands down her arms and took her hands in his. "I will not send you to the Baron; I am not really a gambling man, but I would be willing to wager you are not his niece," Stephen said gently.

"I am no relation to him!" came the fiery reply.

Stephen smiled in the darkness; she might be frightened, but she obviously had some spark within her. The unorthodox way she approached him proved that. "We need to speak, but I do not want to carry on this conversation in the dark. Call me old fashioned, but I do like to see the people I'm communicating with," Stephen said lightly. "If I light some candles, may I have your word you will not bolt?"

"I have nowhere to run," came the honest response.

Stephen slowly let go of her hands. He believed her when she said she would not leave; she would only risk running into the Baron or one of his cronies. He fumbled in the room until he found a candelabrum and lit the candles. As soon as there was light, he walked across to the window and closed the curtains; the night was dark, and any light would reflect far into the garden. He did not want anyone seeing into the room. He saw another candelabrum and lit those candles also before turning to look at the stranger.

He took a deep breath as she stood there, proud and defiant, looking him directly in the eye, but there was fear and uncertainty in her gaze too. He had never been the one for gallant gestures, but the look in her eyes had him ready to fight for her if necessary. He was glad their first kiss had been in the dark; he was not sure if he could have responded if he had seen her age before kissing her. Why was he thinking *first kiss*? He should not be touching her ever again if he guessed her age correctly; she could only just be out of the schoolroom. She was beautiful though. Even in the dim light of the room, it was plain to him she was a real beauty. She had golden blonde hair that was deliciously disarrayed because of his handiwork. Her eyes were not the pale blue that usually came with such blonde hair but a deep emerald green. The colour was mesmerising. Her frame was slender, but not petite, and she stood upright and held her head high.

"Let's start with introductions, shall we? I'm Lord Halkyn, Stephen to friends, and, I think after the last ten minutes we can consider ourselves friends, don't you?" Stephen responded with a slight bow and his usual easy smile.

"I know who you are; the girls advised me that I should seek help from you," she replied, watching him warily. She might have sought him out, but it was clear she still did not know whether to trust him.

"Really? My reputation is obviously better than I thought," Stephen responded mockingly.

"They said you were kind," she said quietly.

Stephen paused; he had never considered himself kind before. He was more likely to be accused of being selfish, self-centred, slightly cold and completely self-indulgent but never kind. His curiosity was piqued. "Let us be seated and you can explain yourself more fully. You can start with an introduction."

"You don't need to know my name," she said as he led her to sit on a two- seated sofa. Its position was such that if the door opened, neither occupant would be seen from the doorway. He sat next to her, but positioned himself on the side nearest the doorway. If they were interrupted again, he would need to cover her with his body to shield her from view.

Stephen sighed at her words. "Let me be clear about one thing: if you want my help, you will have the decency to tell me the truth. If I find you are using me as a fool, I walk out of this room and leave

7

you to your fate. I'm not wasting my time on someone who cannot be honest with me."

His words had the desired effect; she inhaled sharply and paused. She let out the breath in a rush. "I will be honest with you My Lord, if you promise to help me."

"I have already helped, so I think my promise would not add anything to the situation and, as I have already said, my given name is Stephen."

"My name is Charlotte, Charlotte Webster," she replied.

Chapter 2

Charlotte had known she would have to trust Lord Halkyn; there was no one else who any of the girls thought would provide her with help. They were not even totally convinced of Halkyn, but he was described as her only option. She had been grateful for their advice; if she had been left alone, she had no idea what she would have done. This was something completely out of her experience. She had not seen many of the men who visited Baron Kersal's abode, but the ones she had laid eyes on whereof the same level as the Baron: lecherous and lacking in morals. The girls had described Lord Halkyn as kind and considerate in his dealings with them, although he was obviously a rake. Most of the other men had a tendency to inflict pain on the women they used; the girls had said Lord Halkyn had never done such a thing. She had little choice, so she had taken the risk of speaking with him.

She had never behaved so much like a doxy in her life and was relieved the darkness had covered her blushes. If there had been any light, she could not have gone through with the charade. Lord Halkyn had been pointed out to her; luckily he had visited the establishment on two concurrent nights, an unusual occurrence apparently. It was a blessing for Charlotte, though; her time was limited, and she had to act quickly: frightened she most certainly was, but she had to try for freedom.

She assessed the man in front of her. Lord Halkyn might be considered a rake, but he was a handsome one. He had wavy blonde hair, not a dissimilar colour to her own, and deep blue eyes. His mouth was striking; it reminded her of a rosebud and could have looked feminine, but there was hardness around the mouth as if the person it belonged to was bitter. She blushed when she thought what a shame that was; the mouth had brought her so much pleasure for those few moments. It had sent her to a place of warmth and passion. The problem was that now she had tasted what a real passionate kiss was, she was even more convinced she could not go to her fate without a fight.

He was obviously in an unexpectedly strange situation, but he appeared calm; he was just watching her closely. He seemed amused as a range of emotions passed across her face. Charlotte did not know where to start, but as she tried to gather her thoughts, Stephen broke the silence.

"So, Charlotte Webster, shall we start with how old you are or how you came to be in this den of iniquity?" Stephen asked, after giving the girl a few moments. He had enjoyed watching the different expressions flitter across her face, but then he focused his attention. They had limited time, and he needed answers.

Charlotte blushed, "I'm nearly eighteen, and I'm here because of my own foolishness."

Stephen flinched; nearly eighteen was still seventeen. He was more than seven years her senior and probably more than a hundred years her senior in experience if the blushes that kept reddening her cheeks were anything to go by. He cursed silently to himself; this was not good. "Your family?" he asked sharply.

"I have an uncle who has probably disowned me by now. Lord Halkyn, Stephen," she hurried to use his given name at Stephen's raised eyebrows. "I need to leave this place urgently. Every moment I stay here, I am at risk of being discovered, and I can't let that happen."

"So, you need my help, but why should I trust your word? I have known Baron Kersal for a few years. Why should I trust you over him?"

Charlotte closed her eyes; if he did not help her she would be lost, but there was not enough time to explain. While she was still in the house she could not relax. "You have no reason to believe whatever I tell you, but I think you will believe me, just as I trust you. I hope you can tell I am no lightskirt; I am respectable, or I was. Baron Kersal is involved in something that must be illegal; but the girls who work here didn't think you were involved. That was one of the reasons they suggested you might be willing to help. Please can we leave and then I will tell you everything?"

"Why would the girls help you?" Stephen asked. "I've never known loyalty amongst their kind."

"I don't know: perhaps it was because I am so young; perhaps it's because what they've seen happening is beyond what normally goes on in places like this. I don't know!" Charlotte replied, desperation sounding in her voice.

Stephen's mind raced; she had hinted she was no longer respectable, but she had kissed like an innocent. For some reason the thought of her being touched by one of Baron Kersal's cronies made his blood boil. That was, until he realised he was one of those cronies himself. His mouth twisted in a bitter smile; he was probably exactly like one of his immoral associates that she was trying to escape.

He stirred from his musings. "Have you any belongings?"

"Nothing of note; I have my cloak here; that is all," she replied.

"We can leave only if we do so separately."

"No!" came the panicked response. She was sure that if he left her they would search the room.

"I'm not going to desert you, but I can hardly walk out through the hallway with you," Stephen said drily.

"They will find me if you leave me alone!" Charlotte said, panic in her voice.

Stephen sighed, "I will get you out of this building; trust me." He stood and walked to the door; he opened it slightly, but his demeanour changed. As he opened the door he called out, slurring his words and seeming to need the door jamb for support. "Hey, my man! I need my coach, now!"

"Yes, sir," came the distant reply.

"Kersal always has lots of obliging staff," Halkyn said, smiling at Charlotte over his shoulder.

"At least you aren't on horseback!" Charlotte said with feeling. She had not relished a gallop across country on a cold night.

"Perish the thought," Stephen shuddered exaggeratedly. "I like my comforts, my dear."

"I'm not surprised!" Charlotte said primly.

Stephen chuckled; he liked this girl. "We need to get you to a safe place." He walked to the window after blowing out most of the candles. Pulling the curtains slightly, he unhooked the latch and opened the French window. He shushed Charlotte's sharp intake of breath. "You're probably right about not being safe in this house once I leave, so you will have to leave it ahead of me."

Charlotte's heart began to pound. She had felt safe with Stephen, and now she was going to be alone again. She stood, hugging her arms around her shoulders, trying to give herself courage. "Is anyone about?" she asked in a whisper.

"Not a soul in sight. Everyone will soon have tired of Kersal's search and returned to the festivities." Get your cloak and come here," Stephen instructed.

Charlotte did as ordered and moved silently to the window. She was sure her pounding heart would give away how frightened she was.

Stephen glanced at her face and smiled slightly; even in the darkness he could see she was pale with fear. He pulled her to him, wrapping his arm around her shoulders. For some reason he wanted to reassure her. She looked at him warily, but he just smiled down at her. "Keep close to the wall and move towards the front of the house. You chose well in this room; we are almost at the corner of the building. Stay in the shadow of the wall. Wait until my carriage turns this corner and stay in place until I give you a signal."

"What are you going to do?"

"I wouldn't normally go past this part of the house when leaving, so I need to create a bit of a show. Be ready to move when I give the signal."

12

Charlotte nodded her understanding and stood wrapped in the warmth of the arm that draped over her shoulders. Neither moved until they heard the wheels of a carriage stopping at the front of the house. Charlotte shuddered; this was it: her best chance.

Stephen felt the shudder and squeezed her tighter. "If this fails, I will return to the house and get you out, by force if necessary." His words earned him a smile that stirred sensations in his groin totally inappropriate for the situation. He bent down and gently kissed her lips. "Good luck! Now go." And he helped her out the window.

Stephen watched as Charlotte moved along the outside of the building; there was no sound of anyone close by. He closed the window and replaced the curtain, careful to ensure it did not draw attention to the window. He blew the candle out and walked to the door, preparing to give an excellent performance.

He opened the door as the footman approached. He staggered out of the room and bounced into the footman, making them both stumble slightly. "Sorry, my man, a little too much wine and women I think. I need time to sleep it off," he slurred.

The footman grinned and helped Stephen to the door. "This way sir; I'm sure you will feel more the thing in the morning."

"Bloody head will hurt though; Kersal never serves us his best wine," Stephen said, stumbling to the door, almost colliding with a marble plinth and a vase balanced on top. The footman moved quickly and steadied the vase, but still managed to help Stephen along. "He's always been cheap," Stephen muttered as if talking to himself.

The footman choked back a laugh but wisely did not respond to the slur on his master's character. "Here we are, sir."

Stephen paused at the entrance portico; he acted as if the thought of climbing into his carriage was too much, but it was to make sure he was not going to be challenged. He turned to the footman, "My man will help me; here, have this." He handed him a large coin from his pocket.

The footman accepted it with round eyes. Stephen thought it was probably more than the man earned in a month, but it would help with his silence if anything were seen. He reached out his hand to indicate he wanted help from his staff. A footman left the side of the carriage and took his arm. He helped Stephen wobble over to the carriage; when Stephen reached it, he pretended he was going to vomit but dragged the footman down with him. In the confusion, he whispered urgently to his staff member and, when he received a nod of understanding, he let him go. The footman jumped up next to the driver, an unusual occurrence, but necessary.

Stephen stood on the top step of the carriage and hung on with one hand as the carriage started to move. The house footman looked concerned, but Stephen waved at him with his free hand. "Tell Kersal his women are getting as leathery as his wine!"

The words seemed to distract the footman from the fact that the carriage was travelling in the wrong direction. Stephen maintained the pretence until the carriage turned the corner. He waited until he was just out of sight of the doorway and then beckoned Charlotte to the carriage. He hauled her up while the vehicle was still in motion and fell inside with her, closing the door and pulling down the curtain. The steps would have to remain in position until they stopped.

Chapter 3

"Easy!" Stephen smiled with self-satisfaction while Charlotte sat huddled in the corner.

"I'm glad you think so, I think I've aged ten years in the last hour!" Charlotte replied fiercely. She was a little annoyed that Stephen seemed to be enjoying the escapade, while she had been terrified.

"I can assure you that you haven't," Stephen responded teasingly. "Any woman who can behave so like a spoiled miss must be just out of the schoolroom."

Charlotte glared at her rescuer, "You aren't very gallant."

Stephen laughed loudly. "Perish the thought my dear. Half my friends would suffer apoplexy if they thought I'd started being gallant."

Charlotte harrumphed and muttered to herself.

Stephen took pity on her; she had been through an ordeal and, in reality, it was far from over. "Don't mind me; I don't like people much, so I tend to be very dismissive and cynical. I would try and stop it, only I quite enjoy it," he smiled, but he used his winning smile, the one that usually melted his way into any bedroom he chose.

His words piqued Charlotte's attention. "You don't like people? Why ever not?"

"That my dear is a story for another day." Stephen might be willing to tease her out of her annoyance, but he never really pandered to anyone. He was not prepared to sit discussing his lifestyle or opinions. He had far bigger problems to deal with. "Do you have anyone in London who could offer assistance?"

"I don't know a soul. I have never been to London before," Charlotte said, regretting this was obviously the moment she would have to reveal just what a fool she had been.

"Well, where the devil *have* you come from?" Stephen demanded.

"Miss Humphrey's school for young ladies," Charlotte said meekly.

"Dear God, it gets worse! You *are* still in the schoolroom! I thought you'd have made your debut at least!" Stephen exploded. He was angry partly because of the effect the kiss had had on him and the fact that she was an unreachable school miss. He wanted to continue the kisses they had shared, but he was not about to analyse the source of his feelings or why he felt such anger at knowing her age and the level of her innocence.

"I was due to leave in the next month!" Charlotte responded defensively. "Stop acting as if I'm a child!"

Stephen smiled cynically, "But that is exactly what you, are and you should be a hundred miles from here."

"You do say the most ridiculous things," Charlotte responded in exasperation. "What the devil do you think I'm trying to do?"

"What the devil?" Stephen responded in disbelief. "You will mind your language when you are with me, young lady."

"Oh, don't come the prude now," Charlotte said defiantly. "I'm sure you are used to being with women who use far worse language than that!"

Stephen blinked, a little impressed at her spirit; she was still very young to be engaging in a verbal tirade with him, but she was proving she could match him. He soon recovered enough to respond in his usual manner. "Yes, but I usually pay them for spending time with me. I'm sure *you* don't want to be in that situation, do you?"

Charlotte blushed, beaten in the game of words. She sat quietly for a few moments, Stephen watching her closely all the time. She sighed and looked at him in what he was rapidly realising was her usual direct way. "I need to tell you everything, don't I?"

"Yes, you do, my dear," Stephen said, a little gentler than his previous words had been.

"I know I have to, but I have been so stupid I'm ashamed to say the words out loud," Charlotte said with genuine remorse.

"We have all done things that are stupid," Stephen said with a wry smile.

"Oh, I would love to hear your stories one day; I'm sure you had real fun along the way!" Charlotte said, surprising Stephen at her genuine tone of interest in him. She groaned and carried on speaking. "As I've said, the only family I have is an uncle in Lincolnshire. I don't remember my parents; they died when I was very young from some outbreak of fever in the village. My uncle took me in even though he was not married."

"That was kind of him," Stephen said with a shudder.

Charlotte smiled at his reaction. "It was. He really couldn't cope with a young child though; it was not his fault, he did his best. I had to grow up quickly; he could only cope with me if he treated me like an adult. We both decided it was best if I went to boarding school."

"You both decided? How old were you?" Stephen asked in disbelief. If she had been treated like an adult from a young age, it explained why she appeared older, with her words at least. He tried to ignore the memories of her tentative response to his kisses.

"About the age of ten," Charlotte said simply. "I wanted friends my own age; I wasn't stupid. I knew uncle was struggling with me."

Stephen raised an eyebrow, "Too clever for your own good, if you ask me."

Charlotte ignored the remark and carried on. "I enjoyed school. The girls who were there had a similar standard of living to my own: not rich but not poor, so it was happy overall."

"Sounds delightful," Stephen said unconvincingly.

"If you constantly interrupt me with your unproductive remarks, I will never be able to tell you my story. I thought you wanted to hear it? I'm more than happy to stop now!" Charlotte responded tartly.

"Sorry," Stephen muttered. She certainly did not seem to suffer fools he thought to himself as he watched her huff at his response.

"I was due to leave next month, but a few months ago, we got a new member of staff." Stephen raised his eyebrow, but refrained from saying anything. "Yes, you've guessed it," Charlotte said disparagingly. "I was the one who fell for the new footman, or I stupidly thought I had."

Stephen had felt a slight tightening in his chest at her words and had to move in his seat to try and shake off the feeling. "What happened?" he asked.

"Oh, he filled my head with all sorts of nonsense. I've read lots of Romance novels so I should have guessed his words were shallow. What can I say? I was stupid and fell for every one of his silly words, all of his flattery. Oh, how I could kick myself now! Anyway, I didn't have a huge fortune, so I knew I wasn't going to attract a rich husband. I didn't want riches; I just wanted to be happy, and I stupidly thought Christopher was the person to make me happy."

"Go on," Stephen said with gritted teeth.

"He convinced me to run away with him, saying that my uncle would never understand why we wanted to be together. So, we arranged to meet and elope. I wrote a letter to my uncle, apologising for letting him down but telling him what I was doing. The carriage came as planned, and I jumped in without a thought. Only it wasn't Christopher inside waiting to whisk me off to Gretna Green; it was Baron Kersal and one of his trusted girls.

"Did he hurt you?" Stephen asked, vowing silently to kill Kersal if he had.

"No," Charlotte said truthfully. "He'd brought Laura to restrain me, said he didn't want me damaged. I was never to see Christopher again. He is going to stay at the school to wait until the ruckus dies down about me and then start on some other unsuspecting fool," Charlotte said bitterly.

"And what was going to happen to you? Kersal doesn't usually force his women to work for him," Stephen was genuinely confused. It did not sound right. Kersal's entertainments consisted of lots of wine, card games and women, but not kidnapping.

"I was going to be married to one of his so-called friends. Apparently some men like young girls: the more innocent the better, and I would bring Baron Kersal a large sum. From what his working girls told me it's a new line of business for the Baron, but it brings in quite a lot of money. Men will pay to have a reluctant virgin." She had blushed deeply at the words but tilted her chin defiantly.

"You've spent too long with his other girls; you've already adopted the language of the gutter!" Stephen said with a slight smile. His mind was racing; this was on a different level than having a house full of women who were willing participants, for the right amount of money, of course. This was kidnap, ruination and forced marriage. His blood ran cold; what kind of men had he been associating with? He might have some ways that would have decent Mamas ushering their innocent offspring away from him, but he had never done anything illegal. All his partners had been consenting adults. "How do they pick the girls?" he asked.

"They select the ones who don't have a strong family network to protect them," Charlotte responded.

"But you have an uncle," Stephen queried.

"Yes, but many miles away. He never visited, and I didn't go home for the holidays. I was perfect, apparently, ripe for the plucking, as Baron Kersal so delicately put it," Charlotte said with disgust. She had been terrified, but somehow the more miles they covered and the more time she spent in Stephen's company, the more she relaxed. She felt completely safe and at ease with him now.

"I will kill him!" Stephen said. Preying on vulnerable girls was not acceptable in any respectable man's book.

"No, don't!" Charlotte said, all ease gone. "He will know I am connected to you and come and find me. Please before you do anything against Baron Kersal, help me get as far away from him as I can."

Stephen paused; she was in danger. In London she was at risk of seeing someone connected to Kersal. Stephen had no idea how many people were involved, obviously more than a few to carry out such a scheme. The reality of her situation struck him, and then with annoyance he realised he could not just deliver her to some safe place and carry on with his life. What the hell was he going to do with her?

Chapter 4

Stephen was prevented from thinking further by their arrival at his house. He looked at Charlotte and almost groaned aloud; he had not thought this through. He was a single man living alone. The moment she walked into his house she was ruined. He paused before lifting the curtain.

"Raise your cloak hood and don't let anyone see your face until we are inside," he said firmly.

Charlotte nodded, fear again rising to the front of her mind. She knew deep down they had not been followed, but that did not ease the fear, rational or not. She pulled her hood over her head and held it close over her face. She was helped down the carriage steps, and her hand was placed in the crook of Stephen's arm as he walked her inside. The door was opened by Stephen's long serving butler, who made no indication it was a surprise to find a lady arriving home with his master. Charlotte noticed this, and for some reason it annoyed her.

Stephen released her arm when the door closed. "You may take your hood down now," he said to Charlotte before turning to the butler. "Walter, I need you to get the most trustworthy maid from the staff and get her to sleep in the bedchamber with Miss Webster. Please take her to a guest room and, once she has had refreshments, make sure she has everything she will need for the night."

Walter, to his credit, resisted the overwhelming urge to faint at his employer's feet. Never in the whole of his service had he seen a lady brought home who did not spend the night in the master's bed chamber. He had noticed the young age of the girl and for a moment had been disappointed with his employer, but there was obviously something strange going on. He responded as every good butler would, without showing any emotion, then turning to the lady in question, he bowed slightly.

"If you would like to follow me, Miss?" He said in his usual calm way.

21

"But...?" Charlotte stammered, turning to Stephen.

"You need food and rest tonight; it has been a trying day for you. Get some sleep, and we shall talk in the morning. Nothing will happen here that will disturb you, I assure you."

For the second time in as many minutes, Walter had to suppress a range of emotions. His employer showing kindness? Protectiveness even? No, things were definitely amiss. He ushered Charlotte off, and Stephen retired to his study to pour himself a large brandy.

A short time later, Walter found his master rubbing his temples, the brandy glass more than half empty. "Miss Webster is settled My Lord. Maggie will be attending her."

"Who's Maggie?" Stephen asked.

"One of your staff My Lord. She's been in your employ these last five years," came the droll response.

"The day I start noticing the female staff is the day you will resign Walter, so don't start giving me that holier-than-thou, 'you should know the names of your staff, My Lord' rubbish," Stephen said roughly.

Walter smiled broadly, definitely going against any butler rules that existed. "Quite so, My Lord. She's a good girl: honest and very loyal to you, although I can't imagine why."

Stephen grinned at Walter's comment. It was a genuine grin, not one of his usual smiles that were used to achieve an aim. "Neither can I Walter, but I think the girl probably needs a pay rise." Walter had been in his service since they were both young men, rising to butler through hard work and a sudden illness of the previous butler. He was loyal to a fault to his employer but, at the same time, realistic about Stephen's shortcomings. He was older than Stephen and wished his master could settle down and be happy. He very often appeared jade; this was difficult to observe by someone who actually cared for his employer: he cared with something between sibling and fatherly affection.

Walter was an excellent member of staff, and Stephen appreciated his support. This had encouraged Walter into giving more opinions than was usual for a butler, but Stephen seemed to enjoy it and encouraged a sort of friendship between them. This was one of the reasons Stephen used the butler's first name rather than his surname when addressing him.

"May I ask how long will the young lady be staying, my Lord?" Walter asked, trying to be diplomatic.

"Do you know, Walter, I haven't a bloody clue as to what I am going to do with her!" Stephen said, returning to rubbing his temples. "What a damned mess!"

"Could I be of assistance?"

"I will need your help, Walter, when I figure this mess out. No doubt I shall live to regret helping her tonight when I should have walked away and forgot I ever saw her."

"I doubt that very much, My Lord," came the calm response, hiding the nugget of curiosity that had been sown at the thought of his master helping a damsel in distress. He would certainly look more closely at the young lady in the morning; she had achieved something no one else had ever done.

*

Maggie helped Charlotte undress. She had been supplied with a clean shift of the maid's, for which she had been grateful.

"We can have your clothes cleaned and ready for the morning," Maggie assured her. "Then you will feel more the thing. Now let me brush your hair."

Charlotte watched the maid through the looking glass as she tended her. She had had a maid at home and then at school, but Maggie was slightly older than those, being around thirty. The way she fussed and gently dealt with her new charge helped Charlotte relax and feel taken care of for the second time that evening. She became more peaceful as her hair was brushed and tiredness washed over her. It had been a long day; in fact, it had been a long few days. She had not slept very well, being afraid of what might happen to her if she did.

Maggie helped her into bed and handed Charlotte a cup of warm milk. "This will help you sleep, Miss; you look like you could sleep the clock around," she said gently. "I will be staying in the dressing room; I'll leave the door open. If you need me, just shout. I'm a light sleeper, so don't worry; I will hear you."

"Thank you, Maggie, you have been very kind," Charlotte replied sleepily. She was going to have someone nearby, ready to wake if she needed her, someone watching over her. Stephen was in the house, and she knew he would protect her if she needed him. She snuggled down into the large four poster bed. The clean sheets felt refreshingly cool on her skin, and the pillows seemed to hug her head and shoulders. Within moments of handing the empty cup back to Maggie, she was fast asleep, dreaming about kisses from rosebud mouths.

She woke with a start at sunshine flooding into the room. Maggie was up and opening the curtains. She had been downstairs and collected Charlotte's clean dress. "Morning, Miss," the maid said cheerfully.

"Morning," Charlotte replied with a smile. She stretched feeling refreshed, but the reality of her situation soon brought her down to earth. She hoped Stephen would be agreeable to her plans.

She was directed to the dining room for breakfast. It was a large square room, all four sides covered in wood panelling. A large table took pride of place in the centre with a side table running along one wall. A small round side table had been set with two places. Stephen sat at one of the places and stood when she entered the room. "Good morning, Charlotte; did you sleep well?"

"Yes, thank you," Charlotte replied a little shyly. Last night had been mostly in the dark but, this morning with the sun flooding into the room, she had nowhere to hide. Stephen was dressed in his shirt, waistcoat, breeches and banyan, which fell loosely around his body;

no frock coat hid the broadness of his shoulders, or the slimness of his waist. Charlotte gulped as she sat; had she really been so forward with such a fine man?

Stephen watched all her emotions pass over her face. His amusement helped focus his mind; when she walked in it had been a miracle he had not knocked over his chair in surprise. He had thought her beautiful the night before, but this morning she was stunning. Her hair had been dressed by Maggie with small fresh daisies, her blond curls left to naturally fall around her face and cascading from her bun. Her dress was well made and, since it had been cleaned and pressed, it seemed to emphasise her slim figure. Her slight blush only helped to make her look more appealing. He tried to mentally shake himself. When had he become attracted to innocents? If this continued, it was a sure route to the dark side.

"Here, let me get you something to eat," he offered. Anything to keep him occupied and focus his mind.

"Thank you, and thank you for everything," Charlotte replied demurely.

Stephen looked at her, "Have you exchanged places with Miss Webster? Who are you?" He asked with a tilt of his chin.

Charlotte looked confused. "Whatever do you mean?" she asked, her blush deepening.

"Last night I was faced with a fiery tigress. This morning I am faced with a timid kitten. What has happened in the night; where is *my* Miss Webster?"

My Miss Webster, that was a thought she would dream about in the future; but in the meantime Stephen's words had done the trick. She looked him fully in the eyes. "I was hoping you would be lulled into agreeing to my plan. I thought if I were timid, you would agree to it without argument," she said honestly.

Stephen smiled, glad to have the real Charlotte back, "Ah, so you have a plan; at least that makes one of us."

"You haven't any suggestions to make?" Charlotte asked in surprise.

"I have thought of little else, but I'm afraid you will find me sadly lacking; I have no cunning plan up my sleeve," Stephen said with a shrug. His careless words hid his frustration about what to do with Charlotte; the question had kept him awake half the night.

"Goodwin that case I think you will find my proposal perfectly acceptable," Charlotte replied, her confidence increasing, and she began tucking into her breakfast. The long, deep sleep had given her a real appetite.

Stephen watched with amusement as she ate. She really was full of life—a pity he was a hardened cynic. If he had been only five years younger he would have enjoyed courting her, but he was not, so there was no use thinking of what could have been. When Charlotte seemed to have had her fill, he indicated she should follow him.

"We can discuss your acceptable proposal in the morning room."

Charlotte realised Stephen had not wanted to discuss the situation in front of the servants. She was grateful for this. Maggie had been kind, but Charlotte wondered what she and the other servants must think of the situation. Once again she felt like a complete doxy even though she had not spent the night with Stephen; they must think she was some sort of lightskirt.

Stephen led the way to the small room at the front of the house. It was bright and airy, the lemon colouring on the walls and upholstery bringing colour into a small space. Furniture was scattered around the room; the effect was that it looked as if it were done carelessly, but Charlotte could tell that every piece of furniture complemented the others. He had obviously spoken the truth when he said he liked his comforts. Stephen sat on one of the seats, indicating Charlotte should do the same.

"Come, do tell; I am all ears," he said, stretching his legs out in front of him.

"My plan means I need to ask you for further help, but I promise this will be the last time, and I promise to pay you back," Charlotte said in a rush.

"Oh, so it involves my money," Stephen said dryly. "May I ask how much and what the money would be spent on?"

Charlotte flushed with indignation at his words. "I can assure you if there was any other way, I would take it. I need the money to get a great distance away from London."

Stephen relented a little, "You wish to return to your uncle? That is the sensible thing to do."

"No," Charlotte said sadly. "I have managed to sever that tie. The letter I sent to my uncle will have arrived, and he will think I am a fallen woman. He would never accept me in his house again."

"Where are you intending to go then?" Stephen asked. She had already said there were no other relatives.

"I will go to Manchester. I believe it is a large city," Charlotte explained. "If I can borrow the money from you to help with my travel costs, I am sure that in such a city it wouldn't be too long before I found some employment."

Stephen's heart sank. "And what type of work would you be hoping to get?" he asked, trying his hardest to keep the sarcasm out of his voice.

"I would look for a position as a governess," Charlotte replied.

"Without a reference?" Stephen asked, raising an eyebrow.

"Well, if not, there are the new mills. I believe they require large workforces; I'm willing to work hard," Charlotte responded becoming defensive at Stephen's tone.

"Have you ever spun cotton?" Stephen asked the sarcasm fully evident now.

"No, but I can learn!" Charlotte responded tartly. "I will do anything I have to until I am established."

"I'll tell you what you'll do, you foolish chit. You will be turned away from every decent establishment because you have no references. You will be turned away from every mill because you have no experience, and the only option left open to you will be to join an establishment such as Kersal's!" Stephen almost shouted at her.

Charlotte fired up at Stephen's words. "Oh, so what should I do? Accept my fate and return to the Baron and say, 'Oh, sorry. Your offer isn't too bad after all.'? If you think I'm going to roll over and let that immoral criminal win, you have underestimated me. I will find decent work. Now, will you lend me the money to leave London?" She almost shouted in return.

Stephen smiled, "Not until you have come up with a realistic plan."

Charlotte almost growled with frustration. "Mine is the only plan there is, and I am determined to carry it to fruition." If Stephen did not help her, she was actually at a loss as to what to do, but she did not want him to know that.

Stephen stood and started to pace the room. Charlotte watched him, hoping it meant he was going to help her after all, although he looked angry rather than helpful. Minutes passed before he spoke.

"Damn my parents!" he muttered.

"Your parents?" Charlotte asked in wonder. "What on earth have they got to do with this?"

"If they had been decent, they would have supplied me with a convenient sister who could offer you protection and a home until a solution could be found. As it is, I'm their only child, as far as I know anyway, although I'm sure my father must have produced a number of illegitimates along the way," Stephen said darkly.

Charlotte was fascinated; she had known him for such a short period of time, yet she had so many questions she wanted to ask. There was so much in what he said that increased her curiosity about him, but at the moment, she had to worry about her own predicament.

"Of course, your sister would have married by now to a respectable gentleman who lived a hundred or more miles from London. Two hundred miles would be preferable," she replied archly.

Stephen laughed, "Two hundred miles would be best, yes." He became serious, "You picked the wrong man Charlotte; I do not have the respectability to protect you. I do not have a network of close friends I could be honest with who would offer you protection because of my connection with them. They are more likely to condemn you because of your association with me."

The words had been said without any emotion, but Charlotte wanted to wrap her arms around him in comfort. His life must be lonely, she thought. She ached to make him feel better; was she being truly altruistic she pondered or was it that he reminded her of herself?

"You were the one who got me out of that den of iniquity, and for that I will be eternally grateful," she responded honestly. "I created the situation; I have only myself to blame. I foolishly thought I was in love, but now I know how wrong I was."

"Yes, love can cause more problems than it is worth, which is why I've always stayed away from it. Although in your defence it is sometimes surprising how many intelligent people can long for it."Stephen seemed to suddenly be struck by a thought, "Oh, this is priceless!" He chuckled to himself.

"What is?" Charlotte asked.

"I just thought of a perfect solution," Stephen said smugly. "One that will give you the protection of not only one Lord of the realm, but two. He won't be happy about it though, which is even better."

Charlotte was not reassured by Stephen's words, "What are you suggesting?"

"An acquaintance of mine has recently married a young lady who would love you. She is out of the ordinary, but I know she would be willing to help. I don't know why I didn't think of it sooner: Elizabeth would be perfect, or Lady Dunham as she is now," Stephen said.

He was confident Elizabeth would lend her support to the situation; she was the only genuinely decent person he knew.

"And Lord Dunham?" Charlotte asked, referring to Stephen's glee about his acquaintance not liking the scheme.

"Oh, he'll do whatever Elizabeth wants; he's besotted with her!" Stephen responded dismissively.

"I don't know...." Charlotte said, not convinced by Stephen's words.

"It's the best option you have, and they live in Somerset on the Dunham estate. Elizabeth hates London, so they rarely visit, and the friends they have do not mix in the usual circles," Stephen explained patiently. "It will take us a few days to get there; I shall write and let them know of your predicament."

"Are you sure?" Charlotte was still unconvinced but was interrupted by a sudden outburst from Stephen.

"Oh, damnation!" He said roughly.

"For someone who criticised my language last night, you're doing a good job of being gutter mouthed in my presence sir," Charlotte said primly, but there was a twinkle in her eye.

Stephen grinned at her words. "It's not becoming for a young lady to use foul language but, as there is no hope for me, it's irrelevant."

"A poor response, sir, if I may say so! I've already come to expect so much more of you," Charlotte replied. She was not truly offended; in fact it was a compliment that he was comfortable enough to say such things to her.

"Sorry to have disappointed you, but you need to be aware I try my best to disappoint when possible. I've always found life far easier if people have few expectations of one," Stephen responded lightly.

Charlotte guessed the words held a lot of information about the way this man lived. He seemed to want to make sure no one was close to him. It was an odd way to live: a trifle cold perhaps, but she only had to remember that kiss for all thoughts of him being cold to fly out of her head. She tried to get herself back under control.

"So why the outburst?" she asked.

"We shall have to travel on the road for days. We can take the maid with us for respectability, but we need a story, and you need clothes," Stephen explained.

"Oh," Charlotte responded dejectedly. The reality of travelling half way across the country and needing to show respectability sinking in.

Walter entered the room, bringing a morning tea tray, as was usual. Stephen usually needed numerous cups of tea before being able to face the world; he swore tea helped him combat the excesses of his evening pursuits. The conversation he had overheard increased the butler's curiosity even more, but he was a servant employed to help, not ask questions.

When the conversation seemed to grind to a halt, the butler coughed slightly, unable to stop himself being of help. "If I may interrupt My Lord?"

"You've never asked permission before; go ahead," Stephen responded. Charlotte glared at him for his sharp words. "Oh, don't worry about Walter; he has the hide of a rhinoceros, don't you?" Stephen asked pleasantly.

"I find it serves me well in the more difficult employment I have undertaken over the years," Walter replied straight faced.

"See?" Stephen asked Charlotte. "No respect at all."

Charlotte was reassured Stephen was not mistreating his staff. "I've always believed respect has to be earned," she responded, for which she received a smile from both Stephen and Walter.

"Right! Now that my character has been destroyed by you both, would you like to get to the point, Walter?" Stephen asked pleasantly.

"Certainly, sir. I was just going to suggest Lord Dunham had perhaps asked you to escort Lady Dunham's cousin to their abode."

Stephen thought through the proposal and smiled at the butler. "I knew there was a reason I employed you. Excellent idea Walter! No one knows Lady Dunham well; she was raised in the north, so they won't know her family. We can say I collected you from school; even those who think the worst of me would know I wouldn't prey on a schoolgirl," Stephen mused.

Charlotte's heart sank a little at Stephen's words, but she spoke normally. "That would make a good story, but it doesn't solve the problem about my luggage."

Walter coughed a little again.

"Go on," Stephen said, rolling his eyes at his butler.

"If you would excuse me again, My Lord, you have, ahem, used the services of modistes in the past, for, ahem, gifts for some of your friends. Perhaps one would care to visit and obtain Miss Webster's measurements. Usually there are some items that can be obtained quickly." It was obvious Walter was uncomfortable betraying some of his master's lifestyle in front of Charlotte, but he had offered another solution.

Stephen looked stony faced but responded calmly, "Yes, another good idea. Could you send for the most discreet of them and arrange for a full *respectable* wardrobe to be provided?" Walter nodded and left the room to send a message.

Charlotte had no right to be annoyed or jealous. He was a grown man who hardly knew her. She knew she did not have any rights, but if that was the case, why did she feel so desolate, annoyed and jealous at the same time? She could not stop herself making a comment. "I would prefer not to receive the services of a modiste who is used to supply ladies of a certain profession, if you don't mind!" she said haughtily.

Stephen had not wanted his life aired in front of Charlotte like that even though it was for a good enough cause. For some strange reason, he wanted her to think well of him. Her words angered him though, and he responded sharply. "I'm a single man who enjoys the single life to the full. Something which you should be thankful for or else you would be on your way to a forced marriage by now!" he snapped.

Charlotte flushed. "I shall always be grateful for what you have done and are doing to help me, but don't expect me to rejoice when I am put in the same category as a lightskirt!" she snapped in return, sounding as angry as Stephen had.

"No, you are better than that," Stephen sneered. "No lightskirt I have ever known has dragged me into a room and demanded to be kissed. You, my dear, are definitely from a different category."

Charlotte gasped and flushed a deep red. Her eyes stung because Stephen had voiced the sentiments that haunted her before she even carried them out. She *was* a doxy and pretending otherwise left her open to such ridicule as had just been shown.

Charlotte stood with as much grace as she could muster; she did not look at Stephen, but said "Excuse me, please, My Lord," in a shaking voice and left the room.

Chapter 5

Stephen did not see Charlotte for the remainder of the morning. He was aware a modiste had arrived, but confined himself to his study. He was angry with himself at his outburst. He had had no right to respond to her like that, and she had not deserved it. She was a young girl, and he had to keep reminding himself of that. Her verbal sparring made him forget it; she seemed so much older than her years. Yes, that had been explained with her being brought up by her uncle, but that did not excuse Stephen for forgetting just how young she actually was.

Being remorseful was new to him; he normally didn't care enough about anyone for remorse to ever have an impact. There were few people around him with whom he was very friendly, and even fewer he would make any effort for. He had once tried to get close to his friend, Elizabeth, but she had wanted more than he could give her. She was one of those fools looking for love. Stephen checked himself: he did not think she was a fool; she was one of the brightest people he knew. She could make any evening interesting, and he knew she would welcome Charlotte into her home without judgement.

The pair met for their evening meal. Stephen had considered going out but then acknowledged he would be acting like a petulant child, going to his club to sulk. The reality was he did not want to eat humble pie, but knew he must.

Charlotte came into the room in the same outfit she had worn all day. "Please excuse my lack of an evening dress," she said apologetically. "Madame DuPont says she will have everything sent around first thing in the morning."

"Good," Stephen responded. "Charlotte—"

"Before you say anything," Charlotte interrupted. "I have an apology to make. I should not have said what I said this morning. You were right; you are single and entitled to live your life as you please. I had no reason to react the way I did, especially as your lifestyle has saved me from being forced into a life I could not have borne."

Stephen laughed, "I can't cope with the reasonable, understanding Charlotte. I do not know what to say to her when she appears. I much prefer the fiery Charlotte. I also have to admit my own wrongdoing this morning. I behaved like a brute, and I apologise. Now may I have the bane of my life back? I have missed her today," he said with one of his winning smiles. His words were true though; he had missed her company.

Charlotte grinned at him, "Oh, she's never far from the surface."

"Excellent," Stephen responded. "Now. If we get your clothes tomorrow morning, we can leave before lunchtime."

"I will need to pay you back at some point. I would be grateful if you kept a record of all the expense I incur and, when I secure a position, I will repay you every farthing," Charlotte said with a blush. Stephen was a stranger to her after all, and it embarrassed her to owe him so much.

Stephen grunted, "Let's just say that to have spoiled Kersal's scheme, of which I will do more once I see you settled and out of his reach, will be enough recompense for me."

"But—" Charlotte responded.

"No buts," Stephen interrupted."I have enough money to be able to afford a few dresses and a trip to Somerset. Ask one of my lightskirts if you don't believe me," Stephen responded in a way that would hopefully kill any argument. It did; all Charlotte wanted to do was pour her food over his head for reminding her he had been with other women, many other women, but she forced herself to sit still.

*

The following day, they set-off as planned with Stephen and Charlotte in the first carriage. The luggage, Maggie and Stephen's valet Lowe, in the second carriage. Charlotte had insisted they did not need two carriages; the thought of the expense shocked her, but Stephen had told her quite firmly that, on no account, was he going to travel in anything but his usual style.

35

The further they travelled from London, the more lightheaded with relief Charlotte felt. She thought she had been relaxed while in Stephen's house, but as they travelled, she realised she had still been on edge. It was not that she doubted Stephen; it was just being in the same city as Baron Kersal and his acquaintances preyed on her mind.

Stephen was perfectly at ease on the journey. He had good company, a vision of beauty to look at and was in good spirits because of the anticipation of annoying Lord Dunham immensely. He had been an acquaintance of Dunham's for a few years, since Dunham had unexpectedly come into his title. Dunham had become friends with Stephen because they had both been chased by women who wanted to become their respective wives. They also had similar cynical outlooks on life. He did wonder if Dunham had mellowed since his marriage. He had been handy with his fists in the past, something of which Stephen still had all too clear memories. If Michael became very upset at Stephen's sudden arrival, he would have to brace himself for another fight. This time though the shoe was on the other foot; it was Stephen who was protecting the girl, not Michael.

The thought struck Stephen as hilarious. Who would have ever thought he would be acting as a self-appointed protector to an innocent? Certainly not anyone in his circle of acquaintance. It struck even Stephen as strange, but he was not prepared to let her put herself at risk. He would be fine once he knew she was safe; then he would return to London, and everything would return to normal, he hoped.

Each night they stopped at an inn, separate rooms were obtained as was proper. Maggie slept in the same room as Charlotte; Stephen had given her strict instructions she was not to leave Charlotte alone, no matter what the reason. He wanted to ensure her reputation was intact and, although he thought she was safe from any of Baron Kersal's cronies, he wanted to be sure.

On the fourth day of travel, when Stephen was questioning his sanity, they entered the drive of Dunham Park. Charlotte became fidgety. "Are you sure this is the right thing to do?" she asked looking out the window.

"Shouldn't you have asked me that before we set-off from London?" Stephen asked dryly.

"Oh, be quiet with your smart retorts; you know what I mean!" Charlotte responded in exasperation.

"You will like Elizabeth, and she will like you. There is no need to worry," Stephen reassured her, suppressing the grin her words had caused.

They were greeted at the door by a footman, and the butler took them into the large Jacobean building. Its deep red brick looked warm in the afternoon sunshine, but the large building did nothing to calm Charlotte's nerves. She felt Stephen's hand on the small of her back.

"Relax, tiger; it will be fine," he assured her in a quiet voice.

She smiled at his reassuring words, while his touch warmed her and made her feel something else. She was brought out of her thoughts by the appearance of Lady Dunham.

"Lord Halkyn, you are here at last! What a lovely surprise your letter was," the lady smiled at Stephen.

Stephen took Lady Dunham's hands in his and gave her a kiss on the cheek. "Elizabeth you are looking as beautiful as ever, I see."

"Pah!" Elizabeth responded. "You wouldn't have said that an hour ago when I was racing back across the estate, in my breeches, splattered in mud and hoping I would have time to change before you arrived."

"Managing the estate, then?" Stephen asked with a smile.

"Of course! I'm not happy unless I'm on the land. No balls and routs for me, thank you very much!" she responded with feeling.

"It was a great loss to Society when you left London; the entertainments just don't have the same sparkle anymore," Stephen said smoothly.

"Fudge!" Elizabeth replied dismissively. "My removal will have only been noticed by Violet, Edward and yourself. Everyone else had dismissed me as a country bumpkin within a short time of my arrival."

"It was your insistence on talking about crop rotation and planting schemes that did it," Stephen responded in mock seriousness.

Elizabeth laughed but moved to Charlotte. "And you must be Miss Webster. You are very welcome here. Lord Halkyn spoke very highly of you in his letter, and I must say I have been looking forward to meeting you," Elizabeth said easily.

Charlotte curtseyed and smiled at her hostess. "I'm afraid I'm only going to disappoint you; I know nothing about crop rotation or planting schemes. Although I have to admit I know nothing about balls and card parties either, Lady Dunham," she admitted truthfully.

Elizabeth threw her head back and laughed, "Oh, my dear, you don't know how those last words warm my heart. You are going to fit in perfectly here. But you must call me Elizabeth; I don't think I will ever get used to being addressed as Lady Dunham: it sounds so false somehow."

"Thank you; please call me Charlotte," Charlotte replied. She thought she might feel a little less daunted if she did not have to be so formal with Elizabeth. She was a striking woman. She had dark hair and most expressive hazel eyes. Her hair was placed in a high bun, but wisps of hair fell around her face, taking off the harshness of the hairstyle. Charlotte had the distinct impression that Stephen really liked Elizabeth; he seemed to be making a real effort to be genuinely charming with her.

"Are you trying to monopolise my wife again, Halkyn?" came the deep voice of Lord Dunham. This was the meeting Charlotte had dreaded, and the sharp words did not offer any reassurance to her nerves.

"Dunham! Still as miserable as ever, I see. Why do you stay with him, Elizabeth?" Stephen asked.

"Lord Halkyn, you are terrible! When will you ever change?" Elizabeth responded without taking any offence.

"I'm looking forward to the day he oversteps the mark again, and I shall leave him with a permanent reminder of his folly. I know I didn't go far enough the last time," Lord Dunham growled.

"Ha, you're an old married man now; you have me at a disadvantage, since I could not fight you because of my regard for Elizabeth. Although if you ever want an escape from your husband, I would not mind making you a widow, my dear," Stephen said with a straight face.

"Children, children!" Elizabeth interjected before her husband could respond. "Let us not forget our manners in front of Charlotte. My dear, I would like to introduce Miss Charlotte Webster."

"Miss Webster," Lord Dunham bowed.

Charlotte curtseyed in return. "My Lord," she murmured. He was a handsome man, as dark as Stephen was blonde. He had deep brown eyes, which were shooting daggers at Stephen. At the moment, Charlotte could not see why Elizabeth had married him; he seemed stern and forbidding. She mentally questioned Stephen's motives for coming to Somerset, and she had a feeling she would not like the answer.

Elizabeth beckoned to a woman passing through the hallway. "Martha, would you please take Miss Webster to her room to freshen up? Charlotte, Miss Fairfield will see that you have everything you need; she runs this house like clockwork."

Martha came across the hall and escorted Charlotte upstairs. Elizabeth invited the gentlemen into the drawing room. When they were seated, she turned to Stephen. "Now then, My Lord, your friend is a lovely creature, but how did you meet?"

Stephen smiled; Elizabeth was always the one to get straight to the point. "Well first things first: you can drop the 'My Lord' nonsense, especially as you are now the same rank as I, *My Lady*," he said smiling. "Stephen, if you please."

"Fine, although you will always outrank me in my head," Elizabeth said honestly, referring to when they first met, and she was plain Miss Rufford. She was distracted by a snort from her husband. "Now, Michael, don't be uncharitable; you are normally such a good host."

Michael grunted at his wife. "It depends on the quality of the guests we have," he responded uncharitably. He was annoyed with Stephen for visiting. He would never trust him fully after the way he had behaved with Elizabeth previously and was waiting for him to step out of line so he could throw him off the property.

Stephen, true to form, did not leave Michael waiting long, before the usual antagonism started. "Well, today, you have the highest honourable motive for my visit, so make sure you're on your best behaviour. I had thought marriage might have mellowed you, but it appears not to be the case."

"And it appears you have not a shred of decency left in you!" Michael snapped. "What right do you think you have to bring your latest mistress here and parade her in front of my wife? What has Elizabeth ever done to you that would cause you to act with such lack of respect?" He demanded.

Stephen flared up immediately. He was annoyed Michael could think he would insult his wife but, as for what he had called Charlotte, it made him almost shake with anger. "You bloody fool! You know damn well I think higher of Elizabeth than I do of anyone else of my acquaintance! I would never insult her, but you have overstepped the mark. How dare you? Yes, how dare you, whether this is your house or not, insult an innocent girl like Charlotte! You refer to her as if she is a mistress of mine? Have you seen how young she is? What kind of monster do you take me for, that I would prey on an innocent girl and then parade her as if she were a dance hall act? She does not deserve that, Dunham, and I would have expected better of you."

Michael and Elizabeth were both taken aback by Stephen's outburst. He had always been one who was out to have a good time and be easy with everyone in the main. He tried to be controversial, but it was in the pursuit of entertainment. Elizabeth had always thought him a little unfeeling, especially when she heard his views on love and marriage. This outburst, though, was so obviously out of character that both of them were immediately more curious as to who Miss Webster was. They had stared at Stephen almost open-mouthed, but they were both distracted when they heard a noise from the doorway. Both Miss Fairfield and a very pale Charlotte had obviously overheard the full speech.

"Charlotte!" Stephen sprang into action. The look of pure mortification on her face wrenched at his insides, and he vowed he would make Michael pay for insulting her so. "It's no slur on you; it is my past reputation being thrown in my face again. I'm sorry."

Elizabeth gave her husband a furious look. "Charlotte, my dear, I feel we have all got off to the wrong foot. You should have not heard that."

"So it would be fine to say it out of my hearing?" Charlotte asked sounding defiant, but her eyes were just a little bit more shiny than normal.

"No, it certainly would not have been fine," Michael interjected. "I sincerely apologise, Miss Webster for my appalling behaviour. Halkyn is correct; it was because of his, of *our*," he said with a slight smile and apologetic glance at his wife, "past behaviour. I welcome you into my home unreservedly and ask that you forgive my lack of manners."

Charlotte was not immune to a handsome man, especially when he was begging her forgiveness. Michael had changed from an indignant Lord of the Manor to a charming gentleman. She inclined her head. "Thank you; you are very kind," she said quietly.

"I don't usually receive forgiveness so quickly!" Stephen interjected. "Why do you let him off so easily?"

"Probably because he is a respectable husband while you are a complete cad!" Charlotte responded in her usual quick way.

"Why of all the…." Stephen started, but there was no point in him continuing, as his words were drowned out by Elizabeth and Michael's laughter.

Chapter 6

Charlotte was not so flippant and brave during the evening meal. She was seated next to Lord Dunham with Miss Fairfield sitting opposite her. Elizabeth sat at the opposite end of the table to her husband and was flanked by Stephen and a Mr Anderton, Lord Dunham's man of business. This meant Charlotte was diagonal to Stephen and, therefore, had no means of receiving support from him during the meal. She was forced to converse with Lord Dunham and Mr Anderton. Both gentlemen were charming and pleasant, but Charlotte felt completely out of place. Even Lord Dunham asking her to use his given name Michael after the fourth or fifth time she had referred to him as 'My Lord' did not ease her tension. He was not as easy going as his wife, and she dreaded telling them of the situation she was in, and it was a certainty he would find out the truth later.

On the opposite corner of the table Stephen was having a far more pleasant evening with Elizabeth, but he was aware Charlotte was feeling uncomfortable, and he felt for her.

Elizabeth noticed his glances across the table and was even more curious. "Charlotte seems a lovely girl?" she enquired innocently.

"She is, although don't be fooled by her quiet demeanour; she has a lot of spirit. Dunham is overwhelming her at the moment," Stephen replied with a slight frown of concern for Charlotte.

"Spirited and beautiful, she will be a real hit. Has she come out?" Elizabeth probed.

"No," Stephen said, just a little uncomfortable at being reminded of Charlotte's young age. "She got into a bit of a scrape before she had the opportunity."

"I'm curious to hear what has happened," Elizabeth said honestly. "We shall wait until you gentlemen join us in the drawing room. There is no point giving the staff an opportunity for gossip."

"I appreciate that," Stephen replied. "So, how is married life? Not regretting refusing me?" Elizabeth had been the one and only woman Stephen had previously considered marrying. She had refused him because she wanted to marry for love. Instead of being angry at her refusal, it had made Stephen think perhaps he should try to find someone who would love him after all. Those thoughts had obviously not stopped him from his normal pursuits, which had led him to Charlotte.

Elizabeth laughed, "I think my regrets are at the same level as yours," she responded. "We would never have suited."

Stephen smiled, "I suppose not. I could not have coped with turning to mush like Dunham appears to have done." He had noticed the looks Michael had been sending his wife during the meal.

Elizabeth smiled at her husband, a smile that was filled with love and affection. "He is the most wonderful of men. I could not be happier."

Stephen made some disparaging remark, but his words hid the emotions stirred by the look Elizabeth had given her husband. It was not jealousy as such: he did not regret not marrying Elizabeth; she was correct when she said they would not have suited. Looking at Dunham and Elizabeth, for the first time in his life, he saw what true happiness could bring, and he realised he wanted it also. He did not believe he could find it, but even as those thoughts passed through his mind, he looked at Charlotte and wished she were older. She might have been a good match for him, but he could not seriously consider such a thought, as to do so would cause something like regret.

Seeing the way his two hosts felt for each other made him long for the day he would find someone foolish enough to put up with all his faults and love him as Elizabeth loved Michael. He shook himself, thinking he must be getting old to have such melancholy feelings. He needed a night out in one of his clubs and then onto a certain type of establishment. He thought of Baron Kersal. If he was to be honest, he had never liked the man, but Charlotte's situation made him hate him. When everything was settled with Charlotte, Baron Kersal would have a visit he would not easily forget.

Elizabeth led the ladies out of the room and left Michael, Stephen and Charles Anderton to enjoy their port. Stephen used it as an opportunity to find out more about Kersal.

"Did you ever use the pleasures provided by Baron Kersal?" He asked, accepting a glass of port from Michael.

Michael looked at him in puzzlement. "No, why?"

"I just wondered if you know how well he is connected," Stephen said. He was not going to divulge too much information while Charles was present.

"No, I had my vices, but I kept away from men like Kersal. They seemed to be a little too close to being depraved for my liking. I don't think he is well connected; he may have plenty of visitors, but I think that is more to do with the services he is providing. I don't think he is well liked," Michael responded, making assumptions he hoped would be explained.

"You were more astute than I was then," Stephen responded with a grimace at admitting Michael was right about something."It seems he has started to become involved with something illegal."

"I would distance yourself from him. If he is stopped, he won't have any compunction about taking you or anyone else who is in his circle down with him," Michael said thoughtfully, for once not gloating over Stephen's compliment.

"I intend being the one to take him down!" Stephen replied, the frown and firm set of his mouth conveying the seriousness of the comment. He was a man who was rarely without a smile and, even if that smile was sometimes cynical and mocking, it was still a smile.

When the gentlemen rejoined the ladies, Charles moved across to Miss Fairfield and whispered in her ear. She stood immediately and spoke to Elizabeth. "Would you excuse me, please?" She asked her mistress.

"Yes, of course; you aren't working at this hour, are you Martha?" Elizabeth asked her long-time companion and member of staff.

"Mr Anderton would like to have a word with me. I shall retire afterwards if you have no other need for me," Martha responded.

"No, we don't require anything else, thank you. Good night, Martha, Charles. We shall see you tomorrow," Elizabeth replied easily.

The pair left the room and closed the door behind them. "I can see why you keep them on board," Stephen said approvingly at the obvious action. "I'm glad they've left, though; I don't want everyone knowing our business."

Charlotte flushed at Stephen's words. "What he means is my foolishness," she said honestly.

"They would be very discreet, but it would be harder to speak with a large audience," Elizabeth said. "Are we to know your scrape, my dear?"

Charlotte looked quickly at Stephen. "I haven't said a word; don't look daggers at me," he said holding up his hands. "Elizabeth is naturally nosey and, unfortunately, intelligent with it."

Elizabeth laughed instead of being offended. "Be careful, Charlotte; he was always very smooth."

Charlotte wondered about the pair, but could not dwell on it; she had to relay her story again to strangers. Her colour and discomfort increased as she explained herself, but she felt some comfort in the fact Stephen had sat himself next to her on the sofa. It was inappropriate for him to sit so near but, although he was not touching her, she felt comfort in his closeness. She did not elaborate on the way she had sought Stephen's help but told them she had appealed to Stephen, and he had helped her. Between them, they explained how she had been brought there to try and ensure that, if she *were* seen there would be no slur on her character.

Elizabeth and Michael both noticed the unusual action of Stephen sitting next to Charlotte while she was telling her story. He had not touched her but watched her and interjected if he thought she was struggling with the story. When Charlotte finished, he smiled at her in reassurance.

"Kersal is taking a big risk getting involved with such a scheme. They must have men at more than one school," Michael said, frowning.

"I'm not sure how many are involved," Charlotte responded. "I do know there are more than two though; the girls mentioned at least two schools. Apparently the money he is going to make is very good."

"All it will take is for them to pick the wrong girl, and they could be exposed. No one except the immoral would tolerate such an unsavoury scheme," Michael continued.

"He has already picked the wrong girl! I intend making my disgust known," Stephen said grimly, receiving an alarmed look from Charlotte.

"You could endanger yourself," Michael said. "There must be a lot of money being made, as Charlotte says, for it to be worth the trouble. You need to be wary Halkyn; he will not scruple to get rid of anyone who tries to interfere. Don't let your headstrong ways put you in danger; you are not infallible."

Stephen responded with his usual style. "Why, Dunham, are you saying you would miss me if I were done away with?"

"No, but my wife would be upset. Why, I have no idea, but as my wife's happiness is my main concern, I advise you to not get yourself killed," Michael said dryly.

Charlotte gasped and put her hand on Stephen's arm. "No! You cannot; you must not put yourself at risk because of me. I wish I had never asked for your help if the result will be your getting get hurt!" she said in panic.

Stephen covered her hand with his. "Have you so little faith in my abilities?" He asked. His tone was light, but for some reason it meant something to him that she have faith in him.

47

"I am fully appreciative of your capacity to get out of scrapes," Charlotte replied, gaining control of her panic. "I've seen you in action, remember? I fear you would be outnumbered, and in that situation you would be at risk."

"Would you be reassured if I said I will be careful?" Stephen asked.

"Yes, a little, but would you refrain from such actions if I asked you to?" Charlotte asked.

Stephen thought for a moment. "No, but I have considered it for a moment, which is more than I would do for anyone else."

"Well, if you are going to be completely foolish, why should I waste my time worrying?" Charlotte said, the tone of voice betraying the true feelings behind the words.

Stephen appreciated Charlotte's words and smiled at her. "Quite so. I couldn't have put it better myself."

Elizabeth thought it was prudent to intervene, "Before you get carried away with planning the revenge you're going to inflict on Baron Kersal, we need to plan how to help Charlotte."

Elizabeth's words focused the attention of the pair, and they each reluctantly let go of the other. "If you know of how I could get employment, I would be most grateful," Charlotte said.

Elizabeth noticed the firm set of Stephen's jaw, but spoke before he could say anything. "There will be no need for you to seek a position, and you may stay here for as long as you wish," she offered.

"Oh no!" Charlotte responded quickly. "I cannot rely on you for the rest of my days. I must be able to earn my living."

"I would not expect you to be here for the rest of your days!" Elizabeth said with a smile at the naïve comment. "With your looks, all we need to do is have a few dinner parties, and you would be married within the month!" She suppressed the smile that wanted to show itself at the look on Stephen's face. Her own refusal of his marriage proposal had not upset him as much as her last words had done. She was enjoying seeing such a betrayal of feelings, but she had doubts about his suitability for Charlotte.

Charlotte blushed at Elizabeth's words. "I would prefer to find honest work, so I can support myself," she replied quietly but firmly. She could not express that she had already been spoiled for others; she knew she could not have him, but the only man she wanted was Stephen. She did not want to be paraded around the local gentry.

Michael thought it best to interrupt. "You may stay as long as you wish; there is no point rushing into a decision," he said kindly to Charlotte. "In the meantime you do need to write to your uncle and let him know you are safe."

"I can't do that!" Charlotte exclaimed, the feelings of fear and panic overriding her previous reticence when speaking to Michael.

"He is your guardian," Michael explained with a smile. "He will be worried."

"I sent him a letter, saying I was eloping," Charlotte almost moaned. "He will think I'm a fallen woman; he will want nothing to do with me."

"I am sure if he knows the truth, he will understand," Elizabeth soothed. "Guardians have a way of worrying about their wards." She smiled at her husband.

"Especially when they have troublesome wards," Michael groaned in response, but there was no sting to his words.

Charlotte, misunderstanding the words sighed, "Yes, I have been very troublesome."

Stephen decided he'd better be the one to explain the situation to Charlotte, because Michael and Elizabeth were smiling at each other, and it was nauseating him. "Dunham was Elizabeth's guardian," he explained. "She was a complete pain, and he was too pig-headed to act on his feelings."

"I heard that, Stephen," Elizabeth said indignantly. "But your uncle must be worried Charlotte. Why don't you let Michael write to him and explain some of what has gone on and invite him to stay here for a few days? That way you can have time to think about what you really want to do, and the two of you will be able to talk things through."

Elizabeth's words were tempting to Charlotte; it would be a relief if she could sort things out with her uncle. He was her only relative and, although they would never be close, it did bother her to know he would be thinking badly of her. She was mulling over her options when Stephen intervened.

"I should be the one to contact him, not Dunham," he said abruptly.

"We are trying to prove Charlotte is still an innocent girl; a letter from you would suggest she is anything but. I'm sure in Lincolnshire they read the gossip pages, and your name is rarely out of them," drawled Michael, amused that his words caused an immediate angry response from Stephen.

"Why, you...." Stephen started, standing and moving towards Michael.

"Boys!" Elizabeth said firmly. "We shall not have childish behaviour from either of you, if you don't mind."

Stephen stopped and moved over to the fireplace, still fuming at Michael. "It's about time he learned to control his manners and his mouth," he muttered.

"He speaks some truth," Elizabeth said but raised her hand before Stephen could interrupt. "You are a single man, Stephen, and that is the fact of the matter. The letter would be more appropriate coming from Michael."

Stephen reluctantly agreed. It felt as if he was no longer in charge of helping Charlotte, and the feeling unsettled him.

Chapter 7

Charlotte felt more confident about her future when she woke. If Michael could smooth the waters with her uncle, perhaps she would not be cast off as she feared. She mulled over what her future could be while Maggie fixed her hair. She would not be forced to work, but she would be expected to marry. She had always wanted to marry and have a family; it was just that, over the last few days, something had happened that made her think no matter how many men she came into contact with, none would stir the feelings Lord Halkyn had. The reality was that Lords did not normally marry someone who was unconnected with a small or non-existent dowry. A pity when the thought of being loved by him for the rest of her life made her insides warm with pleasure.

She joined the small group in the dining room. She had chosen to wear a pale yellow day gown edged in lace with a scalloped hem. It was feminine and enhanced her colouring. She felt like a young lady rather than a school girl as she entered the room.

Charlotte paused in the doorway at the scene before her. Michael was sitting at the table reading the paper. Stephen was opposite Michael, tucking into a large plate full of food, and Elizabeth was helping herself to some of the bread on the side table. There was nothing remarkable about the scene apart from Elizabeth's attire: she was dressed in breeches, a shirt and braces.

Stephen noticed Charlotte's shocked expression and laughed, drawing the attention of the others. "If it is any consolation, my dear, your expression mirrors the one on my face when I entered the room!" he said easily to Charlotte.

She flushed, a little embarrassed, and felt every bit the naive school girl she was. Elizabeth noticed her embarrassment and responded to it. "Oh, I'm sorry; I've shocked you," she said moving across to Charlotte. "I should have warned you: when I work on the estate, I dress in breeches; I do forget not everyone is used to seeing me like this."

"I'm sorry, I'm not shocked; it's just...." Charlotte stammered, trying to make herself sound less inexperienced.

Michael came to her rescue. "My wife nearly gave Mr Anderton a heart attack the first time he saw her. You will now appreciate that I am married to an eccentric woman. I hope I have your sympathy," he said with a grimace. His expression turned to one of amusement as Elizabeth threw her napkin at him. "Eccentric and violent," he finished.

"Come and sit down Charlotte; help yourself to breakfast," Elizabeth said, purposely ignoring her husband."I forgot to warn you, and I do apologise. Now, I have work to do on the estate that would ruin that beautiful gown of yours. I suggest Stephen take you round the grounds in Michael's phaeton; the grounds are lovely at the moment. I'm looking forward to comparing all the seasons as time passes, but I have not been here for a full year as yet."

Stephen raised his eyebrows at Elizabeth. "And if I had other plans?" he asked. His words brought a deeper flush to Charlotte's cheeks, and he rectified his mistake quickly. "I was going to invite you for a walk Charlotte, but now that our hostess has interfered, you have a choice: phaeton or walk."

Charlotte had been mortified at Stephen's words, but was consoled by his offer. "A phaeton ride would be lovely, thank you."

The group separated after breakfast. Elizabeth promised to be free after lunch to show Charlotte around her house. Michael and Mr Anderton closed themselves in the study. Stephen led Charlotte out to the phaeton.

"I'm sure Dunham won't have sent his best horses around, but we will have an acceptable team to drive us about," Stephen said lightly.

"Any pair of horses would be acceptable to me; I've never been in a phaeton before," Charlotte said with a smile.

"That's what I have to keep reminding myself; you are an innocent in every way," Stephen responded more to himself, but the blush staining Charlotte's cheeks was gratifying. It might be cruel, but he did enjoy teasing her.

"I'm not as innocent I was, thanks to Baron Kersal," Charlotte responded, but regretted her words at Stephen's frown. "Although a lack of innocence does have its advantages when accosting drunken Lords."

Stephen grinned, "I wasn't that drunk. I managed to think up a plan."

"You did, and it was very convincing. I'm surprised you haven't been on the stage," Charlotte said, appreciating the ability to bring him away from the focus on Baron Kersal. The less she thought of anything to do with that man, the better.

"It was far too tempting to be involved with scrapes, both dramatic and farcical, off stage, my dear," Stephen responded.

They rode around the park until it felt as if they had explored every lane. Stephen had not visited before; Michael had not really held entertainments at his home in the years he had held the title. Stephen was impressed with the size and the obvious care of the park; it was clear Elizabeth and Michael worked hard.

Stephen made Charlotte laugh while they drove. She bantered with him at every opportunity, but her lack of experience caused her to blush. Previous to meeting Charlotte, Stephen would have thought a morning spent with a genteel young lady tedious at best. With Charlotte though, he found it refreshing and funny. The blushes frequently colouring her cheeks were endearing, and he returned to the house for lunch feeling relaxed and happy, an unusual emotion for such a cynical man.

Elizabeth, Michael, Miss Fairfield and Mr Anderton joined them for lunch. Michael suggested to Stephen they have a ride out during the afternoon to the far reaches of the estate. Stephen agreed but turned to Charlotte.

"Would you care to join us?" he asked.

"I thought Charlotte could help me this afternoon," Elizabeth said. She wanted to get to know Charlotte a little better without Stephen around, and she was also aware the pair should not spend too much time together. Stephen was a well-known rake and Charlotte an innocent; Elizabeth did not want any scandal for Charlotte while visiting Dunham House. Since becoming the Lady of the House, she did not want to bring any scandal on the Dunham name.

"Of course, I would be happy to help," Charlotte offered. She felt a little disappointed at not being able to spend more time with Stephen, but she could not be so rude as to refuse her hostess such a simple request.

The gentlemen left the ladies, and Elizabeth took Charlotte to her room. "Our time this afternoon will be to your benefit, I think," Elizabeth said indicating that Miss Fairfield should open the doors to her wardrobe. "I need to sort through my clothes, and I think I have a few dresses that would fit you perfectly."

"Oh, no!" Charlotte said quickly. "I cannot accept clothing; you are doing so much for me already."

Elizabeth sat on one of the chairs positioned in front of her fireplace. "I wasn't going to make it public knowledge quite yet, but it is out of necessity I am sorting my clothes. You see, I am hopefully going to give Michael an heir in a few months, and I have an appointment with my modiste to make me a new wardrobe. So, you will be doing me a good deed if you take some of my gowns."

Charlotte smiled broadly, "Oh, you are increasing! What wonderful news!"

Elizabeth replied with a grimace, "I've never quite liked the term 'increasing'; it just seems to emphasise the horrors that are to come. It shall be hard enough when I can no longer wear breeches during the day. My husband is indulgent, but even he would not tolerate me roaming around with breeches straining over a large stomach."

"Does Lord Halkyn know?" Charlotte asked, not quite sure why she needed to know just how close he was to Elizabeth.

"Stephen? No, he doesn't know. He would only ridicule us if we seemed pleased with our news," Elizabeth responded with a shake of her head.

"Why on earth would he ridicule you?" Charlotte asked, surprised.

"We will have a chat about it later; first let us sort out my wardrobe," Elizabeth replied. She wanted a little time to ponder what exactly to tell Charlotte about Stephen. It was obvious the girl was smitten with him, but Elizabeth never thought for one moment Stephen would have any long lasting attachment to someone like Charlotte. She did not want to see her young friend hurt and thought it might be less cruel if she knew exactly the type of man Stephen was.

The ladies enjoyed the afternoon using Charlotte as a doll to dress up. Elizabeth would decide on the dress, and Miss Fairfield would help Charlotte change. Accessories would be added and then a discussion about the outfit would occur between the three ladies. Not all of Elizabeth's dresses suited Charlotte; their colouring was different, so some were rejected, but at the end of the afternoon Charlotte had a substantially bigger wardrobe than she had at the beginning, even outnumbering Stephen's kind contributions.

They sat down to enjoy tea and delicate cakes, and Elizabeth raised the subject of Stephen. Miss Fairfield had left the pair to carry on with her own household tasks, and Elizabeth thought it appropriate they have the conversation while they were alone.

"You asked why Stephen would ridicule us over our pleasure at having a family," Elizabeth started.

"Yes, it seems such a strange thing to do at such a happy time," Charlotte replied, nibbling on a fancy.

"He wouldn't do it to be hurtful, but it is his way," Elizabeth continued.

"He said he is cynical about the world." Charlotte contemplated what Stephen had hinted at to her during their short acquaintance.

"I suppose he is a product of his upbringing or the society he lives in, but he has some fixed ideas about love and marriage," Elizabeth said, trying to be careful with what she said.

"You must know him quite well," Charlotte responded, trying and failing to keep the jealous tone from her voice.

Elizabeth smiled; it seemed like only yesterday she had been in a similar position to Charlotte, trying desperately to hide her feelings about the man she loved and failing miserably. She decided the only way to continue was to be honest. "Charlotte, my dear, what I am going to tell you, I am telling in the hope in the future you will make decisions right for you," she said.

"Go on," Charlotte encouraged.

"I came out very late; I was sent to my guardian, Michael, three years after I should have had my first season. I didn't want anything other than to be able to have an estate and manage it, but I hadn't considered falling in love." Elizabeth remembered her encounters with Michael with a wistful smile.

"You fell in love with Lord Dunham?" Charlotte asked, hoping she would receive the answer she wanted.

"Yes, I did and, luckily for me, he fell in love with me," Elizabeth replied. "But I hadn't realised what demons Michael was struggling with. They don't matter now, but at the time they were very real to him. As a consequence he encouraged other suitors; he thought it would be better if I didn't marry him."

"Why would he do that?" Charlotte asked in disbelief.

"Yes, I have often wondered that," Elizabeth said wryly. "He is a principled man and was acting in a way he thought was best for me. One of the men he encouraged was Stephen."

"Oh." Charlotte replied, her heart sinking.

"I wasn't a huge hit with Society," Elizabeth continued. "The truth be told, it was a nightmare; I hated it, but I think Stephen saw I was different from the others. He was very often faced with women who simpered around him."

"So he fell in love with you as well?" Charlotte asked in a flat voice.

"Oh, goodness me, no!" Elizabeth exclaimed. "This is what I am trying to tell you; he proposed marriage to me, but he doesn't believe in love within a marriage. Actually, I don't think he believes love exists at all. All he wanted was someone whom he thought he would get on with tolerably well, and he even offered to let me continue with my plans and run an estate and suggested we meet up occasionally to ensure the Halkyn line continued," Elizabeth said diplomatically.

"Oh, my goodness! That wouldn't be a marriage; that would be hell!" Charlotte exclaimed.

"Yes, although I did consider it for a while. I realised how unprotected I was, and his name would have offered the protection I needed; it would have been, to some extent, the life I wanted. The problem was, although I hadn't set-out to fall in love, that was what had happened, and second best was just not good enough," Elizabeth explained. "I refused Stephen before I knew Michael could overcome his demons; in fact, I didn't even know about them at that point."

"I see," Charlotte said.

"I want you to understand what type of a person Stephen is. He is very likeable, he is funny and charming; it is no wonder he has women throwing themselves at him. There is a darker side though; he said he would try to be faithful, but he could not give me any guarantees. I did not know how that would have affected me but, believe me, if you are in love with a man and suspect he is not being faithful, it could destroy you," Elizabeth said gently.

"I have not hidden my feelings well, have I?" Charlotte said with tears in her eyes.

"Perhaps I see what you are feeling because I know what it is like," Elizabeth said kindly. "If it is any consolation, I know Stephen likes you; he would not have made any effort at all to help you if he didn't."

"Some consolation, I suppose," Charlotte said with a rueful smile. She wiped her eyes quickly and pulled herself together. "I'm not very good at choosing eligible young men. I think it would be best if my uncle came and locked me away."

Elizabeth laughed, "Well perhaps not that! Don't dismiss the whole male population just because of two characters."

Chapter 8

Charlotte was quiet as Maggie helped her dress for dinner. She normally chatted to the maid, but this time she had a lot to think about. Elizabeth's words had been taken in the spirit they had been given. She was no longer jealous of Elizabeth's relationship with Stephen; she saw now there was nothing to be jealous of. She could see the truth in what Elizabeth had said. Stephen had hinted at his jaded outlook on life; it seemed he was telling the truth and not just saying things to be shocking.

She sighed; she needed a boost of confidence tonight. She looked at her dresses. "I shall have the emerald green one please, Maggie," she instructed.

Maggie paused and then swallowed. "It's not appropriate, Miss Webster," the maid said quietly.

Charlotte knew the dress was not appropriate for a girl just out of the schoolroom. It was a deep green colour not the expected pale shades for a debutante. The neckline was a little daring too, with its ruffled bodice, drawing attention to the breast area. Elizabeth had given it to her for the future; Charlotte knew that: but perhaps it was because she wanted Stephen to want her as much as she did him, or maybe it was just something to hide behind. Whatever her reasoning, she was determined to wear it.

"That is the dress I need tonight Maggie," Charlotte said firmly. Maggie just nodded and helped dress her mistress. The maid had done her duty in offering advice; she could do no more.

The dress suited Charlotte; it brought out the green in her eyes and warmed her skin tone. Maggie had dressed her hair in a simple bun, which on other women could seem harsh, but for Charlotte it appeared elegant. She entered the drawing room with a fluttering stomach but was determined to brazen it out.

Michael looked at his wife in question, but she chose to ignore his glance. They both glanced at Stephen and, although neither of them knew what Charlotte's motivation had been while choosing the dress, they could see it had scored a hit with their friend.

Stephen sucked in his breath when Charlotte entered the room. From the first moment he had seen her, he thought her beautiful but, dressed as she was, she literally took his breath away. His reaction was physical and something else. The tightening of his groin usually occurred when Charlotte was around, but he was a healthy male who reacted to a beautiful woman, and he saw no problem with his healthy male response. Something else had happened though; he was almost overwhelmed by a feeling of possessiveness, which he fought not to act on. He wanted to stride across the room and cover her with a shawl, to not allow anyone but him to see anything but the most minimal amount of her body.

As he watched her move and speak to Elizabeth, he was filled with sadness, another emotion he was unaccustomed to feeling. He could see the woman she was going to become, elegant and beautiful. She would be married to some young popinjay who would not appreciate what he had. Stephen would be left to watch as some dandy turned her head. No, he would not watch, he decided; he would remove himself from her society once Elizabeth started to introduce her to the local gentry. Stephen might not be able to overcome the fact he was too old for Charlotte, but he certainly was not going to stand by and watch her be courted by the young fools who lived in the area. He took a deep breath; it was time he started to plan his return to town.

*

Michael entered his wife's bed chamber after her maid left. He spent most of his time in her room, only using his dressing room to change. It was how they wanted their life to be, as close as possible. It was a comfortable room, decorated in a style they both liked in blues and golds. The bed hangings and curtains had been made to compliment the wallpaper. Elizabeth had always said it was a colour Michael could feel comfortable with; he had retorted any room with her in it was a room where he could be comfortable.

He walked over to Elizabeth's dressing table and placed his hands gently on her shoulders. "Now, what mischief have you been up to with our young guest?" he asked, looking at her through the mirror.

Elizabeth sighed, "I know, she certainly made an impact with that dress didn't she? I thought Stephen was going to jump across the room to get to her!" she replied.

"I hope you are not encouraging her in any wild notions," Michael chided.

"For once I have done the opposite," Elizabeth explained. "I told her exactly what Stephen's opinions were of love and marriage. I thought I was helping to prevent her breaking her heart over him, but it's obvious she is besotted."

"I think you should perhaps have left those things unsaid," Michael said gently.

"I don't want to see her hurt!" Elizabeth responded defensively. "She is a girl who has already had a rough experience; I didn't want Stephen to hurt her as well."

"I understand that, but it's just..." Michael pondered.

"What?" his wife asked, a little annoyed at being challenged.

"I've never seen Halkyn like he is with Charlotte. Did you notice him on the first evening? He sat next to her, giving her support when she told her story. When has he ever done something so openly selfless? I think he may not be as untouched by Charlotte as he would have us believe," Michael said thoughtfully.

"I often see him watching her," Elizabeth admitted. "In fact during our meals, he looks more at her than anyone or anything else."

"Yes, he has never troubled himself over a woman before, so perhaps he is as besotted with her, as Charlotte is with him," Michael agreed.

"What should we do to help them?" Elizabeth asked eager to help her young friend.

"Absolutely nothing," Michael responded, taking Elizabeth into his arms. "You have far too much to do for your husband."

Elizabeth was carried over to her bed and kissed to the point where all thoughts of Stephen and Charlotte were forgotten.

*

Stephen had decided he was going to leave Dunham House and return to London. Then he decided he would wait until after breakfast, but then he decided he perhaps should wait until Charlotte's uncle arrived. She might need his help; her uncle was obviously not the best to decide what Charlotte should do with her future. He would probably agree to her scheme to find employment since he had all but abandoned her at the school. Yes, he would stay until the uncle arrived.

Stephen's internal arguments happened at the same time as a change between himself and Charlotte occurred. He did not understand why or how, but there was a distinct change of atmosphere and contact between the two. Over the following six days Charlotte avoided him whenever possible. If he suggested a ride, she had arranged to go for a walk with Miss Fairfield. If he offered to take her in the phaeton, she found the weather too chilly. If he offered to play a game of chess, cards, or sing while she played the piano, she had a headache and would prefer to read.

She was avoiding him. He should have been relieved; he was leaving after all, but he was annoyed. What had he ever done that would make her want to avoid him? He had only ever helped her; why, he had in fact gone out of his way to help her. With Michael busy, Stephen was left to ponder and fume alone. He would ride out to try and get rid of his dark mood, but the moment he returned to the house and heard Charlotte's laughter or even just her voice, he was in an even darker mood than before.

On the sixth morning Stephen could not stand it any longer. He had tried to persuade Charlotte to join him for a walk, but she said she was intending to read. Not one for inactivity, Stephen decided he was going to get to the bottom of the change in her behaviour.

Charlotte entered the library and closed the door quietly. She leaned against the door, closing her eyes, her nerves stretched to the limit. Avoiding Stephen in order to protect herself was torture.

"Feeling unwell my dear?" came the slightly sarcastic drawl from Stephen.

Charlotte physically jumped at the sound of his voice and flushed deep pink. She had not seen him sprawled in a chair in front of the fireplace. How she had missed seeing him she would never know. Her nerves were usually so in tune to his location it scared her.

"You should have given some warning you were in the room!" she snapped, her shock making her respond more sharply than she would normally have done.

"Why? So you can run away again?" Stephen asked. "I'm afraid I'm getting a little tired of your bad manners, my dear."

Charlotte flushed again, mainly because she had been behaving badly, but it was through self-preservation rather than bad manners. "You consider I am behaving badly because I don't want to spend every moment in your company?" She responded tartly. "Surely, even you are not so vain?"

Stephen blinked; her words hurt him far more than he would ever admit. "I seem to recall there was a time when you were desperate for my company." He stood and walked across to her.

Charlotte stiffened and leaned into the door, as if willing it to allow her to pass through and back into the hallway. "I have already thanked you and will always be grateful for your help," she admitted. "But you will be departing from here soon; I would have thought you'd welcome the release of responsibility for me."

Stephen looked at her; normally he would have welcomed it. Nay, he would never have offered help in the first place, but it always came down to the fact that it was *her*. He wanted to spend time with her. "There is no need to make our time here tedious; we can still enjoy ourselves," he drawled, maintaining the air of someone who did not care by sounding lecherous.

63

His words confirmed what Elizabeth had said, and Charlotte fought to suppress her feelings of disappointment. Being told someone would never be interested in you was less hurtful than having it confirmed. "You do make the most preposterous suggestions!" Charlotte said with disgust.

Although Stephen had meant to be cynical and condemning, he was quick to realise Charlotte was referring to something beyond their conversation. "May I enquire to what other preposterous suggestions you refer?" he asked coldly.

Charlotte was a little overwhelmed by his tone and the cold look in his eyes. She had seen cynicism and derision in his look previously, but it had never been aimed at her; this time it was different. The lines around his mouth were pronounced, and his frown cast deep grooves along his forehead. She took a breath to steady her fluttering insides.

"I have heard from Elizabeth your opinions of love and marriage," she replied defiantly.

For some reason, Stephen could have happily murdered Elizabeth at that moment, but as always, he gave what was expected of him. "And what may I ask was wrong with my proposal? I was giving the woman everything she said she was looking for. If she wanted to chase love like some foolish moon-struck chit, that wasn't anything to do with my proposal. I was honest with her and did not try and flatter her with false words. Some would applaud my honesty."

Charlotte could not resist the urge to probe. "Do you not want to be loved?"

Stephen fought the feelings her words stirred; he would not show the foolishness he had so often condemned. "What would be the benefit? I come and go as I please. I live my life exactly as I want. I have no one telling me they don't approve of my behaviour, that I can't have a mistress if I want one. I do not have to suffer tears and tantrums, which I believe is all that love is," he said bitterly.

Charlotte was shocked but maintained her composure. "How can you say that when you are staying in the house of people who are so obviously in love and happy?"

"They are happy now, but it won't last," Stephen responded tartly.

"Well, I hope your mistresses can keep you warm as you age, because otherwise your bed is going to become a cold and lonely place!" Charlotte said bitterly. She would normally never have uttered such words, but she had felt such jealousy at the thought of Stephen with someone else when he had mentioned having a mistress, she just had to hit out in any way she could.

Stephen used the jealous words to his advantage. He was angry and hurt, something he was not used to feeling, and he needed to be back in control. He moved and placed his arms on the door, either side of Charlotte. "Oh, I think I will have a warm bed for many years to come, don't you?" he whispered, letting his breath tickle Charlotte's ear.

Charlotte sucked in her breath; it was the closest they had been since the first night they met, and the memories of their kisses flooded back to her. She felt her face burning and fought to steady her insides. "Even mistresses have limitations," she said, but her voice was breathless. His eyes were an intense blue, something she had not seen when they had kissed in the dark, and now she felt as if she were being pulled into him.

Stephen was gratified he was having an effect; at least he was not the only one who was suffering. He should stop, if he was a decent man he would stop, but he did not want to, and at the moment he felt anything but decent. "But you have had a taste of what I can offer. Do you not think they would be a little tempted? Are you not a little tempted?" He whispered, his lips brushing hers ever so gently.

Charlotte closed her eyes at his words. All she could feel was his breath and the gentle feel of his lips. He was so gentle there was almost no contact, but it was as if her every nerve was feeling every touch.

"Are you tempted, my little tiger?" Stephen whispered again, a smile playing around his lips, taking away the cynical sneer that was his usual expression.

"Yes," Charlotte moaned, giving in to the feelings he was stirring, the feelings he always stirred. She was too inexperienced to be able to remain firm in the face of such temptation.

Stephen groaned in appreciation at her admission and covered her lips with his. He had not realised how much he wanted to kiss her until his lips brushed hers. At that point he could not have pulled away even if he had a gun to his head. He felt as if he fitted against her, against her mouth perfectly. He had enjoyed her kisses on that first night but, now that he had come to know her, to want her, the kisses were intense beyond anything that had happened before.

Charlotte welcomed his mouth, opening her own for his exploration. It did not matter that he did not love her: he wanted her; she could feel how much as he pressed against her. She pushed against him in return, longing for the feel of him, not knowing what to do, but being guided by his appreciative moans. She wrapped her arms around his neck, no longer leaning into the door, but leaning against him for support.

Stephen let his hands wander. He should behave like a gentleman, but he wanted to drive her as wild as she was driving him. The feel of her fingers pulling at his hair made him want to take her there in the library. His hands explored her back, her bottom, her waist, the edge of her breast. He wanted to touch her skin and was moving to unfasten her dress when noise came from the hallway.

They sprang apart, both taking deep breaths and looking flushed. Neither said a word as they listened. Stephen was the first to collect himself, straightening his waistcoat. "It appears your uncle has arrived, my dear."

"My uncle? Now?" Charlotte exclaimed, her thoughts incoherent. She could not think while she had to concentrate so much on breathing and standing upright. Kissing Stephen seemed to affect her legs, turning them into a substance that could not support her.

Stephen smiled a genuine smile. "You have a moment or two to gather yourself," he said kindly.

Before either expected it, Michael entered the library and looked at the pair. He did not look pleased to find them behind a closed door and without a chaperone, but he pulled the door closed behind him to shield the occupants of the room.

"Your uncle is here, Charlotte," he said abruptly. "Elizabeth has taken him to the morning room for refreshment. I suggest you join them there after you have fixed your hair."

Charlotte flushed and left the room, muttering apologies. Stephen turned on Michael. "There was no need to embarrass the girl!" he snapped.

"There was every need," Michael responded. "Her uncle has arrived, and she hopes he will accept her back into his family. How would it have looked if we had come into the library? How would she have explained she had been compromised, not once but twice?"

"She hasn't been compromised; it was a kiss, that's all," Stephen said dismissively, but the kiss had meant more to him than he would ever admit. He ran his hand through his hair and let out a slow breath, trying to gain internal control. He might sound flippant, but he was feeling anything but inside. Her kisses affected him more than anyone else's had ever done, and he did not know how to deal with the emotions racing through his body at regular intervals since he had met her.

"There is no such thing as 'that's all' when you are kissing an innocent, Halkyn; we both know that. I hope you know what game you're playing," Michael said shaking his head and walking out of the room. He was in no mood to play word games with Halkyn while Charlotte's future was under discussion.

67

Chapter 9

By the time Charlotte joined them, Michael had explained to Mr Webster what had happened to Charlotte more fully than his letter had said. Her uncle was a serious man, greying, with clear grey eyes, in his fifties with no resemblance to Charlotte's fair hair and green eyes. He believed Michael's account, given seriously but honestly about a young girl being the prey of an organised, sinister ring.

Charlotte entered the room hesitantly. She had no idea how her uncle would greet her. She flushed when she saw Stephen already seated. His concern for her had overridden any sense that he should stay away from the interview with her uncle.

Charlotte looked at her relation uncertainly. "Uncle?" she asked timidly.

"My foolish girl," came the reassuring response. "At least we do not have to deal with an imprudent marriage, which your letter seemed to suggest," Mr Webster said, standing to greet his niece. He was a solemn man, but had been convinced by Michael's words that his niece was not at fault.

"Oh, I am so sorry," Charlotte said sincerely. "I was so silly, listening to such empty words and believing them; I have never regretted anything so much in my life. I will never be so foolish again."

"I should hope not," Mr Webster said. He noticed the look that passed between Stephen and Michael, a look not particularly amenable on Michael's part. "So, this gentleman rescued you?"

"Yes, that's correct. I don't know what I would have done if he had not," Charlotte said, barely able to look at Stephen without flushing.

"It must have been a trying time," Mr Webster said, encouraging his niece to talk about her experience, a calculating look in his eye.

"It was. Stephen—Lord Halkyn promised he would get me out of there no matter what," Charlotte said.

"Where did you go afterwards?"

Charlotte noticed both Stephen and Michael stiffen in their seats, but she could not lie to her uncle. "We returned to his house, but he had his butler assign me a maid, and she never left my side. There was nowhere else we could go!" Charlotte said a little defensively. She was aware they had breached what was seen as acceptable behaviour.

"I expect you travelled here in style, not on the stage?" Mr Webster asked, a grim set to his lips.

Charlotte faltered, "Well, yes, uncle, we travelled in Lord Halkyn's coach, but Maggie was with me every time we stopped in an inn. It was all done respectfully."

"I see," Mr Webster said. "And what is Lord Halkyn going to do now?" he asked.

Everyone was immediately on the alert, particularly Stephen. "I don't understand your meaning, sir," Stephen said, calmly enough, but he was watching Mr Webster carefully.

"I am no fool, Lord Halkyn. I have been with my niece barely five minutes and found she has managed to jump from one scrape to another!" Mr Webster said, his manner had changed from forgiving uncle to cold, affronted relative in an instant.

"I have not!" Charlotte said indignantly. "There was nothing else that could be done. As Stephen said, his parents did not provide him with a sister who would have provided complete respectability. Lady Dunham was the nearest thing he could think of."

"He must have been desperate," Elizabeth said apologetically, but there was a twitch of amusement to her lips.

"Madam, I am not finding anything in this situation to amuse me," Mr Webster said sternly.

Elizabeth apologised, and Michael intervened, sounding serious, but there was a twinkle of laughter in his eyes. "I can assure you, we have taken Charlotte's plight seriously and have tried to ensure respectability."

"Thank you, Lord Dunham, but I'm afraid the damage was already done by the time Charlotte arrived here. Travelling across country with Lord Halkyn is not acceptable, and I insist Lord Halkyn do the honourable thing and marry my niece."

Charlotte's eyes flew to Stephen and saw the colour drain from his face. His reaction mortified her and confirmed that, although he might want her, he had no long lasting feelings for her. She reacted immediately.

"No!" She said far more loudly than she had intended.

"I beg your pardon?" Mr Webster said, surprised at his niece's outburst.

"There is no need; it was all perfectly respectable," Charlotte insisted. "Lord Halkyn was the perfect gentleman."

"You travelled for three days with an unmarried man without a proper chaperone. That is not respectable in itself. You must be married; it is the only option you both have!" Mr Webster insisted belligerently.

Charlotte had a sneaking suspicion this was all too convenient for her uncle, but she would not let it happen. "Uncle, if you force this on Lord Halkyn, we are no better than Baron Kersal," she said seriously.

"Don't be ridiculous child," Mr Webster dismissed her. "They kidnapped you and were forcing you into a marriage with a stranger. Lord Halkyn undertook the journey knowing there might be consequences. I am sure he is not so naive."

"He was hardly in a position to do anything else," Charlotte said forcefully. "No one, with any gentlemanly feeling, could have left me in that place. His reward for his kindness cannot be to then force him into marriage. That hardly seems fair; he is condemned if he left me and condemned if he didn't."

Stephen had been quiet throughout the exchange. He had experienced a range of emotions: initial horror at the suggestion

70

had very quickly turned into acceptance. Why not let himself be forced into marriage with Charlotte? He had to marry, and he liked Charlotte a little too much for comfort sometimes, but he was sure, with marriage, his feelings would settle down. It was obvious her uncle was not concerned with the age difference. He decided it was time to intervene.

"Does the idea of marriage to me repulse you so?" Stephen asked Charlotte, trying to sound light-hearted.

"See," Mr Webster interrupted, "Lord Halkyn is not averse to marriage. It is the perfect solution Charlotte; don't be such a simpleton."

Charlotte had been surprised at Stephen's words. She had to know the reason behind such a change in his usual musings about marriage. "Why would you agree to marry me? The situation is not what you anticipated happening when you agreed to help me," she asked, moving towards him.

Stephen regretted speaking as all eyes turned to him. His usual flippancy came to the surface. "We were fortunate we weren't seen, although we could have been; we just don't know as yet. I have to get married sometime, so this is the perfect solution; your reputation is secured, and I get myself a wife."

"A perfect solution!" Mr Webster said clapping his hands.

Charlotte had never turned her gaze away from Stephen while he spoke. Her eyes had widened and then filled with tears, but when she spoke, her voice was firm. "No," she said,

"What?" Mr Webster exploded.

"No, not like this," Charlotte said, blinking back tears and forcing herself to not waver.

Her look of pain hit Stephen like a kick in the groin. He tried to lighten the mood. "Would it be that bad, Charlotte?" He asked, willing her to say yes to his proposal, but refusing to offer anything more to try to persuade her.

"I cannot marry you this way. I need.... I want....Not this way," she stumbled over her words, the tears starting to fall. "Please excuse me." She fled from the room.

There was an uncomfortable moment of quiet broken by an outburst from Stephen. "What is wrong with women? They want perfection when it doesn't exist!" he exploded before storming out of the room.

"Well, I have never seen anything like it before. I cannot understand what has got into Charlotte at all!" Mr Webster said angrily.

"Can you not?" Elizabeth said shortly.

Michael intervened. "I think the whole episode has taken its toll on your niece. We forget how young she is because she has such a mature way about her."

"Yes, but she has just refused a perfectly good marriage proposal, showing exactly what a foolish child she is. I should have sent her to a stricter school or arranged a marriage for her myself; then there would have been none of this."

Elizabeth and Michael exchanged a look full of sympathy for Charlotte. "Mr Webster, you are welcome to stay as long as you wish as our guest, but we would like to offer an invitation for an extended visit to Charlotte. My wife has become very attached to her and has plans to introduce her to local Society. I feel it won't be long before a marriage proposal from Lord Halkyn is irrelevant," Michael said smoothly.

Mr Webster considered the offer for a few moments before standing. "Thank you for your kind invitation. I will not stay; I have acquaintances in the next town whom I would like to call on before my return home. I would appreciate leaving Charlotte in your care for a visit. I can't deny being responsible for her over the years has been a trial, and today I thought that trial might come to an end. With your help I hope she does secure a reasonable marriage; she has very little dowry, so I have realistic expectations on what level of gentleman she would attract. It appears from her outburst she does not wish to be a lady. If you are happy to take the responsibility of marrying off a girl without fortune, I shall happily leave her in your care," Mr Webster said, at the same time being led to the door by Michael.

Michael returned to the room alone a few moments later. He smiled at the expression on his wife's face; she was obviously gritting her teeth. "What an insufferable man!" she ground out. "Could he have treated Charlotte any worse?"

"He did have a way about him, didn't he?" Michael said ruefully.

"That poor girl: no wonder she was susceptible to the charms of the footman; anyone would be preferable to going back home to an uncle like that!" Elizabeth fumed. "And what about Stephen? Could he have offered for her hand in any worse way?"

"Probably, but he would have had to try extremely hard," Michael replied. "He is being a fool; I just hope he realises it in time."

*

Michael found Stephen in his study, swirling brandy in a glass between his fingers. "Helping yourself to my best brandy?" Michael asked, pouring himself a large drink.

"If this is your best, god help you," Stephen muttered.

"Ah, good. Charles must have hidden the expensive stuff," Michael said, sitting opposite Stephen. "I think her uncle came with the intention of trying to marry her off."

"Yes, you were probably the first candidate!" Stephen said bitterly.

"I agree; then finding out I was married, he moved on to the next available person: you," Michael said gently.

"And I foolishly obliged him, for all the good it did me," came the bitter response.

"To be fair to the man, I think most guardians want their wards to marry," Michael said thinking back to his experience.

"When did you realise you had fallen in love with Elizabeth?" Stephen asked.

Michael smiled at the question. "It probably took me two breaths before I was completely smitten, but months of pain before I admitted it. I hope you are not going to be as foolish."

Stephen laughed bitterly, "The great Lord Dunham admitting he made a mistake; I never thought I'd see the day. It is different for me, I am not smitten."

"I see the way you look at her; I see the way you are with her. Don't let the actions of her foolish uncle stop you losing the person you love," Michael urged.

Stephen stood and placed the glass on the small side table. "Have you never wanted someone? What's love got to do with it? She is attractive, and I've spent a lot of time with her, and I forgot myself; but that doesn't mean I love her. Which as it turns out is a good thing: as you heard the girl; she doesn't want me, and I will never beg for anyone to be my wife. I think I shall return to town; there is a bit of muslin I wish to reacquaint myself with. I think it will be best all round if I leave this afternoon," Stephen said and left the room.

Michael sighed and shook his head. He wondered why people never seemed to be able to accept sound advice, failing to remember the amount of times he had ignored equally sound advice when he was acting irrationally. Time had conveniently erased some of the conversations his sister had tried to have with him, which had ended in his refusal to act on his feelings towards Elizabeth. Michael was no different in the fact that it was easier to give advice than to receive it.

Chapter 10

Stephen came down the stairs: he had taken his leave of Michael and Elizabeth; his aim was to leave as soon as he possibly could. His carriage waited for him. The butler handed him his gloves and cane, and he nodded his thanks.

"Tell my coachman I shall be with him shortly," he instructed, before turning towards the staircase. He looked up; he had known she was there. "Charlotte," he said curtly.

Charlotte was flushed and her eyes were red rimmed, but she started to move down the stairs. "You are leaving?" she asked.

"My presence is appreciated more in town; I tire of the country and confined society so easily," Stephen replied coldly, his mouth set in a grim line. He fixed his gloves, barely looking at her. To do so would weaken his anger; she seemed so vulnerable with her tear stained face and wide, sad eyes.

Charlotte winced. "I'm sorry," she said simply.

"What for?" Stephen asked, pausing and raising an eyebrow. He looked at her with derision, something he had never done before.

"For wanting to marry for love," Charlotte replied uncertainly. It sounded weak and feeble in her own ears.

"We may yet meet again," Stephen said coldly. "When I am old and cold because my mistresses don't want anything more to do with me as you so kindly pointed out," he said bitterly. "You may be equally as old and cold because you have failed to find someone who loves you and accepts your lack of fortune."

Charlotte's eyes flashed, "I may not have money, but I can offer love, fidelity and loyalty!" she snapped.

Stephen hid the pain the words caused. "And I am sure you will be able to secure a large house and happy life with those things alone. Good bye, tiger." He bent and kissed her lips quickly but too briefly before walking out of the door.

Charlotte stood alone in the hall, wondering why her legs were not running after the only man she could ever love and why her voice was not screaming, begging him to stay. Instead, at the sound of the carriage moving away, she turned and walked listlessly upstairs.

*

Walter showed no surprise at his master's unexpected return. He was used to the unusual with Lord Halkyn. What took him by surprise was his master's appearance. He looked as if he had not stopped for days: he was unshaven, his clothes were creased, and he was obviously in a foul mood.

Walter made no comment but ordered a bath, organised food and offered the best wine. There was no banter during the evening, an unusual occurrence, but Walter was wise enough to wait until he could find out what had unsettled the usually self-controlled Lord.

The reality of the situation was that Stephen was hurting, and he did not know what to do to stop the pain. He had offered for Elizabeth, but he had not felt anything for her, apart from liking her of course. He had not been disappointed or hurt when she had refused him. In fact, he had decided it might have been the best decision; he wanted someone to look at him the way she looked at Dunham. The way Charlotte looked at him. When he offered marriage to her he had presumed she would accept as her uncle seemed pleased enough. Yet again, though, he had foolishly offered for a woman who wanted declarations of love. Why they insisted on that when he had seen so often that words meant nothing. Time and time again he met married men in the more seedy establishments. They would have their fill of the women there and then go home and tell their wives they loved them and only them.

He supposed Charlotte would not know this; she was very young after all. He cursed himself; he should never have offered for her because of that fact alone. The problem was, he liked her: more than liked her, but it was irrelevant; she would not have him, and he tried to maintain his bitterness towards her. She might never get another offer: she had no dowry, and she had no connections; she was a fool to turn him down, he fumed.

76

Stephen had to admit eventually to himself he was the fool; she was beautiful, funny and had an air about her that would make men want to protect her. Look at how he had reacted to her pleas for help. He had never responded to anyone else in that way before.

He groaned; it was no use: he would not be able to forget her in a hurry. Especially as he was determined to honour his word and bring Baron Kersal to book. He rose early the following morning and made his way to the Bow Street offices. He had never had need to use the service before, but the officers had a good reputation, and he did not know how else he would find help in bringing down the Baron.

He was led into a small office at the rear of a larger one. He had expected the office to be all hustle and bustle, but there was no one about. There were only a small number of Bow Street Officers; he wondered if they were on duty. He hoped they would be able to help him.

He was led into a back office. This was the office of the head of the service; he would not have spoken to anyone else. The gentleman who sat in the office was around fifty years of age. He was tall and slim, slightly stooped, as if the responsibility he held weighed heavily on his shoulders. The smile he offered in greeting, though, was genuine and warm.

"Good morning, Lord Halkyn; to what do we owe the pleasure?" he asked in a more gentle voice than his appearance would warrant.

"Good morning, Mr Frost. Thank you for this interview. I have a problem I need help with," Stephen said, sitting in the chair opposite the desk.

"That's what we're here for, My Lord," came the quiet response. Mr Frost listened while Stephen told him the story from the moment he had been pulled into the room by Charlotte until she was safely deposited in the country. He excluded all the information about the marriage proposal. He decided it was acceptable to omit it; it had no bearing on the case.

"So, you are sure she is safe?" Mr Frost asked.

"Yes, she is now under the protection of good friends and her uncle. She should be safe; Kersal appears to only want girls who are no longer of interest to their families!" Stephen said with disgust.

"It is a sad state of affairs, but I feel Baron Kersal will have the pick of girls across the country. There are many without fortunes who are an inconvenience to their families, but at least Miss Webster was fortunate to find you," Mr Frost said, while thinking the problem through.

"I want to send a clear message out that this is not acceptable," Stephen said forcefully. "I am no angel, but I have never preyed on innocents." He pushed aside the image of Charlotte's tilted head before he kissed her. That was different; she had obviously been in total control. She made that perfectly clear when she refused his marriage proposal.

"Umm, I have two men who have not come into contact with the higher ranks of society; they are very good but not well known. A few of my others may be recognisable to some of the men who frequent this household. I am willing to set one to follow Baron Kersal and see what information he can collect. The other I want you to introduce to the Baron as a friend," Mr Frost said.

"I'm not going back to that place! I will kill him if I see his weasel face again!" Stephen exploded.

Mr Frost smiled slightly at the outburst. "I'm presuming the young lady would not stand as a witness against Baron Kersal?" he asked.

"Of course not. She is an unconnected girl. Who would believe her word against Kersal's?" Stephen sneered.

"Exactly," Mr Frost agreed pleasantly. "In which case, we have to gather evidence that will ensure a conviction. You do realise the consequences for the Baron could be serious?"

"Don't worry: I won't lose courage; I hope he swings for what he is doing!" Stephen said without hesitation.

"In that case I need you to adopt Peters as your acquaintance. Introduce him; get him access to the house. Once he is accepted, there will be no need for you to continue going," Mr Frost assured him.

"Good."

"I shall send Peters around to you as soon as he is available."

"I shall await his visit. I bid you good day," Stephen said with a slight bow. He strode out of the office and walked back to his house.

When he eventually arrived home, he still had not consoled himself that he would have to go and spend time with Baron Kersal and his cronies. He did not analyse whether or not it was that which upset him or the fact he would be returning to the house in which his world had been turned upside down by Charlotte's kiss.

Walter opened the door before Stephen knocked, as efficient as ever. He noticed the frown on Stephen's face but made no comment.

"Walter, I am out to anyone today and for the foreseeable future. I will only see a man named Peters when he arrives. I shall be in my study. Bring up a bottle of brandy. The good stuff, please!" Stephen said sharply, handing the butler his hat and gloves.

"As you wish My Lord. There is already a decanter of brandy in the study, My Lord," Walter informed his master, noting that mid-afternoon was not the usual time his master started drinking.

"That will not be nearly enough," Stephen replied. "Bring another bottle."

"Certainly sir," Walter replied, a frown appearing only when he had turned away from his master.

*

Five hours later, when there had been no sight or sound from the study, Walter made an excuse and entered the room to check on his employer. He had offered food earlier, but it had been turned away with disgust. Only brandy would be accepted, and the butler had retreated.

Stephen was sprawled across the chair in front of the fireplace, one leg over the arm. He held the brandy decanter, no sign of a glass. His cravat and waistcoat were thrown on the floor, his boots kicked off—no easy task without a valet to help. The ever calm butler had to suppress a groan; something was obviously wrong: his employer had never been in such a state.

"Walter, leave me alone!" Stephen slurred after a few moments of peering at the figure in the doorway.

"I just wanted to see if you required anything, My Lord?" Walter said calmly.

"A life without women would be a start. You have my permission to get rid of them all; let's see how good your skills really are," Stephen tried to sound bitter, but his words were so slurred they sounded pitiful.

Walter was irrationally pleased at his employer's words. He had never shown any serious interest in a woman; this could mean he had met someone who meant something to him. Walter did not need to guess who but played along. "Are you sure you mean all women, My Lord?"

Stephen grimaced, "One bloody chit of a woman would be a start."

"I shall do my utmost to get rid of her the next time I see her." Walter wondered if he would ever see Miss Webster again. She had obviously made a huge impression on his master if the scene in front of him was any indication of the impact she had made. The affection he held for his master ran deep, and he really hoped Miss Webster would return to the house one day.

"Do you know, Walter, she wouldn't have me? She turned me down; she has no prospects, no money, but she still turned me down flat!" Stephen said, taking a swig from the brandy bottle.

"You proposed?" Walter could not help the surprise in his voice or asking a question without the correct address. He did not know Stephen had proposed to Elizabeth; as far as he was concerned, this was the first time his employer had proposed to anyone. What was even more unbelievable was he had been turned down.

"Yes, fool that I am. Her uncle was over the moon, but, oh no! That was not good enough for Miss Charlotte bloody Webster: she wanted love. And flowers. And romance!" he said bitterly.

Walter was beginning to form a picture and, although he did not know all the details, some understanding of why the proposal had been refused was coming to light. "Would she perhaps change her mind once she has had time to think about it? She perhaps needs a little time to reflect; women can be such complicated creatures, My Lord," Walter said reassuringly.

"She can change her mind all she likes; this fool is not going to renew any offer. No, Walter, I'm going to stay as far away as I can from any female. They are nothing but trouble. I promise you this: you shall never see Miss Webster in this house again."

Walter reacted quickly but not quickly enough to prevent the brandy bottle slipping to the floor and spilling its contents onto the rug as Stephen collapsed in a drunken stupor. As the butler rang for a footman, he had the sneaking suspicion there was a strong possibility he would be seeing Miss Webster again; he definitely hoped so anyway.

Chapter 11

Charlotte had watched Stephen leave the house and heard rather than seen the carriage pulling away. The staff resumed their jobs, and she was left alone in the hallway. She could have said yes to his proposal; perhaps she should have said yes, but she had not been able to utter the word. Was it wrong of her to want the whole of him? She might be young, but knowing he did not love her, she was under no doubt he would hurt her if she agreed to marriage with him. The thought of him being with another woman because he could not be faithful made her feel physically sick. If she was so affected by the mere thought of it, she refused to put herself in the position of actually living through it.

She eventually managed to walk on shaking legs to her bed chamber and lay down on the warm bed cover. She wanted to wrap herself in the cover and never come out. As much as she could not put herself in the position of an unhappy marriage, a future without Stephen was very bleak.

Charlotte spent the afternoon listlessly looking at the patterns of the wallpaper that hung in the room. The Chinese design looked almost comical sideways, almost comical but not quite enough to bring a smile to her face. She was disturbed from her musings by a gentle knock on the door. She ignored it, but the door opened, and Elizabeth's head appeared in the gap.

"Is there room for someone who can give no useful advice but is worried about you?" she asked.

Charlotte smiled despite the lump of lead that had formed in her stomach at the thought of having to make conversation. "I'm not very good company at the moment; I just want to hide away," she said quietly.

"That I do know something about," Elizabeth said, coming into the room with a huff. "That husband of mine was stupid enough to send me away before we were married, and I almost pined away for want of him."

"It sounds very romantic," Charlotte said, raising herself slightly. It was not acceptable to greet the lady of the house while lying across a bed, no matter what the circumstances.

Elizabeth pulled a chair up next to the bed and sat down. "Romantic? It was the most foolish thing either of us could have done! I can only excuse it by the fact we were neither of us aware of the other's feelings."

Charlotte groaned, "Stephen is fully aware of my feelings. I am not sophisticated enough to hide them!"

"I don't think he is, or he wouldn't have gone off in such a way. Don't forget he probably isn't the right man for you, Charlotte; I think most people who have hearts would struggle with his fixed ideas about love and marriage. I think you did the right thing," Elizabeth said reassuringly.

"It doesn't feel like the right thing at the moment. I just want to see him, want to talk to him, to try and convince him to give love a chance!" Charlotte said, her voice getting some of its usual strength back as she warmed to her theme.

"One thing I have learned," Elizabeth said, taking Charlotte's hands in her own. "One cannot convince someone of something if they have it fixed in their head they are right and you are wrong. I tried that with Michael, but it didn't work, and for once I don't think it had anything to do with him being a stubborn beast," she smiled at Charlotte. "Stephen needs to find out he wants to love and beloved. That is the only way you could both be happy."

"You are correct. I know you are, but it just seems unfair! Why meet a man you fall in love with if you can't have him?" Charlotte asked.

Elizabeth tried to be tactful with her next words. "Forgive me saying this Charlotte; you are still very young. Stephen is very charming and, added to that, he rescued you. Do you not think he has been your knight in shining armour, and it is that which has influenced your feelings? Perhaps if you mixed more in Society, you might meet others you could become attracted to?"

"I could I suppose. I don't know. I know he is a rake; he wouldn't have been at Baron Kersal's if he were an upstanding citizen, but to me he was so considerate. It was easy to forget the reputation the girls had spoken about," Charlotte said.

"Let's arrange some entertainments," Elizabeth said, determined to remove Charlotte's focus on Stephen. "With you here I won't need to do all the work, which will make me very happy where entertaining is concerned. I do need to carry out some level of socialising before I look like a farmyard sow ready to give birth. We can show you the local families, and there are a few eligible young men who will appreciate a beauty in their midst."

"You are very kind," Charlotte said, blushing at the compliment. "Of course, I will help you organise anything you wish, gladly so. You have been so kind to me, but please do not think I will be looking for a husband."

"Oh, believe me, after my experience with Michael's lovely sister trying to match make with every single man within ten miles, I would never inflict the same on anyone else. If you meet someone and fall in love, it will be completely because of your own efforts!" Elizabeth reassured her.

*

Charlotte was to discover, as much as Elizabeth disliked socialising, when she put her mind to something, she carried it out to the full. She hardly had time to miss Stephen she was kept so busy. With the advice of Miss Fairfield, she sent out invitations, organised menus, flowers and seating plans and then had to prepare for the actual entertainments. Admittedly, her first thought in the morning was of Stephen as was the last thought before she fell into an exhausted sleep, but during the day she was kept very busy.

Elizabeth invited Violet and Edward to join their party, and Charlotte liked Violet immediately. She could hardly believe the exuberant woman was the sister of the far more serious Lord Dunham.

Violet entered the morning room during the second week of events. "Yet another bouquet of beautiful flowers has been delivered. I wonder who they can be for?" she asked as she handed them to Charlotte. "Is that the third this morning?" she teased.

Charlotte smiled, but a blush burned her cheeks. "They shouldn't send them to me; Elizabeth is the lady of the house," she said, reading the card and blushing even further.

"Yes, but she isn't unmarried and doesn't have beautiful golden curls and a pretty face to match," Violet said, laughing at Charlotte's discomfort. "Do you think they will resort to duelling for your affections?"

Charlotte laughed at Violet's words, "I doubt it!" she giggled. Receiving the bouquets was flattering, but the gentlemen involved did not come anywhere near to affecting her heart.

"Well, at least your dance card at the ball tomorrow will be full. Always a bonus for a young lady," Violet said, matter of fact.

"I'm quite nervous; it is my first ball, and I would hate to look inexperienced," Charlotte replied, a frown developing.

"You have conducted yourself splendidly over the last two weeks. You will have no problems tomorrow. In fact, if you haven't received at least one proposal you wish to accept, I shall be very surprised and disappointed," Violet said, ever the hopeful matchmaker.

Charlotte laughed, "Elizabeth was right to warn me you would be looking for a husband for me. There is no one I wish to marry." She could have added the word 'here' to the sentence, and it would have been more truthful. There was a man she wanted to marry, but it was just not possible.

"Ah, well, it was worth a try," Violet said resignedly. "But, it does enable me to make an offer to you. We shall be leaving for town in a week and hope you would accompany us. I've missed having some company in the house and having a young girl to take to the entertainments is far better than taking Edward. Would you be interested in joining us for a visit?"

Charlotte was surprised by the offer and a little overwhelmed; she had received so much kindness from this group of people who were strangers to her. Far more kindness and consideration than she had received from her uncle over the years, although he had claimed to have done the best he could.

"It is a very kind offer, and I would love to accept, but would Elizabeth not need me to stay here? I would hate to leave her as the baby's arrival approaches. Also, there is the chance of bumping into Baron Kersal." Charlotte admitted to herself the thought of being in London and meeting Stephen again made her stomach flutter.

"There is lots of time for a visit to London, and you can return here before the baby is born. Elizabeth has Michael, Miss Fairfield and all the staff to fuss over her. She will want you to experience London, I am sure of that. She may have hated it herself, but that is because she loves the freedom the country can give her; I have the suspicion you would enjoy the parties more," Violet said, remembering the persuasion that had to be applied to keep Elizabeth in London.

"With regards to the Baron, he would not dare to approach you once it was known you were a friend of Lord Dunham and staying with Edward and myself. You said he targeted girls who had no connections. It will be made very clear to everyone you are protected and under our care. My husband may be a mild mannered man, but he is no push over. He will make sure everyone knows you are important to us."

Charlotte agreed to Violet and Edward knowing why she was staying with Elizabeth. Although she was embarrassed about her foolish behaviour, she was also practical with regards to keeping it from certain people. She did not believe in telling lies to cover her foolishness. By them knowing of her actions, it seemed she would be able to enjoy a pleasure previously out of her reach.

"In that case, I would love to come," Charlotte said with a smile.

Elizabeth was all for the scheme when the pair approached her. "Oh, it will be just the thing!" she said. "You will love it in London."

"You didn't!" Charlotte said with a smirk.

Elizabeth laughed. "I know; that's because I'm happiest in a field. You will enjoy the dancing, and it will give you chance to receive even more bouquets."

"I shall warn the housekeeper to prepare the vases!" Violet said with a good natured groan.

Chapter 12

Two weeks had passed since Stephen visited Bow Street. He was sick of waiting for a visit from the elusive Mr Peter, but had received a note from Mr Frost explaining Peters had been delayed on another case. He assured Stephen when Peters did arrive things would progress quickly, as he already had his other officer following Baron Kersal. Stephen was annoyed, but there was nothing he could do, so he refused to see anyone and isolated himself in his study and drank brandy.

During the third week, Stephen had finished his evening meal when Walter came in to announce a Mr Peters was waiting to speak to him. Stephen's head felt as if it had been kicked to Brighton and back before being placed back on his shoulders, but he could not turn the officer away. He joined him in his study.

"Good evening, My Lord," Mr Peters said.

"Good evening," Stephan replied. His tone was not unfriendly, but he wanted the business over and done with. "I hope you are here to sort this mess out."

"I will try," Mr Peters replied. He was a young man, dark haired, tall, slim and dressed fashionably, although not expensively. To any outsider he looked like a gentleman, but anyone looking closely at his eyes, would see a hardened, world weary expression no cosseted gentleman would ever have. His age did not reflect the sights he had seen in the city. "I have been told the details of the case, but I would appreciate going over them again with you."

Stephen sighed. He did not need any more reminders of Charlotte than he already had, but he was determined to exact revenge for her sake; he was a man of his word, if nothing else. He commenced his story once more. Mr Peters listened, firing questions occasionally that resulted in Stephen going into great detail of what went on in the house.

"We need to speak to one of the girls," Mr Peters said. "Are you aware of any who would be willing to help?"

"They were sympathetic to Miss Webster, so she said," Stephen replied thinking over what Charlotte had told him. "They pointed me out to her as someone who might help her. They said I was considerate; God help them if I was the best of the bunch!" he said belittling himself.

Mr Peters made no response to the comment but kept the conversation on the matter in hand. "So, there was no one in particular?"

"She mentioned a girl named Laura, I think it was," Stephen said trying to recall exactly what Charlotte had relayed. "I think she was the one who took her under her wing first of all. Yes, it was Laura. She was in the carriage when Charlotte was taken, but I think she was there by force herself. I don't know the girl myself. Well, I may have done, but I don't link her name to a face. It's what single men do, Mr Peters," Stephen said defensively, feeling he had to excuse his behaviour in front of someone who he suspected had never visited such a place for pleasure.

Mr Peters ignored the comment. "We shall see if Laura is available tonight. We both need to speak to her."

"Tonight? I wasn't intending visiting anywhere tonight," Stephen said. His head was pounding; the last thing he needed was to go and drink and pretend to be merry with Baron Kersal when all he wanted to do was crawl into bed.

"No time like the present, My Lord," Mr Peters said, standing. "They will be working on other innocent girls to replace the void caused by Miss Webster's escape."

Stephen groaned; those words were enough to ensure he could not refuse. "Fine, I shall call for my carriage," he said.

The two men set out on the journey to Baron Kersal's home. It was about seven miles from London, so it was away from direct scrutiny. It made the parties and entertainments occurring there easy to be ignored by polite society.

"Who do I introduce you as?" Stephen asked as the carriage drove down the long drive.

"I'm your cousin's son on your mother's side; you've not seen me since I was in leading strings. I'm not doing very well for myself, so you have brought me back to London to show me the sights," Mr Peters said easily. "My given name is Alfred."

"My given name is Stephen. You had better stop referring to me as 'My Lord', if you are my cousin," Stephen said.

The carriage swung around the gravel circle at the head of the drive and came to a stop in front of the large, open doorway of the house. A footman opened the door and pulled down the step. "Well, Alfred, come; this will surely be a night full of sights you will not forget!" Stephen said as he climbed out of the coach.

Peters raised an eyebrow; the sights in a brothel for the rich would be nothing compared to some of the sights he had seen in his twenty three years, but he would refrain from correcting Lord Halkyn. He would not believe him or more likely just not be interested.

Peters stood outside the carriage and straightened his frock coat. He took in every detail as he made a show of fixing his sleeves. The house consisted of two floors, the door and portico in the centre with three windows either side. It was obviously a modern house, built within the last twenty years or so. The sandstone brick reflected the light of the lanterns.

"Alfred, when you are quite ready." Stephen said, his tone a touch sarcastic at what he considered over fussing behaviour by the young man.

Stephen led the way into the hallway, nodding to the footman as he handed over his hat and gloves. A shout from the rear drew the men's attention. Mr Peters noticed Stephen stiffen a little, but a smile was fixed to his face.

"Kersal, how are you?" Stephen asked.

"Halkyn, long time no see. Thought you'd dropped off the face of the earth. Where the devil have you been?" Baron Kersal asked, his red rimmed eyes taking in Mr Peters.

"Had to go and rusticate in the country," Stephen said easily. "I think I'm getting old; the head doesn't seem to clear as easily these days."

"Good God, if you can't take it, there's no hope for the rest of us!" Baron Kersal said with a guffaw. "And who's your friend?" The last was said without laughter. The rule was that not just anyone could attend the Baron's house; he had to be asked for approval. That rule kept the establishment exclusive and more appealing to the gentlemen who visited.

"He's my cousin's son; he attached himself to me while I was in the country. He's a bit green, so I decided to show him London in all its glory. Didn't think you'd object while he's family," Stephen said almost with a challenge. It might be the Baron's establishment, but a Lord would always outrank a Baron and Stephen would always take an opportunity to remind him of that, especially since Charlotte's predicament.

"If he's family, he's very welcome," the Baron said, but he had lost a little of his smile. He did not appreciate being reminded he was lower ranking than someone else. In his home, he was in charge. It was obvious to him Lord Halkyn considered himself above the rules, and he did not like that.

"Go through to the dining room; there is food and drink freshly served. You can have a feast in preparation for later," a lecherous smile suggested exactly what would be on offer later.

Stephen nodded his thanks and led the way into the dining room. He wondered if Baron Kersal had always been such a lecherous toad or if it was he himself who had changed. One thing he had decided was that once this was over, he would never be visiting such an establishment again.

The two gentlemen picked at the food and drink on offer. Peters made no small talk; Stephen had to pretend to be talking to the young man most of the time. He could see that Peters was acting as if he were taking his time over choosing his drink and his food when his eyes were everywhere. Stephen had to acknowledge Peters was very discreet so far.

They were approached by various acquaintances of Stephen's as they sat and ate. Stephen introduced Peters to everyone and made him suffer the brunt of his jokes. He would have done it whomever he was with, but his aim was to let the men know Peters was without money and a relative of his. Stephen did not want the extra complication of the officer being fleeced.

Peters finally put his plate down. "Right, Stephen," he said quietly. "What would you normally do now?"

"I would normally play cards and then finish up in one of the bedrooms," Stephen said unabashedly.

"That is what we shall do then," Peters said, rising from his seat.

Stephen looked surprised. "They will take pleasure in depriving you of whatever money you have with you and more, if you don't watch out," he said. He had seen men lose large amounts during the course of an evening. He normally would not have cared, but the man was in the establishment to help him. He could not in all conscience see him deprived of funds; he did not appear to be able to afford any loss.

Peter's smiled a smile that did not change the aged expression of his eyes, but he looked amused. "Let me worry about my losses; we are here to act as you normally would," he said quietly. A little louder, he said. "Come on, cousin, let's see what you are made of; I feel like playing cards."

Stephen raised his eyebrows but did not falter in replying. "I see now why you have always given your mother reason to worry. They say a fool and his money are soon parted; come then, Alfred, let me show you a master at work."

Peters did not reply but followed Stephen into the games room. He was a man who had seen many gaming hells and had taken part in more card games than he cared to remember. He was not one for disparaging the man with whom he was working, but he was quietly confident he would not be poorer by the night's end.

They walked into the card room adjoining the dining room. It was a room filled with smoke and had a distinct odour of both fear and exhilaration as large amounts were won and lost at the tables. They approached the table where Vingt-et-un was being played and, when the game was opened to new players, they both joined in. Stephen abandoned Peters to his own fate; he gave the young man some credit for knowing what he was doing and concentrated on his own game.

As the games progressed, a small crowd gathered around the table. It seemed the quiet confidence of Peters attracted attention when his small pot of money began to grow. Stephen watched along with the rest of the group while the banker was beaten time after time by Peters. Stephen decided he himself had lost enough for the evening; he did not want to give Kersal or Peters any more of his money. He was impressed by the cool way the officer handled the game and the group. Just because he was new to the group did not prevent them from heckling his attempts to win his game.

After a while Baron Kersal approached the table with a barely suppressed scowl on his face. It would not be good for business if he looked as if he was a bad loser, but he was not pleased. It appeared the newcomer, whom he had not invited, was making a substantial dent into his evening's profits. He was not a happy man.

"Your relation seems to be an excellent card player," the Baron said to Stephen.

Stephen could hardly restrain his urge to pummel his fist into the Baron's face, but a warning glance from Peters reminded him to keep control. "Ha!" he responded, in his usual way. Only those looking very closely would have seen the tick of annoyance in the Baron's cheek. "This is new venue luck. Believe me, his mother and his banker are in despair with his gambling. He shall probably not win again for another six months. It's the same story time after time."

"In that case, I hope he returns to this establishment often," the Baron said, seemingly consoled by Stephen's words. "Too many nights like this, and I would soon be out of business."

Peters looked at the Baron and indicated he no longer wished to play. He left the side of the table and stood facing the Baron, saying quietly. "I have a proposition that will give you my winnings back tonight, if you are interested."

Stephen and the Baron were immediately interested. Stephen hoped the officer still had his senses about him; he had drunk a lot. He tried to be the responsible older cousin. "Now, Alfred, I said I would show you the sights; I didn't say I would get you into trouble."

"Don't worry; it's not illegal. I think you will appreciate it too, cousin," Peters said. His voice was very calm, almost as if he was as sober as the moment they had walked through the door.

Baron Kersal looked intrigued, especially at the chance to get his money back. He indicated the gentlemen should follow him to the side of the room. "What is your proposition?" He asked Peters directly.

Peters looked at Stephen and smiled slightly. "My cousin here thinks I have never lived because I have never been to London, but I want to show him some of the things we get up to in the country. I want my cousin's favourite girl, and I will pay all my evening's winnings if she is allowed to be with us both. At the same time."

The Baron laughed loudly, which was fortunate, as it gave Stephen time to recollect himself from the shock of the words. He had not expected something like that to be suggested and wondered a little more about the officer before him.

"My good man, you will fit in here perfectly!" Baron Kersal said, slapping Peters on the back. "Of course you can have your woman! I'd always thought his Lordship was a bit of a prude; let's see what he's made of! If I wasn't so strapped for cash, it would almost be worth letting you have her for nothing!"

"That won't be necessary," Peters said quietly. "I'm willing to pay for all the services I require, tonight *and* in the future."

The Baron's eyes lit up at the thought of a regular income with a new customer. A large regular income, if his tastes were directed to the more unusual. "Good, which girl is it you require?"

Stephen paused; he hoped Peters knew what he was doing. "I tend to prefer Laura, but I'm not really bothered who it is." He had to give the impression that Laura wasn't that important or Kersal might become suspicious.

"Do you think she's strong enough for an active night?" Peters asked the Baron with a leer.

"She will be. You will see all my girls are capable of whatever the gentlemen want," Baron Kersal replied. He led the gentlemen up to the first floor and into a large bedchamber. The four poster bed dominated the room. The fire was lit, and there was a decanter of wine and clean glasses on a small table. There was one chair, but apart from that the room was empty. The Baron viewed excess furniture as a waste of money.

"Is this room acceptable, gentlemen?" Baron Kersal asked.

"This is fine; all we are missing is the lady to make sure our night is a success," Peters said, handing over a substantial amount of his evening's winnings. Stephen noticed he had kept an amount back, which the Baron did not seem to notice. As he was being paid around ten times what he was normally paid for the use of one of his girls, Stephen doubted he would care that he had not actually received all the money back.

The two men were left alone, the Baron assuring them Laura would be with them soon.

"I hope you know what you're doing," Stephen said quietly.

Peters smiled slightly and nodded. He moved to the bed and started to close the bed curtains.

"What are you up to now?" Stephen asked.

"Rooms like this will usually have peep holes, so some of the men who can't afford a woman or who prefer to watch rather than take part can look on. I don't perform for anyone."

Stephen had a sudden sick feeling to his stomach. He was not sure whether it was because most of his acquaintances had probably seen him perform at one time or another or whether it was because he was not sure what the night was about to bring. Whichever it was he longed to be hundreds of miles away from this house. Where, he could not openly acknowledge because to think of that, to think of *her*, while he was about to do goodness knew what was a slight on her innocence. It was going to be a long evening.

Chapter 13

Charlotte had dressed carefully for the ball. She loved the dresses she now owned through Stephen's and Elizabeth's kindness. Stephen. If only she could dance with him, she thought with a sigh. They had jumped a few stages of a normal relationship, straight to kisses and marriage proposals and heartache. Not the stuff of romance novels where the hero woos the heroine and there is a steady progress of the romance, she thought ruefully.

The preparations for the ball had been different from the other entertainments. Charlotte knew both Violet and Elizabeth hoped she was going to make a match of it with someone in the area. Elizabeth had confided one day that, although she was no matchmaker, she was hoping Charlotte would settle in Somerset, so Elizabeth could enjoy her company for longer. The two had grown close over the weeks of her visit, and Charlotte had to admit being able to see Elizabeth every week would be a real temptation when thinking of a place to live.

She could have laughed off the matchmaking if she didn't think there was going to be an approach to Lord Dunham for her hand in marriage. She was flattered she had been welcomed into local Society, although she acknowledged it was her connections with the Dunhams that ensured she would be accepted. What Charlotte failed to realise was that her admirers were genuine. She had no fortune, but she was a beautiful girl, and her liveliness and kind nature were very real added attractions to the young men of the area.

Mr O'Hara was the most persistent of her admirers, and she worried in case she was being rude by her behaviour towards him. She was doing her best to make him understand she was not interested in him romantically. He called every day; he sent flowers every morning, and he asked for the first dances whenever there was opportunity. Tonight, again, he had secured the first two dances. Charlotte had been unable to refuse; she did not want to encourage him, but she could also not refuse the request of dancing if she hoped to dance with anyone else. It would be a poor reflection on herself and her hosts. She had decided, though, she had to tell him he must not continue with this attention. Others in the wider social circle were beginning to speculate on a match between them.

Charlotte smiled to herself as Maggie stood behind her, performing her usual magic on Charlotte's hair. A few months ago, Mr O'Hara would have been everything she had ever wanted. He was handsome, funny, kind and thoughtful: everything a good husband should be. He had only one fault and that was he was not Lord Halkyn. No matter how perfect Mr O'Hara was, how comfortable his income was, how nice his house in Bristol was, he was not Lord Halkyn. He could not make her heart race; could not make butterflies appear in her stomach, or make her blush at a look or a word. He would never be someone she could fall in love with; she liked him, but she did not love him.

She stood before the full length mirror in the corner of her bed chamber. Tonight she had to be polite but clear; she would set him straight on her feelings. Her appearance gave her courage; her dress was a pale green silk. It suited her blond colouring perfectly and brought out the colouring in her eyes. She was not officially out yet, but Violet had suggested she come out in London while visiting with them. Officially, she should not have been attending such a grand ball but, because she was unknown in the area, Elizabeth had insisted it was a minor technicality to which Lord Dunham had shaken his head in despair.

Her hair had been expertly curled by Maggie and ringlets allowed to fall, framing her face and tickling her neck. Maggie had a wonderful technique of arranging her hair so it bounced as she walked. Elizabeth had given her a small necklace of silver chain with an emerald droplet. It was perfect for a girl not long into Society. Her apparel was completed with the pale green ribbon securing her hair.

Charlotte smiled at herself; she looked every inch the lady, not a young girl virtually on her own in the world and lucky to be in such fine surroundings. It still made her shudder to think how different her life could have been but for Lord Halkyn's help. He would never realise how much happiness he had inadvertently brought her; she had never experienced family life such as she was now involved with every day, and she loved every moment.

She thanked Maggie and left her bed chamber. It was time to join Elizabeth, Michael, Violet and Edward in greeting the guests. She was nervous but excited too. Her first ball, in such a fine house, with nearly all of the people she cared most about gathered around her.

*

The music struck up for the first dance, and Charlotte was approached by Mr O'Hara. He led her onto the ballroom floor, and they began their journey down the long set. They chatted when they met in the dance, mainly about the ball and those present. Charlotte knew her moment had to be chosen well. When they reached the bottom of the set and waited to rejoin the dance, Mr O'Hara changed the tone of the conversation slightly.

"You look beautiful tonight Miss Webster," he said with a smile. He was dressed finely himself: a dark frock coat, contrasting with a royal blue waistcoat. His cream breeches and white stockings set off his outfit. With his dark hair and dark eyes, set against his pale complexion he looked every inch the fine gentleman he was.

"Thank you," Charlotte said demurely. Compliments were always something she did not quite know how to respond to, not being used to receiving them.

"I am the luckiest man here tonight," Mr O'Hara continued his flattery. "I can see all the others glaring daggers at me as we dance."

Charlotte laughed. "I think you exaggerate, Mr O'Hara," she said, dismissing his words.

"I don't think so; I can almost hear their mutterings!" Mr O'Hara continued determined to woo his chosen one.

They rejoined the set, and Mr O'Hara continued his bantering, sometimes making Charlotte laugh, sometimes making her groan at him. He pretended to take offence but laughed when she appeared concerned she had insulted him.

As the dance came to an end, he took Charlotte's hand. "We have the next dance, but could I persuade you to miss it?"

"Of course, are you unwell?" Charlotte asked with concern.

"No, I would like to speak with you. I realise I can't take you out of the ballroom, but if we could sit by this window, I shall obtain some refreshments, and we can take the opportunity of speaking without the interruption of the other dancers," Mr O'Hara said, leading her to an empty chair.

Charlotte did not want a tete-a-tete, but she realised it might be the only opportunity to speak to him in relative privacy. The windows along the ballroom were slightly inset, creating a small seating area in front of each window. As it was the early part of the evening, some of the windows were still closed, something that would change as the heat increased.

Charlotte sat compliantly and waited while Mr O'Hara gave instructions to a footman to bring them some wine. Charlotte was not sure about drinking wine, but the footman had disappeared before she could utter any objections. Mr O'Hara sat in the chair next to her; they were in full view of the ballroom, so it was perfectly acceptable.

"You do know I want to take your hands; no, I want to take *you* into my arms at this moment," Mr O'Hara said quietly enough that no one passing could overhear.

Charlotte blushed, but her voice was firm, "Mr O'Hara, I am not used to such talk; please let us not be silly and spoil what is promising to be a lovely evening."

Mr O'Hara smiled, "You wish me to hide my feelings? Miss Webster, ever since I met you, I have wanted to shout them to the whole world, and I am not a man who is used to feeling so strong an emotion as this."

They were interrupted by the footman returning with two glasses of wine. Charlotte grasped hers gratefully, all worries gone of drinking something that she was unused to, as she took a large gulp. Mr O'Hara's words were making her slightly uncomfortable and panicked.

"Mr O'Hara, please do not utter such things!" she pleaded, after allowing herself a moment to get over the burning of the wine as it travelled down her throat.

"Why not? Why can I not be honest before the woman who I wish to address as something more than Miss Webster?" Mr O'Hara asked.

"Because I do not return those feelings!" Charlotte said bluntly.

Mr O'Hara looked surprised but not disheartened. "I realise I am being forceful with you; we have barely known each other more than a few weeks, but in time you could develop feelings for me. If we could make things more official, we don't need to marry immediately; we could take our time."

Charlotte finished off her wine quickly and set her glass down on a conveniently placed side table. "Mr O'Hara, I'm flattered; I truly am, but I don't wish to marry you, not now, nor at any time in the future."

"Give me time; that's all I ask," Mr O'Hara persisted.

Charlotte frowned; he was being too insistent, too intense for such a location: they were in a public place. People might notice. Her fears were confirmed when they were interrupted by Violet.

"Ah, there you are, my dear," she said speaking to Charlotte. "Elizabeth would like to introduce you to a latecomer; he is hoping you still have room on your dance card."

Charlotte rose, feeling the effects of drinking a glass of wine quickly, but managed to remain composed. She was grateful for the opportunity to leave Mr O'Hara; she was dismayed when she saw his frown at the information a guest wanted to dance with her. "Of course; please excuse us, Mr O'Hara; I hope you enjoy the remainder of your evening." She hoped by her words he would get the message she would not be seeking out his company again.

Violet linked her arm through Charlotte's as they skirted the dancers. "I thought it time to intervene," she said smiling at people as they passed.

"Thank you; it was most opportune," Charlotte responded gratefully. "Mr O'Hara was becoming a little intense."

"Yes, it looks as if you have made a conquest there my dear," Violet said happily.

"Unfortunately, he is not listening to the fact that I do not wish for him to be anything more than an acquaintance!" Charlotte said firmly.

"Oh, that's a shame," Violet replied. "He would have been such a suitable young man."

"It appears I still prefer someone who is most unsuitable," Charlotte said sadly.

Violet patted her hand in sympathy. "Work hard to forget him; let the others have a chance to show what happiness they can offer. Excitement is fine, but marriage needs to be based on trust and affection. To not be happy in a marriage can make the soul wither and die; I have seen it happen time and again; please don't let me see that happen with you, my dear."

Charlotte sighed, "I know: I am trying, honestly; just no one seems to compare to him."

Violet handed Charlotte over to Elizabeth and was introduced to Mr Dawson, an old friend of Lord Dunham's and a very dear one of Elizabeth's. He seemed a pleasant gentleman and offered to take Charlotte in to supper when he realised her dance card was full. She agreed to this, as she had immediately warmed to this gentleman who would be staying with them for the coming week.

Charlotte put Mr O'Hara to the back of her mind as she danced with her other partners. They flirted, and she laughed, not taking their words seriously but in the spirit most of them had been given. She was realistic; she was not an heiress, so although she was a popular dance partner, she would not be seen as a serious consideration by many of those gathered here. That was perfectly acceptable; she was not looking to marry. At least, no one from Somerset anyway.

Mr O'Hara appeared by her side when the supper gong was rung and was deeply offended Charlotte would not be going into supper with himself, even though no arrangement had been made to this end previously. He glared at Mr Dawson as he held out his arm for Charlotte.

"It seems I should watch my behaviour tonight, or I am liable to be called out by your young man," Mr Dawson said, good naturedly as they entered the crush of the supper room.

"He is not my young man," Charlotte replied. "Until tonight, I thought he was very pleasant and amenable, but he is rapidly becoming the annoyance of the night," she said with feeling.

Mr Dawson chuckled and shook his head. It seemed that Elizabeth had found herself a like-minded friend, one who said exactly what she was feeling. When he made sure Charlotte was seated comfortably, he offered to get her a drink.

"Would you be kind enough to bring me a glass of wine?" Charlotte asked with a faint blush at Mr Dawson's raised eyebrow. "I really feel I need one after Mr O'Hara's behaviour."

Mr Dawson nodded and brought over two glasses and then returned to bring some food. Charlotte picked at the food while being entertained by Mr Dawson. He was very fond of Elizabeth and Lord Dunham, and took pleasure in telling Charlotte some of their earlier escapades, those which were suitable for a lady's ears. She drank the wine and asked for another; the wine and Mr Dawson's charm were making the night seem pleasant once more.

The dancing started again, and Charlotte was entertained by her partner; she felt light headed, but freer, more open to the compliments and empty flirting; she found everything very funny.

After two dances, she needed to sit down. She excused herself and sat in one of the window bays and watched the dancing. It was a lovely evening. She felt in need of something to drink, so skirted the edge of the dancing and made her way to the refreshment room. She could have sent a footman but wanted to move around. The table was laid out with a footman busy serving. She obtained a glass of wine and moved out of the room. She drank quickly; she was due to start another dance when the music ended.

Drinking the wine quickly soon turned out to be a mistake; Charlotte felt a little dizzy and instead of drawing attention to herself moved out into the hallway. She needed to sit where she could let the dizziness pass and compose herself and get ready for her next partner.

She made her way to the morning room and was about to close the door when Mr O'Hara pushed his way in and closed the door behind him. Charlotte exclaimed in surprise, but Mr O'Hara spoke quickly.

"Shh, unless you want to bring half the house running," he said quietly. "I just wanted to talk to you."

Charlotte was silent; she was a little afraid. Her lack of experience putting herself at a disadvantage against an amorous man.

"I can't leave you tonight with no hope of there being something between us," Mr O'Hara said, touching Charlotte's cheek gently. "I want to marry you, Miss Webster; I want to spend the rest of my days looking after you."

Charlotte closed her eyes; it would be so easy to say yes. She was sure he meant his words; he was such a steady young man. She would be secure, she would be looked after; why could she not agree to the match and be done with it all?

Charlotte's action of closing her eyes must have appeared as an encouragement because Mr O'Hara moved towards her, taking her in his arms. He bent his head to touch her lips with his, just as Charlotte opened her eyes in surprise at his movement. She stilled as he bent to kiss her; he was gentle, reverent almost, his eyes closed, savouring the moment.

The first instinct Charlotte had was to pull away with indignation at such forward behaviour, but she paused. Everyone was telling her to forget, to marry someone more suitable, to put her happiness first. So, instead of pulling away, she moved her arms around Mr O'Hara's neck and pulled him towards her; just had she had done on that fateful day at Baron Kersal's. Mr O'Hara groaned with pleasure at her movement and pulled her tightly to him; her breasts were pressed into his chest, and he held onto her as if he would never let go. Charlotte responded to his kiss for a few moments and then slowly her movements stilled. She let go of his hair she had been grasping and let her hands fall by her side.

Mr O'Hara pulled away at the change and rested his forehead on Charlotte's; he was breathing deeply, and his pupils were dilated. "What's wrong?" he asked gently. "Have I pushed you too fast? You have made me so happy in the way you responded; I hope you will see how well we suit."

Charlotte pulled away. "I am truly sorry," she said simply. She was. She should not have used him in such a way; she had responded to his kiss to compare it to another's, and there could be no comparison. She had been completely spoiled by Stephen for anyone else.

Mr O'Hara looked confused. "I don't understand; you acted as if you wanted my advances. Are you teasing me, Miss Webster?" His tone had changed slightly; he sounded angry.

"I'm sorry," Charlotte repeated. "I was not teasing; I was trying to force myself into liking you."

Mr O'Hara flinched at her words. "You were trying to *force* yourself into liking me?" He said incredulously.

"I'm sorry," Charlotte repeated quickly. "I'm not saying this correctly; I can't seem to explain myself, but I didn't want to hurt you."

Mr O'Hara looked as if he were going to burst, but the morning room door opened, and Lord Dunham and Mr Dawson walked in.

Lord Dunham took in the pair, a frown developing as he noticed Charlotte's obvious distress, and Mr O'Hara's barely suppressed anger. "May I ask what is going on here?" he asked in general.

"I was making an offer, but I've been told clearly that it's not welcome!" Mr O'Hara said bitterly.

"You have made a proposal to Miss Webster without seeking my consent first?" Lord Dunham asked calmly, but there was a reprimand in the words.

Mr O'Hara flushed. "I was going to seek your approval tomorrow!" he snapped.

"I suggest you visit me tomorrow, at the earliest opportunity," Lord Dunham said.

Charlotte gasped at Lord Dunham's words; he surely wouldn't force her into a marriage with Mr O'Hara? The gentleman nodded his assent and left the room. Lord Dunham turned to Charlotte and, although he noticed how pale she had gone, he was annoyed she had put herself in such a position.

"I would have expected you of all people to be more aware of the dangers of putting yourself in a compromising situation, Charlotte," Lord Dunham said with reproach.

Charlotte's pale face was suffused with a blush of mortification. "I came in here because I was feeling dizzy. He forced his way in, but I did not insist he leave, and for that I am truly sorry."

"You would have been if anyone else had seen you," Lord Dunham said.

"Please My Lord, M-Michael," Charlotte stuttered at the look she received from the man before her. "You aren't going to force me to marry him are you? I know you could, but please...."

"I suggest you return to the ball and enjoy the remainder of the evening, if you can," Lord Dunham said with a more gentle tone. "We shall talk again in the morning."

"That's what worries me!" Charlotte said, but left the room.

Mr Dawson and Michael were left looking at each other; Mr Dawson had the ghost of a smile hovering around his lips. Michael groaned, "Don't you dare laugh. John!" he said with feeling.

"It reminds me of when Elizabeth was introduced into your life," John smiled at his friend.

"Yes, but this is worse; Charlotte is in love with Halkyn. I had hoped that Halkyn would come to his senses and realise what he had and make up for his previous mistakes, but it seems he is a bigger fool than I thought. He refuses to change his ways and the one he has hurt is the one who cares for him the most. We've been hoping, for her sake, she would be tempted by someone more suitable, but after tonight it doesn't seem so," Michael said with feeling.

"Oh, good God, you'd better tell me more!" John said in mock horror.

Chapter 14

Charlotte would not have been any happier if she had known of Stephen's activities at the time she was kissing Mr O'Hara. He was waiting in a bedchamber for a lightskirt, no she would not have been pleased at all.

Laura came into the room looking wary and afraid. Stephen felt sorry for the woman, partly because of the support she had given to Charlotte. He walked across the room and embraced her; while he was holding her stiff body, he whispered in her ear.

"Do not worry; we are not going to harm you, but we need to speak to you, so please play along." Laura relaxed into him at his words, and Stephen let her go. He took her by the hand and made a big show of introducing her to Peters. "This is my relative, Alfred. He seems to think we have been boring in our previous rendezvous, my dear; I hope you will show him the contrary is true." He squeezed her hand in reassurance, and Laura seemed to understand.

She approached Alfred and wrapped her arms around his neck, nibbling on his jaw. "Oh yes, My Lord, we will certainly make sure he goes out of here knowing exactly what sort of pleasure is available."

She unfastened Alfred's frock coat and helped him out of it. She lay the coat over the chair and then turned to Stephen. "You too, my sweet," she said playfully and helped him out of his frock coat. Both men were helped out of their waistcoats and then she took off their cravats. Both men allowed her to do as she wished. Once their cravats were gone, Alfred turned to Laura.

"On the bed, wench!" he said, not unkindly but firmly. Laura looked a little worried, but Alfred moved across to her. He took her hands in his and pulled her towards him; he whispered something and then kissed her fully on the lips. Laura relaxed into Alfred and allowed herself to be picked up and carried to the bed. She opened the curtains slightly and clambered onto the mattress.

"Come on boys," came the muffled voice behind the thick drapes. "Come and show me what you're made of."

Both men climbed onto the bed and without making it obvious, made sure the curtains were closed, ensuring no one could see in through them. The three made sure they moved around to create the illusion they were engrossed in carnal pleasure. Stephen left it to Alfred to whisper to Laura the reason they were there. Her eyes widened at the information, but she turned to Stephen immediately.

"I wanted to ask you about Charlotte. Is she well?" she asked, keeping her voice low.

"She is well and safe and will never be at risk from Kersal again. It was a kind thing you did to help her," Stephen said.

"She was so young and so scared in the carriage, but she tried to hide it and gave Kersal a right tongue lashing. He looked as if he wanted to gag her, but I wouldn't let him. It was my job to make sure she was returned here unharmed, and I did," Laura whispered. "I know it's happened before, but I've never been involved. It has always felt wrong, but once I'd seen that child, I couldn't stand by and do nothing. We do this but we get paid and agree to it to a certain extent; she wasn't given any choice or a way out."

Child. Stephen almost flinched when Laura said the word, how could he have proposed marriage to a child? He was as bad as Kersal. He tried to dismiss his thoughts and focus on the matter at hand. "Her friends thank you and want to stop Kersal," he said quietly.

As the conversation progressed, Stephen came to the conclusion it had to be the most surreal conversation he had ever experienced. It consisted of whispers interrupted by noises from Laura, Alfred and himself. There was also a lot of movement around the bed by the three of them, all without actually touching each other. They had to give the impression of having an enjoyable experience.

Laura had confirmed what Alfred had said: there were peep holes in all the rooms. It had sickened Stephen further, but she also suspected that, once the people who had chosen to watch their session realised there was nothing to see, they would be left alone. They continued with the farce purely to be on the safe side. Laura's safety was vital.

She had a lot of information to give, most of which Stephen could not hear as it was whispered to Peters. He fired questions at her on regular intervals. She seemed relieved to be able to speak to someone in authority about the goings on. Even though she was a working girl who would never be accepted into civilised society, she had standards and morals. Kersal it seemed was turning most of his girls against him, but Laura was not sure if anyone else would be prepared to give them more information to help the case.

"We will gather what we need; your information is just setting me on the right track," Alfred assured her. "It will save me a lot of time."

"So you can then return to your own world well away from this hell," Laura had whispered to him, sounding bitter.

Alfred had looked a little surprised at her words, but soon regained his usual calm expression and leaned in to answer her. "We are both involved in different types of hell," he said calmly. "Mine isn't any better or worse than yours, but it is every bit as much a hell, believe me."

Laura did believe him and did not know really why she snapped at him. She could see in his eyes the horrors he had seen. She was attuned to people, she had to be in her profession, and she could see the gentleman before her had been involved in far more than any reasonable human being should have been. She trusted this man and would help him in any way she could. The kiss he had given her at the start of the evening she would remember for a long time to come. It would help when she had to blank her mind to everything happening to her, for if she did not close her mind to what she did, she would have gone insane a long time ago. The memory of his kiss would provide a place in her mind to which her sanity could retreat while her body was being abused.

Alfred's questions seemed to last forever; Stephen was becoming bored with the situation. He was relieved when Alfred thanked

110

Laura for her help. She nodded her head and began to take off her dress.

"What are you doing?" Stephen asked in disbelief.

"They won't expect me or you to climb off the bed fully dressed," she said simply. "Don't take them for fools; they aren't. They may be a little drunk, but they aren't stupid."

Stephen sighed in resignation. He was not embarrassed about getting undressed, but it was a damned inconvenience. Laura pulled the pins from her hair and ruffled her curls. As the three continued to undress, Alfred reached inside his pocket. He brought out a small pouch.

"Here, this is yours," he said quietly to Laura.

"What is it?" she asked, not reaching out to take it.

"It is your reward for your work this evening," Alfred said simply.

"Reward? I'm a working girl Alfred; I shall get my pennies after the evening has finished. Don't feel obliged to pay twice; I'm sure you've already had to pay handsomely," she responded a little tartly.

"You would receive a reward for the information you supplied. I won't be able to give it to you in the future, so you may as well have it now," Alfred said, throwing the pouch on the bed.

"So you won't be back?" Laura asked; for some reason the thought left her with a dead weight in her chest.

"No, we won't be back to this place ever again," Stephen responded with venom. "Take the money Laura; you've earned it." He got out of the bed covers, dragging his clothing behind him. "Well, my dear, that was a bloody good time even if I do say so myself!" he said arrogantly, moving over to the table containing the wine and having a large glass. He appeared quite happy with the evening's entertainment. After having his fill of wine, he sat down on the chair and started to dress himself. "Come, Alfred!" he shouted. "Even you must have had your fill by now."

Laura picked up the pouch and emptied it quietly into her hand. She looked questioningly at Alfred. "This is too much; a reward is usually a few pounds. I couldn't earn this much in three years even if I worked every night," she said simply.

"I won most of it tonight," Alfred said with a shrug.

"And the rest?" Laura asked, looking into Alfred's eyes.

"We all need help sometimes; use it well and get away from this business," he said gently.

Laura knelt up on the bed and wrapped her arms around Alfred's neck. She had on no corset, and she pressed her breasts into his shirt front. "Thank you," she whispered, before leaning in and kissing him fully on the mouth.

Alfred should not have allowed such a kiss to take place. He was on duty and she was a working girl. If he was found out, he could lose his job, but the amount of feeling given with that kiss almost took his breath away. He responded like a starving man being offered a banquet, pulling Laura to him and kissing her fully in return. They separated, both gasping for breath, wide eyed and flushed.

"I won't ever see you again, will I?" Laura said.

"It would be best if you didn't; in my line of work there is a high casualty rate," Alfred said, matter of fact.

Laura cupped his cheek in her hand. "In another life I would have taken care of you," she said simply.

Alfred turned his head and kissed her hand. "In another life I would have let you," he replied and got off the bed without looking back.

Both men dressed without speaking and left the room. Laura hid the pouch and dressed slowly, tears running down her face. She shook herself once she was presentable again; there was no point repining over something she could not change. She had been given the opportunity to leave this establishment, and she would pick her moment and go without looking back. She had done enough here.

Stephen and Alfred returned to Stephen's house. Both travelled in silence thinking about the night's events. The carriage arrived at the house, and Walter opened the door. It might be the middle of the night, but the butler looked no different than if he had opened it during the afternoon.

"Walter, go to bed!" Stephen said gruffly, but not unkindly.

Walter bowed his head slightly. "Do you require anything else, My Lord?"

"Strong brandy," came the usual response of late.

"Already in your study, My Lord. If there is nothing else, I shall bid you gentlemen good night."

Stephen led the way into his study and poured two large glasses of brandy. He took a large drink and slumped into one of the chairs in front of the fire. "Thank God that is over."

"It was worth it," Alfred said, sitting opposite Stephen, when invited to sit down. "She knew a lot more than I expected. My colleague Corless has been working on the outside, following the Baron, noting who he meets and building a picture of his activities. With the work that Corless is doing we should have enough to move in quickly."

"Good! I would hate to think he was left to roam the streets for much longer. I didn't realise just how much I hated him until tonight."

"I realise it was difficult, but at least you returned. When all this comes out there will be speculation as to who informed on him. Your appearance tonight will probably mean you are excluded from suspicion," Alfred explained.

Stephen looked Alfred squarely in the eye. "What about Laura? Will she be safe?"

"I don't know," came the honest reply. Alfred appeared to have his usual control, but a slight gritting of his teeth betrayed some emotion he was hiding. "I gave her enough money to enable her to get away and support herself for a time, but she will have to pick her moment, or she will put herself in danger. She is intelligent and has survived in that world until now. I am sure she will be fine."

"I hope so; I would hate to think, in stopping Kersal, we have put someone else in harm's way," Stephen said. "So what happens now?"

"You leave the rest to us," Alfred said with authority. "Mr Frost will inform you when there is something to report. But until then, be assured work will be going on to stop this ring." He rose. "It's time I returned to my lodgings. Thank you for your assistance, My Lord."

Stephen stood and shook the officer's hand. He had gained respect for the calm Alfred even in such a short period of time. "Well, I can't say it was a pleasure, but I hope we've done enough to help you. Good luck."

Alfred left Stephen alone. Stephen sat back down with his brandy. His duty was done; he had done everything he could so another girl such as Charlotte would not face the same horror. Charlotte. He should be celebrating, he told himself. He no longer had to think about her; there were no further ties between them: he could forget her.

He poured himself another brandy; it was going to be a long night.

Chapter 15

Charlotte awoke with a headache. It was no surprise; after all, she *had* drunk four glasses of wine! She got out of bed quickly; it was a late hour, and she wanted to get the interview with Michael over as soon as possible. She dressed and went directly to the dining room. The relief that filled her when she realised Michael and Elizabeth were still resting flooded through her so much she greeted Mr Dawson with a large smile.

"Good morning, Miss Webster," Mr Dawson said, standing as she entered.

"Good morning," she replied. "I feel I could eat the whole of the breakfast spread out on this table!" Charlotte said.

"Be careful, Miss Webster: many more nights drinking lots of wine and then eating large breakfasts and you shall no longer be the belle of the ball," Mr Dawson teased.

"Good," Charlotte said firmly. "After a fiasco like last night, I don't know how anyone comes through a season without getting into trouble. I don't think I could."

"You will soon be able to keep the likes of Mr O'Hara in check, I'm sure," Mr Dawson said reassuringly.

"I've had so little experience of Society," Charlotte said honestly, feeling, if she had a full season, she would feel constantly out of her depth.

"You remind me of Elizabeth; and she managed to get through, just. I'm sure you will be fine," Mr Dawson said, amused.

"If Lord Dunham doesn't force me into a marriage first," Charlotte muttered darkly.

"He's a fair man," Mr Dawson said in defence of his friend, but his tone was gentle. He could see Charlotte was remorseful and worried.

Charlotte's anxiety increased when she found out later Michael was in his study with Mr O'Hara. She returned to her bed chamber not wishing to have to make conversation with anyone and spent her time pacing the room, dreading the time when she would be forced to face Mr O'Hara and potentially be forced into a marriage she did not want.

She was eventually asked to go and join Michael in his study. She entered, looking every bit the scared, very young woman she was. Michael had to suppress a smile at the fear in her face; it was slightly flattering to be able to instil such emotion in someone since his wife would be more likely to laugh at him than be scared.

"Come in, Charlotte; please be seated," Michael said kindly, his compassion overwhelming his amusement.

"Thank you," Charlotte replied quietly. She sat facing Michael, the emotions she was feeling clearly expressed on her face. Michael waited while she composed herself. She sighed and took a breath. "I need to know: are you going to force me to marry him?" she said in a rush.

Michael laughed loudly. "No talk about the weather first?"

Charlotte smiled, despite her fears. "If I am going to be condemned, I'd rather know now. Idle chit-chat about the weather can wait."

Michael admired her direct way. "I spoke to Mr O'Hara this morning."

"I know; it took such a long time!" Charlotte said with feeling.

Michael suppressed a smile. "Maybe so, but I needed to give him a piece of my mind about his behaviour last night."

Charlotte flushed at the memory. "I was foolish. I should have asked him to leave."

"Why didn't you?" Michael asked. He certainly had given the young gentleman a set down O'Hara would not forget in a hurry; but if Charlotte did like him, he would not discourage the match.

116

Charlotte thought for a moment, wondering whether or not to be honest with Michael. She would have been if it were Elizabeth asking the same question, so she decided to trust her host even though most of the time she was a little bit in awe of him.

"At first, I didn't know what to do. I've never been in that situation before." She flushed a little; that was not exactly true, and Michael knew it. When her uncle had arrived, she had been found in the library kissing Stephen. That seemed different somehow: she was not afraid of Stephen; she had been a little afraid of Mr O'Hara. With Stephen she had only ever felt protected.

Michael correctly interpreted the blush, but did not think there was any use going over old ground. He had said his piece at the time. "Go on," he encouraged.

"When he started to say he wanted to marry me I thought about everything everyone had been saying about Stephen," Charlotte said candidly. "I know enough of his reputation to understand why everyone has been telling me to forget him."

"You turned down an offer of marriage from him," Michael gently reminded her. If she was longing for Stephen, she could have had him weeks ago.

"I know and, as silly as this may sound, I still think it was the right decision. I want to be loved; I want to be married for *me*, not just for convenience. Does that make sense?" Charlotte asked.

"Yes, it does, but how does Mr O'Hara fit in?" Michael coaxed.

"He is a nice gentleman; he is perfectly eligible: I do see that," Charlotte admitted. "I have listened to everyone about how unsuitable Stephen is, so I thought perhaps I should give it a chance."

Michael's heart sank a little; he would have to ask, but he really did not wish to know. "What happened?"

Charlotte really flushed this time. "I didn't encourage him, honestly; but all at once he was kissing me. My first reaction was to push him away; I would have done if I hadn't had everyone's voices in my head, telling me to forget Stephen and meet a respectable young man."

"And?" Michael asked.

"So I kissed him back," Charlotte said in a rush.

Michael inwardly groaned; he should appreciate this as practice before he hopefully had a houseful of daughters, but he wished his wife was having this conversation instead of him. He could imagine how she would laugh later when he relayed the story, not about Charlotte's embarrassment but of his own.

"Has it convinced you Mr O'Hara is the man for you?" he asked.

"Goodness no!" Charlotte exclaimed. "The kiss was nice—well, it was not bad, but it was nothing like.... It wasn't.... Have you ever kissed someone and wondered how you could ever want to kiss anyone else because that kiss was like an explosion of everything good?" Charlotte asked, her intensity making her overcome her bashfulness.

It was now Michael's turn to flush slightly, but his reply was honest, "Yes, I have."

"Well, you will know exactly how I feel about Mr O'Hara then. He is nice, but he's not *him!*"

"I do understand, but Charlotte, there is no guarantee Lord Halkyn will ever cross your path again. I am sorry to be blunt, but I doubt you will ever hear him renew an offer of marriage even if your paths do cross." Michael said the words gently, but he needed to make Charlotte realise, if she was hankering after Halkyn, she had already had her chance.

Charlotte looked crushed. "I know the decision I made was the correct one, but it doesn't mean to say I don't know what I have lost. I'm trying to be pragmatic by thinking I didn't have the chance of a life with him before, so I shouldn't be upset now."

"Is it working?" Michael asked with a twinkle of amusement.

118

"Not a tiny bit!" Charlotte said with a groan, but she smiled at Michael. "Thank you for not forcing me into a marriage I would not have been happy in. I refused Stephen because I would not be happy, so I could not agree to marriage to someone whom I didn't care for. I do like Mr O'Hara, but I need to be loved and to love no matter how out of the ordinary I may sound."

"As my wife and I are of the same opinion, I cannot criticise you, but I do hope you meet someone who will offer you the happiness you are looking for."

"What about Mr O'Hara?" Charlotte asked.

"I've told him if you had a change of heart overnight, I would invite him here immediately, but I would not expect him to pester you in future." Michael could see the relief in Charlotte's face once she realised her actions would not force her into a marriage with the young man. He felt sorry for the girl, but there was nothing he could do to help.

They were interrupted by a knock on the study door. The butler entered at Michael's command. "My Lord, I am sincerely sorry to interrupt you, but there is an urgent item of correspondence that has just been delivered. The rider is waiting for a response and has insisted you see the letter most urgently; otherwise, I would have not disturbed you," the butler explained apologetically.

"Don't worry; we were just finishing up here," Michael said with a smile at Charlotte. "We had nothing left to discuss but the state of the weather."

Charlotte smiled at the quip but was soon on her guard. Michael had taken the letter and sliced it open. As he read, the colour had literally drained from his face and he frowned. Charlotte leant forward in her seat desperate to know what the letter contained that could have such a grave impact on her host.

When it seemed Michael had forgotten he was in the room with anyone else, Charlotte said quietly, "Is it bad news?"

119

Michael stirred himself and looked at the girl sitting before him. Was it only seconds ago he was joking with her? "Charlotte, you will have to excuse me. This letter contains information I have to act on immediately: it will change my upcoming plans; it will change all of our plans."

"It's not....Is he well?" Charlotte asked, feeling completely selfish at thinking only of how the news might affect her, but she could not stop herself from asking the question.

Michael smiled slightly. "It has nothing to do with Lord Halkyn; he is well as far as I am aware. Please excuse me for a moment. I will join everyone in the drawing room in a short while and inform you of the contents of this correspondence."

Charlotte left the room both relieved and worried. Lord Dunham was such a calm, commanding person, the news must be serious to have shaken him so much.

As the butler closed the door, leaving Michael alone in his study, he sat forward in his seat and placed his head in his hands. When he read the news he had been gripped by such fear, it would have brought him to his knees had he been standing. He had to protect her; there was no other alternative, but he had almost failed her once before; what if he failed this time?

*

Michael sent word everyone should gather in the drawing room. This was a strange summons, so everyone was a little uneasy. Eventually they were joined by Michael, who looked grim but in control. He approached Elizabeth, sitting next to her and taking her hand in his.

"I'm afraid, Violet and Edward, I'm going to have to ask you to postpone your trip to London; and, John, if you can stay on here, I would be much obliged."

Normally John would have been flippant with his friend, but he could sense his unease under his grim demeanour. "I am at your service, Michael. What is it?"

"Yes, what has happened?" Elizabeth asked.

"I've had some news today I hate having to tell you, Elizabeth, because I know it will unsettle you," Michael said, bringing his wife's hand to his lips and kissing it.

"What is it?" Elizabeth asked gently. She was concerned for her husband; she had always disliked seeing him worried, especially when it was on her account.

"I've received communication to say that George Watson was not on the ship when it arrived in Australia," Michael said quietly.

The news stilled the people in the room. It was obvious everyone, apart from Charlotte, knew the meaning of the name, but she kept silent. When people such as Mr Anderton and Miss Fairfield take sharp intakes of breath at the mention of a name, Charlotte knew it was not the time to ask for explanations.

"I don't understand," Elizabeth said frowning. "I'm presuming by your demeanour he did not die on the journey?"

"No," Michael confirmed. "Apparently, Miranda was very sick by the time they reached Australia; she had not travelled well. There had been an outbreak of fever on board. She was very ill but lucid at the time they docked. When it was realised that George was missing, she took great pleasure in saying he had never been on board. He had escaped before the ship set sail."

"Why did he not take Miranda with him?" Elizabeth asked quietly.

"She cursed him to the others, saying he had only looked after himself. Although if he had taken her, there would have been more chance of them being caught, so it's just one more example of their selfishness," Michael said bitterly, remembering the lengths the brother and sister would go to in order to gain something for themselves.

"So, he didn't leave this country?" Violet asked.

"No. All this time, we have been under the impression they were both out of the country, and the reality is he could be anywhere,"

Michael snarled, angry he had tried to be fair, and now his family, his wife and unborn child, were in danger.

Edward intervened, "We will stay as long as needed. You will need help in trying to track him down; send word to Bow Street."

"I will, but he could be anywhere!" Michael said.

Elizabeth squeezed her husband's hand. "Tell us the truth Michael; what else did the letter say?"

Michael sighed after a moment. "Miranda was quite clear George's aim was to finish what they had set out to do: to ruin you. She did not survive long after that; the authorities thought it was the thought of her being able to gloat to them that kept her alive. She enjoyed being able to tell them they were all incompetent fools."

"He can't ruin Elizabeth now; she is a married woman," Violet said, pointing out the obvious difference in circumstances since the last time George and Elizabeth had met.

"We know what he wanted to do; it's obviously still his aim. He could be here now! Damn them for not finding out sooner! You have been in danger for weeks!" Michael exploded.

Everyone jumped at the outburst, but Elizabeth responded calmly to her husband. "I am surrounded by people; my socialising can easily be cut short because of my condition. I'm happy to confine myself to the locality and not put the baby at any risk. He will be found."

"Michael, she will not be left alone for a moment," Violet assured her brother. "Charlotte, could you please accompany me? I have some errands I need help with if we are to stay here indefinitely."

"Certainly," Charlotte replied, and the two ladies left the room together.

Violet led the way to her bed chamber and sat at her dressing table. She invited Charlotte to sit on the chaise lounge at the end of the bed. "My dear, I think you should consider returning to your uncle while all this is going on."

Charlotte was shocked. "I don't understand. If you want me out of the house, of course, I will go, but is there nothing I can do to help? It seems from what has been said the more people remaining here the better. If I can be of assistance, I will."

"You are a dear girl; I was hoping you would say that, but you may not when you realise what we are up against."

Violet told Charlotte about Elizabeth's cousin, his wife and brother approaching Elizabeth to try and obtain her money. When she refused, they had plotted to have her compromised by George, the brother. That way she would have been forced into marriage, and they would have had access to her fortune.

"They drugged her and took her to an inn. Only for her cousin being afraid for his life when Michael got to him, Elizabeth would have been ruined by George. Michael never talks about it, but Elizabeth once told me if Michael had arrived even five minutes later, it would have been too late."

Charlotte was horrified at the thought. It was far worse than anything she had been through, and that *still* gave her nightmares. She wondered how Elizabeth could seem so at peace. "My goodness! What happened to her cousin?"

"He was killed; George had a gun, and it went off in the fight after they were discovered. Miranda and George were held until the magistrate could be found, and then they were put on trial. We thought they would be hanged, but Michael asked for the sentence be transportation to Australia for their crimes. He didn't think Elizabeth would rest easy with their deaths on her conscience. It has all taken so many months, we thought everything was settled until today. George will be a desperate man: everyone will understand if you want to leave; you must consider what we will be facing by staying here."

"No!" Charlotte said firmly. "I would not dream of leaving now. You need the help of everyone here, and I will do whatever I can to help."

"Thank you, my dear; the more people around Elizabeth, the less likely it is he will approach her.

Chapter 16

For a week after Stephen had attended Baron Kersal's den of iniquity, he did not leave the house. His food intake was limited, but his brandy intake was steady. He rose late and refused to see anyone; he remained undressed and unshaven, something previously unheard of. Walter had watched his employer without comment but had started to secretly dilute the brandy. He could do very little, but he was determined to try and prevent his master from drinking himself to death.

All the staff were worried, as his Lordship had always been in control. They might not have agreed with everything he did, and they all longed for the day when he would settle down, but they had not expected this. Walter had informed the key staff Lord Halkyn had been refused in a marriage proposal, and they all came to the correct conclusion their employer was in love and suffering the consequences of rejection. The only person still in denial about being in love was Stephen himself.

He did not know what to do with himself. Until he had finished his business with Peters, there had been a purpose. He had said he would seek revenge on Baron Kersal, and that is what he had done. He could do no more. The problem was once his task was complete, all he could think of was Charlotte and how she had refused his proposal. He was bitter and angry, but instead of doing his usual trick of going out to experience every social activity polite society could offer and quite a few it could not, he could not find the motivation to do anything. So, he sat at home, dwelling on a pair of green eyes in a beautiful face and tried to deaden any feeling by drinking himself into a stupor.

A week into this, the pain had subsided into a bitter case of self-pity, another emotion Stephen was unused to feeling. He was withdrawing into himself, and he did not know what to do to return to his former self. He questioned himself time and again, how could such a girl get under his skin so much? She was barely out of the schoolroom; he should have run in the opposite direction as soon as he discovered that: but instead, he had been drawn to her, had found could not leave her or forget her. Every time he closed his eyes, she was there, pulling those faces that showed each emotion she was feeling or coming out with a comment that would surprise him and set him rocking on his heels, unsure of what to say in return.

Walter entered the study quietly; any slight noise gained an abusive outburst these days. He suppressed his frown as he approached Lord Halkyn, who was slumped in the chair, looking barely conscious.

"My Lord, a letter has arrived," Walter said gently.

"Put it on the fire when you light it; it will have more use there," Stephen slurred, not opening his eyes.

"I think it may be important, My Lord," Walter persisted.

"Have you a hidden talent, Walter?" Stephen asked, still slurring, but the sarcasm was clear. "Have you started being able to see through parchment, or do you just read my letters?"

"Neither, My Lord," Walter responded calmly.

"Well, then, throw the bloody thing away!" Stephen muttered angrily.

Walter decided to take another approach. "The letter has Lord Dunham's seal."

Stephen froze, opened his eyes slightly but then shrugged. "There is no reason why Dunham would be contacting me."

"Perhaps Lady Dunham is ill," Walter suggested, purposely not mentioning the name both men were thinking about.

"She's as strong as a horse, that one!" Stephen responded, but he sat up in the chair and ran his hands through his hair.

Walter decided to use the information Stephen had muttered in one of his drunken rants about love, marriage and children. "Ladies who are in a delicate condition can sometimes ail more than they normally would. I do hope she is well. By all accounts she is a fine lady, but not to worry: I shall destroy the letter as you have requested, My Lord."

"Has anyone ever told you that you could not be devious if your life depended on it?" Stephen muttered, but there was the ghost of a smile on his lips.

"I believe Napoleon did not fear for his country's defeat when I offered to help with our nation's defence," replied Walter seriously.

"And instead I've been cursed with you," Stephen muttered. "Give me the letter."

Walter handed over the letter and waited while Stephen opened it and read its contents. He saw Stephen sit up further and grip the letter with more force. When he had read and reread it, he crumpled the paper as he slammed his fist down. "Damn the man for being so bloody noble!" He cursed.

"My Lord?" Walter asked gently, almost regretting forcing the letter onto his employer.

"Bloody Dunham! Why couldn't he be like the rest of us and want to see the people that wrong us hang for their crimes?" Stephen growled. "I need tea, Walter! I need to be able to think. Bring lots of tea!"

Walter left the room with a sense of relief. He was not sure of the contents, but its initial impact had been for his master to want to be sober, which was a step in the right direction.

*

Far too much tea later, along with some ham and bread and, though Stephen did not feel completely sober, his head was clearer than it had been for days. He pondered what Michael's letter said.

There is no one else we would trust; and with your recent involvement with Bow Street, I hope it will give you an insight into how best to use them. Elizabeth is in real danger: this man has nothing to lose; he has lost everything and has no family left alive to my knowledge. For the first time in my life, I am afraid of the consequences. If he should reach Elizabeth before we track him down..., these thoughts and worse have kept me sitting awake at her bedside since I received the news. Please find out what you can and send a reply at the earliest opportunity. He would not have initially known where Dunham Park was located, so I am presuming his first approach would have been to the London house. Act quickly, Halkyn, please.

Michael had enclosed full particulars of the dates when everything had happened, the trial and the sentence. He had finished by giving a full description of George.

Stephen had at first ranted at Michael's stupidity. This is exactly why he did not want to tie himself to someone whom he loved; if they were ill or worse, how did one continue afterwards? His thoughts were that of someone defensive and still in denial. When he again looked over the letter, his concern for Elizabeth grew. Dunham had been a hit with the ladies in his prime, but one of his attractions was that he was confident about his abilities. He was not one to show fear or uncertainty in public.

Stephen realised the letter must have cost Michael a great deal of pride to write. His panic came through the words as clearly as if he were standing before Stephen, and that was what caused the frown on Stephen's face. Elizabeth was in danger, and she was one of the most genuine people he knew. He considered her a friend—her more than Dunham—and for that reason he would help all he could.

Charlotte was not mentioned in the letter, and it frustrated Stephen, but he should not have expected she would have been. A man almost out of his mind with worry over his wife and unborn child would not think of mentioning his house guest. Even if she were the last person Stephen actually wanted to know about. She could even be engaged by now; Elizabeth had said she was going to introduce her to Society. Well they would be welcome to her. He'd like to see what the gentlemen of Somerset thought of a Miss who was determined on romance without a dowry to encourage it!

Stephen almost reached for the brandy bottle, but stilled as his hand touched it. If he started again he would be no help to

Elizabeth. He owed her friendship enough to stay sober. He rang the bell and, while waiting for Walter, scribbled out a note.

Walter entered the room, and Stephen handed him the sealed letter.

"I need this delivered to Mr Peters tonight. Into his hand and only into his hand no matter where he is. Pay whoever or whatever you have to in order that he receives it. I am at home to Peters at whatever time he calls, day or night, and tell Lowe I need to bathe, to have a change of clothes, and a shave!" Stephen commanded, rubbing his hand over a chin that bore evidence of almost a week's worth of stubble.

"Yes, My Lord," Walter replied and left the room. He was going to brighten the day of Lowe the Valet, who had been in a decline since Lord Halkyn had refused to dress.

*

Peters had been shown into Stephen's drawing room as the clock struck midnight. He had been hard to track down but had been finally caught up with near the docks, not usually a place to be alone on a dark London night.

Stephen stood when the gentleman entered. "Thank you for coming," he said, reaching out his hand in greeting. "I did not expect to be seeing you quite so soon again."

"No, My Lord," Peters said. "I take it from your letter this has nothing to do with the Kersal case?"

"No, although I hope that *that* matter will be drawing to a conclusion soon?" Stephen asked.

"It will, but we are waiting for the right moment before we act," Peters replied, giving nothing away.

"Good," came the quiet response. "You'd better sit down; I have a job I hope you can help with," Stephen said, and proceeded to tell Peters all of the details in the letter. He did not show Peters the document; he felt Dunham's emotions were exposed in that letter, and he did not want a stranger to see that.

Peters listened in his usual quiet way, interjecting questions when he needed clarification. At the end of Stephen's tale, he thought for a moment. "I think Lord Dunham is correct; he will have gone to the house in London first. It is the easiest to reach; he must have escaped from the docks, and he could just disappear into the crowds in London whereas it would be far harder to do that in the country."

"Do you think he will still be in London?" Stephen asked, knowing it was only a faint hope.

"It depends how long he decided to hide after he escaped from the ship. He wouldn't want to hide for too long, especially if he has no money. I will start in the morning."

"Will you question the staff?" Stephen asked.

"Not necessarily," Peters replied with a hint of amusement in his eyes, but it did not quite reach his mouth. "He may not have approached the staff, but there are many other ways to find out if he has been near the house."

Stephen nodded, and the men parted. There was nothing else Stephen could do but send out a short letter to let Dunham know the search was in hand.

*

Peters returned to visit Stephen after two days. It had actually been a relatively easy task but one that gave him no pleasure. He knew his news would increase concern, rather than reassure.

Stephen was in the study; it looked like he had been pacing when Mr Peters entered. He nodded to the gentleman to sit down and offered him refreshments. Mr Peters declined and took out his notebook ready to relay the information he had gathered.

"George Watson, or a man very closely matching his description was seen in the area of Lord Dunham's London house over three weeks ago," Mr Peters said calmly.

Stephen took a long breath. "Three weeks? That must mean he's in Somerset by now," he said grimly.

"It is a fair assumption, My Lord," Mr Peters responded. "He was seen watching the house and then fell in with a group of tramps that frequent the area. Their mornings are spent knocking on the basement doors asking for scraps of food. He spoke to some of the junior staff in the house. They did tell him about the family and about Dunham Park."

"Stupid idiots!" Stephen exploded. "Why on earth did they think he was asking after the family? So he could call on them when they returned to town?"

"They are young girls of twelve, first time away from home and living in a large house. They are proud of the family they serve. It's not an unusual question in any respects; the tramps would want to know if the families were at home or not."

"What possible benefit would that information be to them?" Stephen asked.

"If the family are at home, there are more parties, which means more food, meaning more waste. They eat better when a family is in residence."

"Oh." Stephen was generous to charitable causes, but he had never thought of the practicality of needing to gather food on a day to day basis. "Did he give anything away?"

"Not really," Mr Peters replied. "He mentioned he had worked for Lady Dunham's family in the north and was hoping she would give him a job on her estate. He came across as a man down on his luck; he gave no other information, which is no surprise."

"So, that was three weeks ago," Stephen mused. "How long would it have taken him to reach Dunham Park?"

"Probably well over a week; he would have likely walked and probably at night. Let's not forget he is a man on the run. If he was caught and his true identity discovered, he would be hanged."

"Let's hope that happened," Stephen said gruffly.

"We would have heard," Mr Peters said reasonably.

"He must be in the Somerset area," Stephen said, a sinking feeling developing at the thought Elizabeth was truly in danger. There was another niggle that would not subside, however he tried to ignore it. Charlotte was in that area, as was a man who was on the run and determined to damage the family in residence. Elizabeth was in danger, but Charlotte was also at risk because of her residence there.

Stephen rang for Walter. "I need to send a letter to Lord Dunham. He needs to know they are at risk. Would you take it and act as protector for Lady Dunham?"

"Me?" Mr Peters asked in disbelief. "I am working on other cases My Lord."

Stephen sighed. "I do not wish to appear overbearing, but one, no two of my friends could be in danger; I trust your ability. I will pay whatever it takes for this to be your top priority."

"It isn't about money," Mr Peters scowled at Stephen. The aristocracy always thought it came down to money.

"I apologise; I did not mean to offend, but I need your help," Stephen said quietly. He had seen the fire in Mr Peter's eyes and had withdrawn his overbearing manner.

A small cough came from the door of the study. Stephen raised his eyes at Walter. "Yes, Walter?"

"My Lord, I beg pardon in overhearing some of your conversation, but if I could offer a suggestion?" The calm butler asked.

Stephen looked at Mr Peters. "He's only asking permission because you are in the room; normally he just offers the suggestion whether I want to hear it or not."

Mr Peters looked slightly amused, but refrained from saying anything. Walter coughed again; Stephen was sure it was to hide a laugh, but the butler's face remained impassive. "Your flattery overwhelms me, My Lord, but as I was saying, I feel Lord Dunham may appreciate it if both of you gentlemen could go to the estate."

"Both of us?" Stephen asked in disbelief, but his heart had started to pound at the thought.

"Yes, My Lord. Trusted friends are hard to find, and the more people in the house surrounding her Ladyship, the safer she will be. Staff cannot be present all the time."

Stephen thought for a moment. He wanted to go. He had wanted to go as soon as Walter had suggested it, but it would put him in Charlotte's company again. He dismissed his pounding heart. He was a grown man, one who could respond to the needs of a friend without having to be afraid of the effects a seventeen year old chit would have on him.

Stephen turned to Mr Peters. "Will you accompany me, please? I realise you have other work, but is there any possibility you could accompany me? My friend is in danger."

Mr Peters nodded; he would have to pass his work to a colleague. He would owe Corless an unlimited amount of drink for the favour, but he wanted to help Lord Halkyn. The appeal in Lord Halkyn's request damped down the previous inappropriate comments he had made. Peters responded quietly, "Yes, give me two hours, and I will be ready."

Stephen nodded and turned to Walter. "Arrange the carriage Walter, and let it be clear: we will be travelling as fast as it can bear."

"Yes, My Lord."

Chapter 17

The family had quickly developed a routine and, although Elizabeth hated not being able to wander across the fields, she held to the restriction of staying on the immediate parkland. Edward, John, Michael and the male staff were all happy to accompany her on long walks around the estate. Miss Fairfield, Charlotte and Violet took carriage rides and walks around the formal gardens with staff to accompany them. When she was within the house, there was always someone with her. It was a prison, but a necessary one.

The tension in the household could be felt, but everyone tried to get on with life as best they could. Michael and Elizabeth had talked behind closed doors, their conversation being upsetting to both, but important. They both realised the threat was serious.

Charlotte did all she could to make herself useful to Elizabeth. If she had felt her presence was not welcomed, she would have returned to her uncle's home, whatever the consequences, but her presence was needed. She made up a third person on many of Elizabeth's short outings. They had come to the conclusion that by being in a pair, there was the likelihood they were still vulnerable, but by being in a threesome, there was less chance of them being approached. More people, therefore, helped.

Mr Anderton and the senior staff regularly undertook searches of the property and buildings to ensure no one was hiding anywhere. Everything was being done to reduce the chance of George being able to get close enough to reach Elizabeth. No one let themselves hope he was not in the area. If he could avoid deportation, he could certainly find his way to Somerset.

The second Sunday morning felt more normal than the first had. Elizabeth insisted she wanted to go to church as normal; it would cause speculation in the local population as to why Lady Dunham was not attending church, which she wanted to avoid. As the church was on the edge of the parkland this did not seem an unreasonable request by Elizabeth. It was agreed Michael, Edward and Violet would arrive at the church first, to enable the men to search the grounds. Mr Anderton and Mr Dawson, along with the staff, would carry out a thorough search of the house while the group were absent. Elizabeth would travel with Charlotte and Miss Fairfield in the carriage and hopefully every part had been thought through.

Charlotte stood by Elizabeth as she waved Michael, Violet and Edward off. Elizabeth sighed as she remained at the entrance of the house, waiting for her own carriage to be brought round.

"Are you feeling unwell?" Charlotte asked. There was no use in asking if everything was fine; it had obviously not been fine since Lord Dunham had received the letter.

"I admit to having my nerves stretched to the breaking point," Elizabeth said with a smile that was part smile, part grimace. "I am longing to get on the back of a horse and ride in a straight line until it can run no more. I had thought London could be confining; I never expected the country to be so."

"I'm sure he will soon be found," Charlotte sympathised.

"I hope so," Elizabeth replied with a groan. "We should be receiving reinforcements soon," she said more gently. "Lord Halkyn and a Bow Street Officer are on their way here; in fact they should be arriving anytime. Michael had a word to say they were on their way. I hope it will not cause you distress; I will understand if you wish to leave when he arrives."

Charlotte had flushed deeply at Elizabeth's words. Stephen returning to live in the same house? The man she had refused and who had taunted her as he left. How could she face him again? *Could* she face him again?

She shook herself inwardly. Of course, she could face him again; he was the man she thought of every time she had a spare moment. He would be cruel no doubt, dismissive as he had been when they parted, but oh, she would relish being able to see him again. She had missed him so much.

"I do not wish to leave," she said quietly after a moment or two.

Elizabeth squeezed her hand. "I am grateful you don't, and I hope Stephen appreciates what a gem you are when he sees you this time."

The carriage arrived, and Charlotte climbed in, a little distracted. Stephen would not appreciate her still being here; he was obviously coming down to help, not to see her. She had to remember that to keep herself in check.

Charlotte paused; the dishevelled man was pointing a gun at her and had a finger over his lips in a shushing motion. She froze: she had never been faced with a gun being pointed at her; even Baron Kersal had not used such extreme measures. The man indicated with the barrel of the gun she should continue into the coach and take a seat.

Charlotte moved slowly, eyeing the door opposite. If she threw herself out of the door behind her, she would surely injure Elizabeth and, although they were in danger, she could not risk hurting the baby. The man noticed her looking at the door and smirked.

"It's locked," he hissed in a whisper. "Sit, and you may live."

May live. Charlotte started to shake; suddenly the danger she was in was very real.

Elizabeth followed Charlotte into the carriage, wondering what had made her pause. She gasped when she saw George sitting opposite Charlotte, now with a second gun in his hands, one pointing at Charlotte, one at herself.

"Get in the carriage quietly and without fuss, and your little friend will live. For now," he whispered roughly.

Elizabeth seemed very calm as she continued into the carriage. "There is one other," she said to George. "Have you got a third gun to threaten us with, George?" Her tone was sarcastic, and Charlotte was shocked yet impressed that, in such extreme circumstances, Elizabeth could appear so calm.

"I am going to make you pay for all your insolence, don't you worry!" George hissed at her.

Miss Fairfield had reached the entrance of the carriage and had seen the scene before her. She waited, not wishing to move quickly in case Elizabeth or Charlotte came to harm. George turned to her, but kept his guns on the two already seated.

"Move slowly back out of the carriage and fold the steps and close the door yourself. Don't let a footman near or you will need a new mistress," George commanded.

Miss Fairfield paled at his words. "You will not get away with this," she said quietly, her voice shaking.

"If I don't, then the heir to the Dunham estate will be lost before he's born," George said. At Elizabeth's gasp, he turned his head slightly but without taking his eyes off Miss Fairfield. "Yes, Elizabeth, I know about the baby: the one that should have been mine only for that interfering guardian of yours. Now, Madam, when you leave the coach, give the driver the instruction to turn left out of the main gate and drive fast until he hears further instructions."

"He's been told to only go to the church," Miss Fairfield said firmly, her hands were shaking, but she was not going to let Elizabeth down.

"You shall have to persuade him, or this little girl will lose her life and then so will your precious Elizabeth. As for you, I shall be watching, and if you move from the spot outside the house until the carriage is out of sight, I may have to shoot Elizabeth. Not so that she will die immediately, since we have some unfinished business, but enough to cause her and the baby pain. Now leave!"

Miss Fairfield left the carriage and with a shaking voice, she commanded the footman to stay where he was while she lifted the steps and closed the door. She saw George appear in the window where she could see him, but no one else. She stepped back and motioned to the driver.

"James, there has been a change of plan. For her Ladyship's safety you need to drive fast and turn left when you reach the main park gate. Continue until you hear further instructions from within the carriage," came the slightly shaky instructions.

"But, Miss Fairfield, that won't take us anywhere near the church. His Lordship was very clear," James queried with a frown. "Is her Ladyship well?"

Miss Fairfield was not about to lie. "For the moment; James, please do as I ask: it is of the utmost importance."

Something must have registered on Miss Fairfield's face, for the coachman nodded and clicked the reins to start the horses. She stood and watched the carriage moving quickly along the drive; the further it travelled, the more she started to shake.

The second the carriage window was out of sight, Miss Fairfield ran into the house. "Phelps!" she shouted for the butler. "Phelps, where are you?"

"Miss Fairfield?" came the calm voice of the butler. He had never heard Miss Fairfield raise her voice in all the time he had known her.

Miss Fairfield gasped for breath. "Get Mr Anderton or Mr Dawson, or both, quickly! George Watson has Lady Dunham!"

Phelps did not need any further explanation. The name had been seared in the memories of the staff. The normally calm butler shouted instructions to footmen, and a frenzied search of the house and outlying buildings was commenced to find the two gentlemen.

Miss Fairfield stood, hugging her arms around herself in an attempt to stop the shaking. She had to be calm; she had to be able to repeat everything that had happened. Every second that passed, though, caused the panic inside her to increase, as each moment meant the carriage was moving farther away from the house. It seemed an eternity before she heard running footsteps on the gravel outside followed by the appearance in the hallway of Mr Anderton and a footman.

Miss Fairfield turned to the man who so often had been her antagonist and promptly burst into tears. The action made Mr Anderton pause for a moment before crossing the hall and wrapping his arms around Miss Fairfield.

"What is it? What has happened?" he asked, in a tone more gentle than he had ever used before. He sensed the tears were from fear, and he needed to be able to calm her in order to help.

"Charles, I have let her down!" Miss Fairfield moaned into his shoulder.

Mr Anderton suffered the second surprise in as many minutes; never had Miss Fairfield used his given name. "Miss Fairfield, Martha," he whispered. "You have not. Tell me quickly what has happened, and we can go to her. I need every detail though."

By this time Mr Dawson had also joined the crowd in the hallway, and Miss Fairfield gathered herself together enough to tell the gentlemen what had happened. "Like a coward, I did exactly as he instructed!" she cursed herself.

Charles turned to Mr Dawson. "I will follow the carriage on horseback; you get to the church for his Lordship and Mr and Mrs Parker. We need to cover all the routes. Phelps, I need horses! Now!" There was a flurry of activity behind Charles and Miss Fairfield, but he still held her shaking form.

Charles bent to Miss Fairfield's ear and whispered. "I will bring her back; I promise. Trust in me, Martha."

Miss Fairfield pulled herself away from the comfort of Charles's arms and looked into his serious face. It was as if the last months had not taken place. "I do trust you," she said simply.

With a nod Charles was through the door, Mr Dawson on his heels, and the sounds of horse hooves on gravel indicated they were on their way.

Phelps returned inside and approached Miss Fairfield. "A brandy, Miss Fairfield, to enable you to be ready for her Ladyship's return?"

Miss Fairfield nodded mutely and followed the butler into the drawing room. She could not consider any other outcome.

*

Elizabeth and Charlotte gripped each other's hands as the carriage moved forward. George saw the action and sneered. "You've brought this on yourself my, dear Elizabeth. If only you had agreed to marry me at the start; but no, you had ideas of grandeur. Just look where it is has got you, living the last few moments of your life in a carriage, racing away from your husband. He won't save you this time."

Charlotte gripped Elizabeth's hand even tighter at George's words. Elizabeth felt sickened but squeezed Charlotte's hand in return to reassure her. She looked at George squarely "You will not get away with this," she said. Her voice sounded calmer than she felt.

George laughed, "Elizabeth, I don't want to get away with it. Have you forgotten because of your husband I am a wanted man? If I get caught, I hang. If I don't get caught, I live on the streets until I starve, or I catch some deadly disease. No, I have no future here or anywhere else! So, my dear, I have nothing to lose, but you and that interfering husband of yours will be brought down to my level before I go. You will know what it is like to know you have no future, to know you have lost everything!"

"It isn't our fault you are in this situation," Elizabeth insisted. "If Miranda and Herbert hadn't lived beyond their means, they would have never made contact with me. Neither of them held any affection for me. I did not seek them out; I just wanted to be left alone to live my own life."

"Yes, you wanted to manage the estate. Herbert's estate, but when it needed help you did not want anything to do with it. If you had agreed then, we would all be living happily in Lancashire."

To Charlotte's horror, Elizabeth snorted. "You may have been living happily, but I certainly would not have been."

Charlotte was surprised and breathed a sigh of relief when George laughed at Elizabeth's outburst. "You always did have spirit. I would have liked to tame it; I see your husband hasn't been able to."

Elizabeth fell silent for a few moments and then looked at George more calmly. "Your argument, if that is what you can call it, has always been with me. Charlotte has nothing to do with this. She is only involved because of her friendship with me. She shouldn't suffer because of that."

Charlotte did not know what Elizabeth was going to say, but she gripped Elizabeth's hands. "Stop Elizabeth; we are in this together."

"How sweet," George sneered at Charlotte. The young girl gulped at the man before her; she was convinced neither of them would leave the carriage alive.

Elizabeth turned to Charlotte. "You should not be forced to face this. It is my fate being decided, not yours." She turned back to George. "Please let her go."

George laughed, "While your little friend is here, you will behave yourself."

"I will do everything you ask me to do; you don't need Charlotte," Elizabeth said firmly.

"If I don't need her, I should kill her now," George said, aiming his gun directly at Charlotte's head. The gun had been hanging a little loosely over his arm, but now he was gripping it tightly.

"No!" Elizabeth said quickly. "If she lives, I will do anything you ask but not if she dies."

"It doesn't really matter either way, but I feel generous. Stand up," George commanded Charlotte.

Charlotte was convinced he was going to shoot her; he had convinced them he had nothing left to live for, so why would her life be of importance to him? She felt strangely detached as she struggled to stand in the fast moving carriage, letting go of Elizabeth's hand in the process. If she were to die in this carriage, she would do it bravely. She fought against the fear she felt and focused her mind on those blue eyes she craved so much to see again and the rosebud mouth that had given her so much pleasure when it had kissed her. Stephen would be her last thought, the only thought that took her into the afterlife.

George placed one of the guns down, but threatened Elizabeth. "If you move I shoot you in the stomach, understand?"

Elizabeth nodded. She would have already acted if she were not expecting a child. She wanted her baby to live and had to do anything she could to try to make that a possibility. She sat still, hoping George would release Charlotte.

What happened next happened so quickly Elizabeth barely had time to take in a breath in horror. George seemed to push Charlotte against the carriage door; Charlotte lost her balance, and George moved quickly, unlocking the door and releasing the handle in one easy motion. Charlotte's body tumbled out of the carriage; she was obviously unable to save herself because of the speed and the way she had been pushed. There was no scream as she fell to the ground.

One of the rear footmen shouted something, and the carriage slowed. George cursed and grabbed his second gun. He raised it to the roof of the carriage and pulled the trigger. The shot went harmlessly through the roof, but it was enough to scare the horses and the men at the front and rear of the carriage. It confirmed to them all something was very wrong and their mistress was in danger. George shouted through the open door to keep going. As the carriage rumbled along at speed, he grabbed for the door as it swung and slammed it shut.

Chapter 18

Elizabeth sat motionless. She had just killed her friend. How could she ever live with herself after this? How could she ever face Stephen again if Michael had been right and Stephen had real feelings for Charlotte? She had just been the cause of her death, and he would never forgive her. She would never forgive herself.

"That's quietened you. I should have done it at the start!" George gloated at the expression of horror on Elizabeth's face.

"Have you no feelings?" Elizabeth said bitterly.

"No," George replied with a sneer.

Elizabeth looked at the man before her. She had no idea how he had gained access to the carriage, especially the way he looked, dirty, unkempt and wild. He must have been determined in his aim; he must have the same madness Miranda had suffered from. Miranda. Elizabeth thought back over the actions of the brother and sister; she did not feel any pity, just anger at the way they had presumed they could use her as a commodity and then discard her when she was no longer useful to them.

She realised George was right: he had nothing to lose, which put her and her baby in an unenviable position. He was going to kill her; whether or not he forced himself on her did not seem to matter to him. It had mattered the last time, but then he had needed her to marry him; but this time there was not that option. She had discussed every eventuality with Michael in detail; they had both wanted to be prepared for the worst. Elizabeth set her shoulders; she knew what she had to do.

George flicked the lock on the door when Elizabeth slid across to the window. "Don't get any ideas!" he snarled.

"I wouldn't dream of it," Elizabeth replied calmly. "I am merely trying to get closer to look out of the window. I'm feeling rather sick from being jostled around. A side effect of being with child."

George grimaced, "Why is nothing ever easy with you?"

Elizabeth actually smiled at that comment in genuine amusement. "My husband would have some sympathy with you in that regard," she said. George grunted, but was not drawn. Elizabeth had to keep in control; she did not know how long she had to act before he decided the moment was right to kill her. "I am sorry about Miranda."

"She may be on the other side of the earth, but she will soon have the people around her dancing to her tune!" George said with a little pride.

Elizabeth knew once she started there was no going back. She took a breath. "George, Miranda died when she reached Australia."

"You lying bitch!" George spat and smacked Elizabeth across the face.

Elizabeth's head spun, but she continued. She put her hands on the seat to steady herself. "I'm not lying. She survived the journey and was able to gloat to her captors that you had escaped, but she died soon afterwards. They wrote to Michael and informed him you were on the loose."

George's face twisted at Elizabeth's words, but he paused before speaking. "I wondered why you were so well protected."

"Did you watch me for long?" Elizabeth asked, a chill creeping down her spine at the thought of being watched by such a man.

"A little while. Enough to know it was going to be difficult to get to you, but I still did it, and today I will get my revenge once and for all."

"I'm sorry, George, that things worked out the way they have, but it is time you gave up. No one else needs to die today if you stop this now," Elizabeth said coaxingly.

"I decide who dies and when!" George snapped.

"I'm afraid you don't, George, not anymore," Elizabeth said with determination.

The shot rang out of the carriage, and the horses once again were frightened by the sound. James the driver struggled to maintain control, which was not helped by him being overtaken by three men on horseback. He was about to curse the riders until he recognised one was Lord Dunham and another his man of business, Mr Anderton. He pulled the carriage to a halt, but shouted to Lord Dunham gunshots had been fired.

Michael had heard the shot and for the second time in his life he thought he would faint. He'd had to grip hard on the reins while the feeling passed. He had no idea what was going on inside the carriage, but he could not wait to find out. If Elizabeth were dead, it would not matter if he followed the same way. He jumped off his horse, almost before it came to a halt and grabbed the carriage door.

John and Charles both shouted to Michael, but he did not hesitate and yanked the door open. He clambered inside immediately. The two men followed and both visibly sagged with relief to see Michael holding onto Elizabeth as if he would never let her go and the slumped body of George Watson on the opposite seat. The pool of red was spreading from his chest; his gun lay loose, unused, across his lap.

Eventually Elizabeth moved, to look at Michael, "I want to go home, but we have to find Charlotte first," she said, her eyes threatening tears, but her will refusing to let them fall.

"Where is she?" Michael asked, stroking his wife's hair.

"I don't know: somewhere along the route we have taken. He threw her out of the carriage while we were travelling at speed, Michael. I asked him to let her go, and he pushed her out! She must have been killed, but we must find her body. I've killed her just as if I pushed her out myself," Elizabeth choked.

Michael was appalled by what he heard, but he continued to stroke Elizabeth's hair. He rested his head on her forehead. "We will find her," he said gently.

Michael helped Elizabeth out. "James, the carriage contains the body of George Watson. Please take it to the magistrate and inform him what has happened. If he needs to speak to me, I shall be at Dunham House. Lady Dunham will be travelling back on my horse, at a slow pace. Which route did you take?"

"We came around the estate on the East road and then followed the Melksham Road, My Lord," James explained.

Michael turned to Charles and John. "Charlotte was purposely thrown from the carriage by Watson; we are looking for her body," he said quietly, hoping Elizabeth did not hear. Both men looked grim but nodded and mounted their horses. "If you go ahead of us and look for her, we will follow in your wake. I don't wish to travel any faster than a slow trot with Elizabeth on the horse. I think she had suffered enough exertion for today."

The group split, and Michael and Elizabeth followed the others at a more sedate pace. For a while, neither spoke, each in their own nightmare. Eventually though, Michael squeezed his wife and kissed her head. "I would not have got through this day if anything had happened to you. When Charles and John burst into the church, I thought it was too late then. You are so precious to me Elizabeth, and yet I feel so helpless sometimes."

Elizabeth leaned back into Michael's shoulder. "I knew there was real danger this time, but we had prepared. I just wanted to protect Charlotte...." she sobbed.

"They will find her," Michael soothed, but he had little hope of her being alive. The human body did not often survive being thrown from a carriage at speed.

They arrived back at Dunham House to see John and Charles's horses still at the front of the property. This gave them hope; if they had brought her, they would want to go straight inside rather than to the stables. Michael gently lifted Elizabeth down and led her inside. There was a lot of bustle in the house. Phelps, as ever, met his master at the door.

"Phelps, where are Mr Anderton and Mr Dawson?"

"They are in the drawing room," came the reply. "I shall supply refreshments, My Lord."

"Thank you," Michael responded walking with Elizabeth into the room, his arm never leaving the hold it had on her waist. He was not sure he could ever let her out of his reach again.

Miss Fairfield sat on a chair facing the door with Mr Anderton standing over her. Mr Dawson was near the fire with a glass of brandy in his hand. Violet and Edward sat next to each other on a sofa.

"Elizabeth!" Miss Fairfield cried, almost leaping across the room to her mistress. She acted completely out of character by grasping Elizabeth and holding the younger woman to her. "I thought I had sent you to your death! I am so sorry that I obeyed him; I keep going over what happened again and again. I should have taken the risk and acted!" Miss Fairfield babbled so far out of character that Elizabeth smiled at her companion.

"Martha, I have returned safely. You did the right thing. He had a gun pointed at us; he was determined to shoot if he thought it needed," Elizabeth soothed. "Please do not concern yourself. You could not have acted in any other way. I would have hated for you to have been hurt by being foolhardy."

"It will be a long time before I can bear to let you out of my sight again," Miss Fairfield said with feeling.

"Elizabeth, sit," Michael commanded gently.

Elizabeth did sit down without argument at her husband's command, an unusually meek action, but she turned to Mr Anderton and Mr Dawson. "Charles, John, did you find her?"

A look was exchanged between the two men, Mr Anderton spoke first. "There was no sign of her."

"No sign of her?" Elizabeth asked in disbelief. "How can that be? Where could she possibly have gone?"

"Elizabeth," Mr Dawson said gently. "We cannot be sure, but the only sign of anything was some blood on a large stone. We checked the area thoroughly, but there was no sign of her. We have no idea where she is."

"She can't have just disappeared!" Elizabeth almost wailed. "Oh, how am I going to tell Stephen?"

"Tell Stephen what?" came a voice from the doorway.

Elizabeth gasped, "Stephen! We were not expecting you yet."

"Obviously," Stephen said abruptly. "Now can you please explain what has happened that is so bad you are afraid to tell me?"

"Halkyn, my wife has been through enough today," Michael said sharply.

"And I see that Miss Webster is missing, so I am guessing she has had some involvement with the events of the day," Stephen responded brusquely. He could not help himself; his feeling of panic was increasing by the minute.

"We were taken by Mr Watson," Elizabeth started to explain quietly. "He was determined I was going to die today, and I didn't want Charlotte involved, so I asked him to release her."

"So, where is she?" Stephen persisted, his heart pounding with apprehension, but the only outward sign of his discomfort was a deep frown as he stared at Elizabeth.

Elizabeth's eyes filled with tears. "I'm sorry Stephen; he pushed her out of the carriage!" she sobbed.

"He did what?!" Stephen shouted. "Where is she?" He felt as if a hand had gripped his chest and was squeezing the breath out of him.

"We don't know," Mr Dawson intervened.

"You don't know?" Stephen said incredulously. "A girl is pushed from a moving carriage, and you can't find her?"

"They saw some blood," Elizabeth sobbed.

"This gets worse," Stephen ground out. Mr Peters stood behind him the whole time but took the opportunity to step forward.

"Where was the blood?" he asked.

Michael looked at the stranger. "I presume you are the Bow Street Officer?"

"Yes, My Lord. Peters, at your service. I'm presuming the threat from Mr Watson has been removed?"

"Yes, he was shot and killed today when his attempted kidnap of my wife and Miss Webster failed," Michael explained.

"Good, at least there is no further danger from him. If someone could direct us to the location where the blood was seen?" Peters persisted.

"I will take you," Mr Dawson said, moving towards the door.

The three gentlemen left the room, and the remaining occupants fell into a silence finally broken by Violet. "I don't understand; how was he killed?"

"Not now, Violet," Michael said gruffly, still trying to protect Elizabeth from going over the events of the day.

Elizabeth moved slightly away from her husband. "It's fine; I will need to speak to the magistrate at some point anyway. He was going to kill me; he said he was. As he said, he had nothing to lose anymore. Michael and I had talked through every possible eventuality we could think of, one of which was if I was in one of the carriages with him."

"Good thinking, Michael," Edward said with approval.

"Once I was alone, I thought I might have a chance of finishing it, but I didn't want anyone being caught in the middle. When the opportunity was right I managed to pull out one of the guns that had been hidden in the carriages. Four guns in each carriage, one on the window side of each seating bench. I needed to prime it before I

149

pulled it out, but because of their position I was able to do that without his notice. When it reached the point I thought there was no other way I could persuade him to stop, I took the gun out and shot him," Elizabeth said with a shudder.

"You did the right thing; the man was mad," Edward said reassuringly.

"I know it was the correct thing to do if I was to have any chance of surviving, but it doesn't alter the fact I have killed someone. I shall have to live with that until the day I die," Elizabeth said sadly. "The expression of shock on his face I shall never forget."

"You had no other choice," Michael soothed. "We went over this beforehand. You would only act if there was no other way."

"I know, but at the moment, it doesn't make it easier. Would you mind if I retired to my bed chamber? I suddenly feel the need to lie down," Elizabeth said quietly.

*

Stephen's horse needed to rest, but he pushed it on. He had to find her; she could not be dead. People tumbled out of carriages and survived; they had to. If she had not been at the location where she fell, perhaps she had been hurt and wandered off in a daze. They needed to find her before nightfall; she could be feeling disoriented. Once he found her, he would tell her how worried he had been about his tiger, and she would laugh at him and her eyes would twinkle as she smiled, and his chest would feel less tight, and he would be able to breathe properly again. He had to find her.

Mr Dawson led them to the road, it was a rough area and, at the side of the road, there were a number of stones. One clearly had fresh blood on it. The three men dismounted and looked at the stone as if it would reveal its secrets.

Mr Peters was the first to move, beginning to search the surrounding ground. After a few moments he straightened. "There is no other indication of blood, which is a good sign," he said.

"She can't have gone far; she was injured and on foot," Stephen said grimly.

"If she walked somewhere, she will have left some sort of trail. Look for any disturbance on the ground; footprints would be ideal, but I don't think we'll be lucky enough to find them. Look for broken branches over there in the woodland, or grass that has been flattened. Anything that would suggest someone has walked through it," Mr Peters directed.

Both men followed his lead and searched the area in detail. Every possible route was checked and rechecked for any sign Charlotte had moved that way.

After half an hour Mr Peters called them together. "She did not leave here on foot," he said, completely sure he was correct.

"How did she leave then? She was alone and thrown from a carriage, for goodness' sake!" Stephen snapped, his nerves stretched beyond the breaking point.

"Someone must have come to her aid," Mr Peters replied calmly, ignoring the tone of voice from Stephen.

"This isn't a well-used road by the state of the road and surrounding area," Mr Dawson suggested, looking at the growth of grass between the ruts in the road. Nothing could grow on the busier roads.

"Then that should make things easier," Mr Peters said. "I suggest you two gentlemen return to the house, and I shall continue my enquiries."

"I'm coming with you," Stephen said belligerently.

"If she is injured, which the blood on the stone would suggest, she will need care when we return. From the look of the others, no one there is in any fit state to look after an injured person. If you go back and rest, she will be able to rely on your help and support, should she need it," Peters' voice was calm but firm.

Stephen listened and, after a very short time, he nodded his agreement and climbed onto his horse. "Peters?" he said.

"Yes, My Lord?"

"Thank you."

Chapter 19

Charlotte awoke to the sound of whispered voices. She opened her eyes slowly, trying to remember what day it was. She was sure it could not be morning, but she did not understand why she would still be in bed.

"She's awake," a voice said, and there was a flurry of activity at the bottom of her bed.

Charlotte tried to move her head, but a sharp pain at her left side made her wince.

"Don't move my dear; you've been in a fall. You had us worried for a time, but the doctor was sure you would wake," came a soothing voice.

Charlotte struggled to recognise the voice, but she did not. The face that appeared over her was unfamiliar, and Charlotte frowned. "Where am I? What happened?" she asked, reaching to feel the side of her face. The woman who tended her was around forty and rather rotund, but her heavily lined face was filled with nothing but concern for her young patient.

"All in good time, all in good time," the soothing voice continued. "We can go over that when you feel more like yourself."

Charlotte felt the pad of a dressing on her left cheek, which carried on to the side of her eye. She struggled to try and remember what had happened to cause such an injury. "Where am I?" she persisted.

"You are safe, in a farmhouse, just a mile or two outside of the village of Colerne."

Charlotte frowned. Safe. She had felt safe recently. The feeling puzzled her; why had she needed to feel safe? It caused another feeling, one she could not quite grasp; it was just out of her reach. She was in a farm outside of Colerne. It was a place she had never heard of.

"I'm sorry: I must appear rude; I don't remember ever visiting Colerne," she explained, frowning as she tried to remember.

"You probably haven't ever been here. You took a tumble a few miles away. We found you on the road and brought you back to the farmhouse. There was no sign of a horse, so it must have bolted when you fell. You need to rest; you've had a bump to the head."

"It's all so unclear," Charlotte muttered, but the thought of resting was tempting; she felt very tired.

"You go to sleep, and we can talk more later, but before you do I need to ask you one thing: do you remember your name?"

Charlotte smiled slightly, even though every movement seemed to hurt. "Of course, I remember my name," she replied sleepily. "I'm Miss Charlotte Webster of Miss Humphrey's school for ladies."

*

It was two long days before Peters returned to the worried residents of Dunham House. Stephen had been acting like a caged animal, pacing each room and needing to almost be physically restrained by Lord Dunham to prevent him taking off on a search of his own.

Peters looked exhausted when he returned and accepted the glass of brandy Lord Dunham offered with a grateful look. Stephen had to bite back his impatience while the officer took a large swig.

Elizabeth entered the study where the three men were gathered and approached Mr Peters. "You look fit to collapse but, before we arrange food and rest, please tell us what you found."

Peters breathed heavily. "She is alive," he said simply.

Elizabeth sank down in her seat, suddenly realising she had been holding her breath. "Thank God," she whispered, fighting back tears of relief.

"Why did you not bring her back?" Stephen demanded roughly, almost joining Elizabeth in shedding tears, he felt so lightheaded.

"She is being cared for by a family on a remote farm. They must have come across her quite soon after the accident happened," Peters explained, ignoring Stephen's outburst. "They used the farm cart to transport her back and called the doctor when they returned. She was unconscious and had a head wound, so they didn't have much hope of her recovery."

Stephen took a sharp intake of breath. "But she lives?" he asked hoarsely.

"She lives, and she has regained consciousness, which was in doubt when they first found her," Peters explained. "She has a wound to the head. The doctor told the family she was very lucky."

"She was to be alive after falling from a carriage at high speed; it is little short of a miracle," Michael said.

"I've spoken to the doctor and took the liberty of explaining a little of what happened," Peters continued. "Without giving any details that would cause gossip of course," he assured Lord Dunham.

"Of course," Michael replied. He had barely met the officer, but he had total faith in his abilities. It could have something to do with the seriousness of his eyes or the gravity of his demeanour. Whatever it was, Michael would have trusted him with anything.

"What did the doctor say?" Elizabeth asked, dreading the news that her friend could be permanently injured.

"He said the fact the push from the carriage was so unexpected probably saved her life. She had no time to respond, to tense before she hit the ground, so the injury was minimal. In his opinion normally she would not have survived. He said with the continued help of God, she will be fine," Peters explained.

"The man is a fool!" Stephen snapped. Until he had Charlotte back under the same roof he was under, he would not settle, and he would not apologise for his poor behaviour. The last two days had been the worst of his life, and he needed to see Charlotte and tell her of his feelings. He finally realised he could not live without her in his life, and the need to tell her was driving him insane.

"We shall make arrangements for her return as soon as the doctor says she is well enough to be moved," Michael said, ignoring Stephen's outburst. He had some sympathy with what he imagined he was going through.

"There is something else," Peters said cautiously, not meeting the penetrating glare emitting from Stephen.

"What is it?" Michael asked.

"She told them she is Miss Charlotte Webster from Miss Humphrey's school of ladies," Peters said calmly.

"What?!" Stephen exploded.

Peters did not flinch, but this time met Stephen's eye. "She has lost the last few months' memories. Whether it is permanent or not, the doctor does not know. He said time will tell."

Elizabeth turned to Stephen. "She will remember you as soon as she sees you," she assured him. Her heart had twisted to see the pained expression on her friend's face.

"Will she?" Stephen asked. For once his bravado deserted him, and he realised he could have lost her even though she was alive. The feeling she could forget him stung like nothing else he had ever experienced. He was desolate.

"Of course," Elizabeth said firmly. "One does not forget such strong feelings, no matter what may happen."

"If I may interrupt, Lady Dunham," Peters said. "The doctor advised only the minimum of visiting initially. He does not know what damage too much activity or excitement will cause to her brain."

"We shall do nothing that would risk harming her," Elizabeth said firmly. "I will visit her first, and slowly she will return to us." She turned to Stephen, "Patience, my friend: she will come back to us; I know she will."

Chapter 20

Two days later Elizabeth set out with Violet to visit Charlotte. They carried with them flowers, fruit and cakes, along with the good wishes of most of the household. As they travelled in the carriage, the sight of Stephen prowling over the parkland stuck in Elizabeth's mind. He had promised not to visit Charlotte, but she could see such a promise had cost him dearly.

They arrived at the farmhouse to be greeted by two barking dogs. The farmer's wife came out to chastise the animals and greeted the two ladies with a smile. "Welcome to my home; I'm Mrs Hurst," she said as they introduced themselves. "I'm not sure if Miss Webster will remember you; she is wearing herself out trying to remember everything since she realised there are gaps in her memory."

Mrs Hurst led the way through the large farmhouse kitchen that housed a cast-iron range, a huge table and as many pots and pans as would grace any large residence. Beyond the kitchen was a small hallway from which stairs led upward and a doorway to the parlour. Mrs Hurst indicated the ladies should precede her.

"Please make yourselves comfortable; Miss Webster will be along shortly," she explained.

Elizabeth and Violet settled on two of the chairs and waited. Very soon the door opened, and Charlotte entered. She looked pale and a little drawn; the bandage on her head was very much in place, and she moved more slowly than she had previously.

She smiled shyly at the two ladies before her. "Mrs Hurst said I have spent some time staying with you, but you will have to forgive me; I don't seem to be able to remember," she explained with embarrassment.

"It doesn't matter that you can't remember us," Elizabeth said quickly reassuring her. "We can become acquainted again. What is important is that you are well."

"Thank you. I am improving all the time," Charlotte responded demurely.

"Oh, Charlotte, I am so happy to see you!" Elizabeth suddenly exclaimed, the relief of seeing her friend alive overcoming the need to be restrained and quiet.

Charlotte laughed at the outburst. "Thank you. I will continue to try to remember everything. I am truly sorry I can't," she said with a little frustration.

"Perhaps you are trying too hard," Violet offered. "It may come back naturally with time."

"That's what the doctor said," Charlotte confessed, "but I am impatient. I'm having the strangest dreams, you see, and until I remember, I doubt I will be able to understand them."

"Perhaps we could help?" Elizabeth offered.

Charlotte flushed a little. "I think if I voiced them, you would think me mad," she said. "It is more feelings I experience than actual events."

"You forget we do remember the last few months," Violet said. "But we will not hurry you; you can tell us another day."

Elizabeth gave Charlotte the presents and started to name everyone who had sent their best wishes. "Miss Fairfield sends her love, and I know she will want to visit soon. Lord Dunham wishes you well. Lord Halkyn is keen to see you back at Dunham House, and Mr Anderton sends you his best wishes," she said.

"They are all very kind," Charlotte said. "Please send my thanks and my apologies."

"So, no names sound familiar?" Elizabeth asked.

"No," Charlotte said sadly.

"Well, my dear, we shall leave you now to rest, but if you have no objections we shall return in a few days to see how you are faring," Violet said, aware she did not want to overtire the patient.

"You would be most welcome," Charlotte responded politely.

158

The ladies left the farmhouse and were silent for the first part of their journey. The silence was finally broken when Elizabeth sighed.

"Poor Stephen," she said with feeling. "I do not know how he will deal with seeing her with Charlotte having no memory of him."

"I do feel sorry for him, but maybe all is not lost. It is still early days," Violet reassured Elizabeth.

"I hope you are correct. I don't know how Stephen will cope if she has forgotten him completely," Elizabeth mused.

*

Over the following two weeks Elizabeth visited her friend every other day. Each time she was accompanied by either Violet or Miss Fairfield. Although Charlotte always seemed glad to see them, there didn't seem any progress in her memory recall.

One day Elizabeth arrived alone. "Good afternoon, Mrs Hurst; how is your patient today?"

Mrs Hurst smiled at Elizabeth, "She is looking forward to seeing you, as always, My Lady."

As soon as Charlotte had been discovered at the Hurst's farm, arrangements had been made to compensate the Hurst's for their trouble. They objected initially, but Elizabeth had, in her easy way, persuaded the family to accept payment for their care of her friend.

Elizabeth had been troubled since finding Charlotte and felt the need to speak to her alone. She had insisted before Charlotte was brought back to Dunham House, she had to know what had gone on in the carriage. Elizabeth was not sure Charlotte would easily forgive her for the part she had played in the incident.

Charlotte greeted Elizabeth when she entered the parlour. "Good afternoon," Charlotte smiled. "Mrs Hurst has been showing me how to bake, so I hope you are hungry."

"I am always hungry for cake!" Elizabeth said, sitting down on the chair.

"As long as you remember while you are eating it, it is my first attempt, for you might think there may be room for improvement," Charlotte said with a grin.

The ladies ate their cake and drank tea while Elizabeth told Charlotte of the activities of Dunham House. She always mentioned Lord Halkyn, but there was never any sign Charlotte remembered anything. When she finished her drink, she placed her cup down and folded her hands in her lap.

"Charlotte, I need to clear up something with you. It may cause you pain, and if you don't want to see me after today I will understand," Elizabeth started.

"Why would I not want to see you?" Charlotte asked puzzled. "You have been very kind to me."

"Because I was the cause of your fall!" Elizabeth blurted out.

Charlotte frowned, "I thought there was a criminal involved? Mrs Hurst told me the officer who discovered I had been brought here said we had been held against our will. The criminal who was trying to hurt you pushed me out of the carriage while it was in motion. How could that be your fault?"

Elizabeth sighed, "The gentleman was keeping the information to a minimum to prevent any scandal being linked to my name, but it is only fair you know the truth."

"I'm listening," Charlotte responded, sitting back in her seat.

Elizabeth explained who George was and the history of her family. She went on to tell of the days up to the coach ride to attend church and what had happened inside the coach. Finally, she explained what had happened when she had asked George to release her friend.

"I had no idea he would respond in such a way, but I should have known he was at the point where he just didn't care anymore," Elizabeth said. "The sight of you falling out of the carriage I will never forget for as long as I live. I had thought every eventuality had been discussed between myself and Michael, but we hadn't thought anyone with me would be put in such danger. We had wanted to prevent anyone else getting hurt."

Charlotte thought for a few moments before she spoke. "I hoped that, by hearing the story, it might help, but my memory seems to be stubborn," she started with a small smile. "With regards to your involvement, please don't let it worry you; you acted in such a way to try to save me. Neither of us could have known what he was going to do. It wasn't your fault."

"You are generous," Elizabeth said. "I just did not want us to become friends for a second time without you knowing the truth."

"What happened to George?" Charlotte asked.

"I shot him," Elizabeth said quietly.

Charlotte started to laugh, "Oh, my goodness! Don't ever let me get on the wrong side of you!" she said with a giggle.

Her words lightened the mood, and Elizabeth left the farmhouse feeling as if a weight had been lifted off her shoulders. Charlotte could forgive her, which would go some way to enable her to start forgiving herself.

*

Eventually after some weeks, Charlotte began to look more like her old self; Elizabeth made a proposition. "You are stronger than when we first started to visit; why don't you return to Dunham House and continue your stay with us?" she asked.

"But I don't remember my stay," Charlotte responded.

"I know, but perhaps if you return to familiar surroundings, it may help you remember," Elizabeth suggested. "After all, you have only known this farm since your accident."

Mrs Hurst agreed wholeheartedly with the scheme. She was fond of her young guest but realised she would be more comfortable in a larger house with what she considered to be her own people.

161

All was arranged, and Elizabeth and Miss Fairfield accompanied Charlotte on her return to Dunham House. Charlotte spent her time looking out of the window, trying to distinguish something familiar in the countryside.

"Don't push too hard," Elizabeth said soothingly. She could see the impatience on her friend's face.

"It is so maddening to know those around me will have memories that I won't!" Charlotte said.

"Are you still having the dreams?" Elizabeth asked. They had not been mentioned since that first visit.

"Yes," Charlotte replied. "They are feelings more than images. I feel safe when I can see a figure, but I have no idea who it is. Then I feel sadness, as if there is no hope, but about what I have no idea. There are horses and a carriage, and I'm afraid, but I expect I am remembering the accident. It is very confusing," she explained with a shrug.

Elizabeth wondered if the figure was Stephen, but she could not say anything to Charlotte. It was not her place to interfere. She had told Stephen he was welcome to stay as long as he wished, but once he had seen Charlotte, she was not sure if he would stay in the area. She did not know if he would be able to tolerate the torture of seeing Charlotte as a stranger.

Charlotte joined the family after lunch. She had been tired from the journey and rested before meeting the rest of the party. She felt a little overwhelmed on entering the drawing room but was greeted with smiles from the assembled group. There was one gentleman who did not smile but watched her intently as she approached Elizabeth.

"Do you feel rested?" Elizabeth asked, indicating Charlotte should join her on the sofa.

"Yes, thank you," Charlotte replied with a smile.

Elizabeth introduced Charlotte to everyone. She was hoping for some sort of recognition, but could detect none from her friend. She felt real sadness for Stephen as she saw the way he looked at Charlotte: as if he had been starved for months, and she was the solution to his hunger.

Stephen could not have taken his eyes off Charlotte if he tried. She looked paler and thinner than before, more demure than his tiger, but she was still beautiful. She was still his Charlotte, although the irony was not lost on him. She was less his now than she had ever been; she had no memory he could tease her with. Only his memory held the kisses they had shared.

As soon as he could he left the gathering. Charlotte was not really taking part in the conversation, but she was listening intently to everything that was being said, obviously hoping something would help. He could not bear to be in her company with the difference in her. He missed seeing the way she had looked at him, the way he had been able to make her blush.

Charlotte noticed Stephen leaving and for some reason had felt the urge to follow him. She could not explain why. As soon as she could she left the gathering, hoping to find Stephen and try to find out why she felt drawn to him.

She met him at the bottom of the stairs; it was obvious he was going out riding.

"Are you leaving the gathering, Lord Halkyn?" she asked, not really knowing what to say.

"Yes. The social niceties bore me," Halkyn said in his usual bored tone. It made him wince when she used his formal title.

Charlotte frowned at his response, but he did not think he had offended her; she was obviously thinking deeply. "No, you don't like society much unless it is on your terms do you?" she asked hesitantly.

Stephen's heart skipped a beat; was she remembering? "Tell me more," he said quietly.

Charlotte continued to frown. "I'm sorry, My Lord; it was a fleeting moment, more a sense of something than a true recollection."

"It's unimportant," Stephen responded coolly. "If you will excuse me, Miss Webster, I have many miles to cover."

"Are you leaving?" Charlotte asked. His words had caused her heart rate to increase. For some reason she could not explain, she did not want him to go.

"No, fool that I am, I am not leaving," Stephen said with derision at his weakness, at being unable to leave the person causing him pain. "I need a long ride is all."

"Forgive my delaying you," Charlotte curtsied and moved to one side to let him pass.

"You are forgiven, tiger," Stephen said and, without a backward glance, he left the hallway.

Charlotte stood frozen to the spot, frowning at the empty space Lord Halkyn had filled. It was many moments before she shook herself and returned to the drawing room. She was distracted all afternoon but was left to mull over her thoughts, as everyone hoped her distraction was a sign she was remembering.

Chapter 21

Stephen avoided Charlotte as much as he could over the following few days. He cursed the fact he was making himself miserable by staying, but he kept negotiating with himself as to how long he should remain. It had initially been until Charlotte was settled, then it was until her colour returned. He knew once that happened, there would be another reason he could not go. He could not leave her; yet he could not bear to be near her either.

He ignored the puzzled looks he received from Michael and Elizabeth, but he could not change his actions. Seeing her look at him as if he were a stranger twisted his insides as much as if he had been stabbed. When she spoke to him so formally, he wanted to shake her until she remembered, so he avoided her.

Charlotte knew Lord Halkyn was not happy in her company, and it puzzled her. The move to Dunham House was working in some respects; it was feeling more familiar, and some things were coming back to her. Very often it was just feelings or a fleeting remembrance of something, but she felt sure what she was remembering were true memories, which made his behaviour all the more confusing.

She walked the grounds every morning, trying to put the things she felt in some sort of order. At times she did feel as if she was trying to process too much information, but somehow it was important she did not just let memories come back naturally.

One morning she walked through the rose garden deep in thought. She did not notice Stephen was walking towards her as he was obscured by a hedge of roses. She turned and let out a little cry, startled at his sudden appearance.

"I did not mean to frighten you," Stephen apologised. He had not known she was there or else he would have walked in the opposite direction. He did not like to put himself under her scrutiny.

"You do not frighten me, My Lord," Charlotte responded. "I was startled out of my thoughts, that's all."

"You are probably the only schoolroom miss who isn't frightened of me," Stephen responded coldly.

"I'm no longer a schoolroom miss and apparently haven't been for some time. Although I can't remember it happening, I've been told that, while I have been staying at Dunham House, I celebrated my eighteenth birthday," Charlotte responded tartly, but then she calmed down. "I've never been frightened of you. I have always felt safe with you, haven't I?"

Stephen paused before answering. At first he thought she might be remembering something, but he came to the conclusion she was purely fishing for clues, and her memory was not returning. He decided he was not going to indulge her. "Have you? I can't understand why."

"Because you protected me," Charlotte said with a frown. "I just can't remember why."

"Oh, well, never mind; I'm sure it wasn't important," Stephen said with disdain. "If you will excuse me, Miss Webster; as much as I find your company delightful, I must continue my walk."

Stephen turned and moved away from Charlotte. She was not aware of it and would never be unless she eventually remembered the circumstances, but she would have the unlooked-for privilege of being the only person whom he had ever protected now and in the future. He would certainly reject any similar situations; it had caused him nothing but heartache, which grieved and annoyed him, especially since he could not put it all behind him and walk away.

Charlotte looked at his retreating back with a frown. Something was not right. This was not how they were with each other. She could not quite grasp the memory, and she almost screamed with frustration. She stomped after Stephen, determined he would not speak to her in such a way; she knew he had not done so in the past.

Charlotte caught up with Stephen by picking up the hem of her dress and running. It was not a dignified way to conduct herself, let alone seeking out a man, but she was determined to speak to him.

166

Stephen heard her approach; she was sure of it, but he did not stop. Charlotte reached out and grabbed his arm; later she would be mortified about her forward behaviour, but for now she just reacted.

"Yes, Miss Webster?" Stephen said in a bored tone, finally admitting defeat and halting.

Charlotte was a little breathless and gasped to catch her breath. "Why are you doing this?" she asked.

"Doing what?" came the bored response. Stephen was a master at making people uncomfortable if he chose and, for some reason, he could not help himself with Charlotte.

Charlotte glowered at him. "This is not you!" she snapped. "You have never spoken to me in the way you have since I returned."

"Has your memory returned, Miss Webster?" Stephen asked with a raised eyebrow.

"No," Charlotte said honestly. "I just know this wasn't how we spoke in the past. Why are you being so unreasonable now?"

"Because I don't know how else to be around you." Stephen said the words before he could stop himself. The look of pain on his face went a long way to confirm the truth of his speech.

"Please be as you were previously," Charlotte said gently.

"I cannot!" Stephen said with derision, quickly getting himself under control.

"I don't understand why not," Charlotte said, almost pleading for some information.

"I suggest you ask Elizabeth; she is always keen to talk," Stephen said harshly. "Now if you will excuse me once more." He bowed his head slightly and started to walk away.

Charlotte spoke without thinking. "I miss you, Stephen. I have missed you from the day you left me in the hallway and returned to London."

167

Stephen swung around and faced her. "What did you say?" he asked quietly.

Charlotte was frowning, "I don't know where that came from, but I remembered something. Your given name is Stephen; I called you by your given name!"

"Anyone could have told you that," Stephen said dismissively. "What did you mean by the rest of it?"

Charlotte tried to explain, "I get feelings and the occasional image. It is hard to make it all clear, but I had a moment just then. I was in the hallway, and you were leaving me. Why were you leaving me?" she asked.

"Because it was the best thing to do for the both of us," Stephen replied. He had been filled with hope when she said his name, but then a sickening realisation struck. If she started to remember, she would remember refusing his marriage proposal, and they would be no better off. He had been a fool. He needed to leave. "It looks as if your memory will come back after all. I am happy for you, Miss Webster." He turned and walked away.

This time Charlotte did not try to stop him. Instead she watched his retreating back with a small smile on her face. Her memory was finally returning.

*

Stephen almost walked into Michael in the hallway when he entered the house.

"Halkyn?" Michael said at the troubled expression on Stephen's face.

"I shall return to London later today," Stephen said shortly not appreciating being brought out of his reverie.

"Would you join me in the study for a moment?" Michael asked, not waiting for an answer but leading the way out of earshot of the footmen on duty.

168

Stephen groaned but followed. "What's wrong, Dunham? Afraid you will miss me?" he asked sarcastically.

"I'm just wondering why the sudden change of heart," Michael said ignoring Stephen's tone.

"I'm tired of the country," Stephen lied.

"What has happened with Charlotte to make you want to leave?" Michael asked patiently. He knew he had been as annoying when he was in denial about his feelings for Elizabeth, so he could not criticise the man in front of him who was so obviously suffering.

"Why does it have to have anything to do with Charlotte?" Stephen responded.

"Because I see the way you look at her, as if the fact that she does not remember you causes you acute pain," Michael replied truthfully.

Stephen sighed, "Her memory appears to be returning."

"And that is a bad thing?" Michael asked in confusion. He would have expected Stephen to be desperate for Charlotte to return to her old self.

"Her memory is returning, so she will remember what delights your darling wife told her about me; she will also remember refusing my offer for her. It suddenly struck me it would be best if I left now," Stephen responded with a shrug. "I'm not prepared to watch her withdraw from me a second time."

Michael thought for a few moments. Halkyn was not the most noble of men, but since Charlotte had come into their lives he had seen a change in his acquaintance. He was convinced that Halkyn was in love with Charlotte, and he had also seen what a good effect she had on him. He wondered if there was hope for Stephen after all of her affection softening his bitterness.

"Convince her her memories are wrong," he finally said.

"What?" Stephen asked, wondering if his host had lost his mind.

"Convince her you are worth more than the rumours and tittle-tattle. Woo her," Michael said with a shrug.

"I've never chased anyone in my life!" Stephen snorted.

"I would wager you never looked at anyone as you look at Charlotte or had your insides turned inside out when you think about leaving her, either," Michael said calmly.

Stephen flopped into a chair. "Dammit, I must be getting soft in my old age; am I so transparent?" he asked, running his hand through his hair in frustration.

Michael laughed, "Unfortunately I think I recognise the signs because it wasn't too long ago that I was in a similar situation. Different reasons but the same outcome."

"Curse women. I have fought this since I reached maturity," Stephen muttered.

"Why fight it? Isn't she worth it?" Michael asked surprised.

Stephen looked at the man before him. Dunham had been an acquaintance and then a rival of sorts, but Stephen had never expected him to become the friend and confidante he appeared to be now.

"She is worth ten of me, and it is only when I forget myself I can imagine a life with her. When I am being truthful with myself, I acknowledge she would be better off without me," he said quietly.

"She could do a lot worse than you," Michael responded truthfully.

Stephen laughed, "Yes, I could offer her money and a title, but what if I got sick of her, Dunham? What if I broke her heart?" he asked seriously.

"The fact you are asking those questions probably means that you wouldn't," Michael responded reasonably.

"Probably isn't good enough," Stephen said, standing. He needed to get away.

"Don't leave today; think about it for a day or two, and then make a decision. Give yourself the chance to think before dashing off; you could regret leaving for a long time," Michael said.

"Your children will hate you," Stephen responded with a grimace.

"What on earth has this to do with any future children I might have?" Michael asked in confusion.

"Reasoned arguments are a dead bore. You will bore them senseless. At least they will be able to turn to me to bring some excitement into their lives and allow them to be devils," Stephen drawled. "I will give your advice some thought, although the fact it looks like rain may have more to do with my decision than your persuasion."

"As you wish," Michael responded amused. Pride would not let Stephen act in any way other than he was used to people seeing, but Michael had seen a glimpse of the man underneath, and was no longer worried about his young guest.

Chapter 22

Stephen hid himself in the billiard room. He needed to mull over Michael's words and try to come to terms with his own feelings. He was not necessarily ready to declare his undying love to Charlotte or to even recognise love was what he was feeling. He was aware, though, that he had never before had the feelings he experienced while being with Charlotte. No other woman he had ever met previously moved him in the way she did. He had only kissed her twice, but both kisses were burned into his memory, unlike the hundreds, possibly thousands of kisses he had experienced prior to meeting Charlotte.

He had no idea why his feelings had developed. He had met far more sophisticated women in his time who could banter with him enough to have him roar with laughter. He had experienced women who were expert in satisfying him in bed. Innocence had always bored him; it was too much like hard work to show them his preferred way of doing things, and he had therefore never dallied with someone as innocent as Charlotte. There was also the risk of being forced into a marriage he did not want if he dallied with an innocent, another reason why he should have avoided Charlotte.

He slammed the ball into the opposite corner pocket. Perhaps he was turning into the type of low character who was attracted to Baron Kersal's more immoral schemes. He snorted with disgust, he might have a colourful background, but he would never sink so low as forcing himself on an innocent.

Forcing himself on an innocent. He could not stop the smile spreading across his face when he thought of the first words Charlotte had uttered to him. He had never been begged for a kiss in such a way before. He had had women throw themselves at him, but that had never stirred anything in him apart from contempt for the marital state, because they were usually married. No, Charlotte had been different from the start. Her unique mix of innocence, fire and helplessness had been a mix he had been unable to resist.

Another ball was slammed into the pocket; it was not just that. She had looked to him for help and been sure he was capable of giving it to her. She had trusted him and been confident in his ability. Her courage had remained steady while she was in his company, and it had been because of his ability she had felt that way. No one had ever relied on him before; no one had ever wanted his protection in such a way. No one had ever rejected him because, although she cared for him, she believed he did not care enough about her and was not going to settle for his indifference.

He still smarted from her rejection of the marriage proposal. Her uncle had been quite rightly over the moon at the proposal but not Charlotte. Oh no, she had wanted his love not his proposal. Another ball was rocketed into the waiting pocket. She had turned down the most eligible offer she was ever likely to get, and yet he could not condemn her for it. She had principles and even at her young age, had the courage to stand by them.

"Should I warn Lord Dunham he may need to purchase a new billiard table?" Charlotte asked from the doorway. "I'm not sure his current one can take such harsh play." She smiled with amusement at Stephen's startled expression. She had watched him for a few moments before speaking, unable to take her eyes off his face.

"Are you following me, Miss Webster?" Stephen asked, overcoming his surprise quickly and returning to his usual uninterested manner.

"Perish the thought that such an action would have on my reputation if the company suspected such behaviour," Charlotte responded easily. "I was merely attracted to the sound of a billiard table in pain."

Stephen smiled slightly, "I wasn't aware billiard tables were susceptible to pain. I would have been less brutal if I had realised."

"I would expect no less; you are not a cruel man," Charlotte replied, entering the room. "Now, are you going to teach me the rules, or am I going to have to stand and watch you play alone all day?"

Stephen's eyes narrowed. "Billiards isn't a pastime for a respectable young lady," he said shortly, wary of what Charlotte was trying to achieve.

"I have a feeling my respectability has been hanging in the balance for some time now," Charlotte responded with a shrug. She entered the room fully and picked up a cue, weighing it in her hands. "I feel one game of billiards isn't going to affect it one way or another."

Stephen laughed despite his reservations. This was the girl with spirit he had seen in the beginning. "In that case, Miss Webster, allow me to show you."

Charlotte smiled at the sight of Stephen relaxing. She had sought him out, but it was for her benefit as well as his. She remembered things when she was near him, so she needed to be near him. "Prepare to be beaten, Stephen."

Stephen ignored the change from the formality of his title, which she had used since the accident, to his given name. She was remembering, but perhaps he should enjoy her company until she remembered everything. He indicated she should join him at the table and started to explain the rules of the game.

*

Elizabeth was attracted to the billiard room by the laughter coming from within it. She recognised it was Charlotte's laughter and was curious and troubled her friend was in the room. When she entered, the surprise at the sight before her was clearly written on her face. Charlotte was fully participating in a game of billiards with Stephen. The pair were fooling around, obviously not taking the game seriously, hence Charlotte's laughter.

The pair stopped their antics as soon as they noticed Elizabeth's entrance, Charlotte flushing a little, and Stephen scowling at Elizabeth. "Elizabeth," he bowed slightly at her appearance.

"Stephen. Charlotte," Elizabeth responded, not quite coolly but frosty enough to express her displeasure at such a scene. She did not want to see her friend hurt by Stephen again.

"Stephen has been teaching me the fine art of billiards," Charlotte said lightly, but her blush was evidence she was aware of Elizabeth's disapproval.

"I was hoping you would accompany me on a visit to some tenants," Elizabeth explained to her friend.

"Of course," Charlotte responded, immediately putting down the cue. "I shall fetch my pelisse and bonnet and meet you in the hallway in a few moments," she said quickly, dipping a quick curtsey to Stephen before turning her back to him and hurrying out the door.

Elizabeth turned back to Stephen when they were alone. "Do you think it is wise being unchaperoned with Charlotte for such a long time? I could hear her laughter before I reached the doorway."

"We were having a game of billiards with the door open. It might be a sign I'm getting old, but it's not the most ideal location for anything untoward to happen," Stephen drawled.

Elizabeth ignored the mocking tone Stephen used. "I think highly of you Stephen, but I hope you are not going to hurt Charlotte again," she said in her usual direct way.

Stephen bristled, "I seem to recall I offered her marriage, and I was the one who was refused. Perhaps she is the one who would hurt me?"

"Yes, but you offered marriage without love!" Elizabeth responded quietly. She knew Stephen's cynicism where feelings of love were concerned.

"Do you know, Elizabeth, I have considered you one of my friends in this fickle world we live in, but it appears I may have been mistaken. Your husband has more faith in me than you do."

"Michael? What has he said?" Elizabeth asked.

"He suggested I court Charlotte, that I don't let the past hinder what we could have in the future. I seriously considered it for a moment, but with friends like you around, I haven't got a chance, have I? You will always be the spectre of the past, reminding me what I strove to be, never allowing any of us, particularly Charlotte to forget what a monster I was. You are in danger of sounding like the bitter, spiteful dames who frequent society all too often!" Stephen moved around the billiard table and approached the doorway.

"I think you should stop pretending to be my friend Elizabeth. If I offended you so much by my foolish marriage proposal to you that it has coloured your opinion of me, just be honest enough to say it. I don't want to continue presuming you are my ally, when in reality you so obviously dislike me," he finished bitterly.

Elizabeth opened her mouth to reply, but Stephen had moved past her and left the room. A movement from behind the doorway caught Elizabeth's eye and she was mortified to see Charlotte's pale face emerge.

"Charlotte..." Elizabeth started.

"Are you jealous that Lord Halkyn likes me?" Charlotte asked quietly.

"Jealous? No!" Elizabeth exclaimed. "I don't want him to hurt you: that's all."

"Why would he hurt me?" Charlotte asked, her demeanour stiff and aloof.

"He did once before," Elizabeth said gently. "His views are....We spoke about it in the past."

"Of which I cannot remember, but I am remembering feelings, and I know he would not intentionally hurt me," Charlotte replied.

"I hope your confidence in him is not misplaced," Elizabeth responded, a little defensively.

"It isn't," Charlotte replied firmly.

Chapter 23

Elizabeth sought out her husband when her duties to her tenants were completed. She felt like the spiteful dame Stephen had compared her to but was sure she was right to be cautious for her friend. That did not ease the tension remaining between Charlotte and herself all through the visits they had undertaken.

She explained to Michael what had occurred, and her heart sank further as he shook his head at her words. "I was only trying to act in Charlotte's best interests," she finished defensively.

"You should have left them alone. Now Charlotte is aware of some of Halkyn's past, and it may influence her as it did before," Michael replied calmly, but it was obvious he was disappointed with Elizabeth's actions.

"Surely she needs to know the truth?" Elizabeth asked in disbelief. Her husband was so committed to doing what was right in every area of his life; she could not believe he was suggesting she should lie.

"We all change, Elizabeth. You must have seen the changes in Halkyn from the first moment he introduced Charlotte to us. He is not the man who offered for you!" Michael responded, unable to stop his teeth grinding a little at his last words.

Elizabeth moved to her husband and wrapped her arms around his neck. "My feelings have never changed since I first fell in love with you. I could never have been tempted into marriage with Stephen," she said, reaching up to kiss him.

Michael returned the kiss but pulled away after a moment. "Just remember how you reacted when you realised there were difficulties in the way of our happiness. You fought against them, and perhaps Charlotte is doing the same," he offered, smiling at his headstrong wife.

"But Stephen's view on marriage...." Elizabeth started.

"He told me he was afraid if they married he would hurt her," Michael interrupted. "Those are not the words of someone who is untouched by love."

Elizabeth groaned and put her head on her husband's shoulder. "I am a fool. I may have damaged my friendship with them both."

"Leave them be, and they will work it out and forgive you along the way," Michael said reassuringly, hoping his words held enough conviction.

*

Charlotte had mixed feelings about the conversation she overheard. She had returned to ask Elizabeth a question about the possibility of donating a quilt from her bedroom to some tenants but had not uttered a sound once she realised the conversation had been about herself and Stephen.

Herself and Stephen. It seemed her feelings were correct; they did have some sort of history. It had not sounded as if the situation had been destined for a happy ending. It was so frustrating to not be able to remember everything yet, although memories were coming back, more than she was admitting to anyone else. Her feelings for Stephen were strong; she had the suspicion she would always feel safe while he was around, and she also felt loved by him, which was in direct contradiction to what Elizabeth had hinted at.

Elizabeth was obviously questioning Stephen's commitment. Charlotte did not seriously think Elizabeth was jealous; anyone seeing her with Lord Dunham could see she was besotted with her husband, but there was obviously a reason she thought Stephen would hurt her. She puzzled over it during the following evening. There was no sign of Stephen that evening, which made the meal overly long in Charlotte's view. She was so used to his presence, to know that every time she looked up, his eyes would meet hers, she felt quite miserable without him.

Then Violet and Edward announced it was time they were returning to London. "I miss my social whirl," Violet explained with a smile. "I had hoped we could still take Charlotte with us, but I think a little longer here would be of more benefit."

"I was to come to London?" Charlotte asked. "I don't think I have ever been there before."

"You spent a night there some time ago," Elizabeth supplied. "But there was no time for socialising; you were collected from just outside of London and the morning after brought to visit us."

"Really?" Charlotte responded, clearly distracted by the new information.

Elizabeth was relieved Charlotte did not ask any more questions. She could not lie to her friend but, at this point, did not want to start explaining the history of her arrival with them.

*

The following morning Violet and Edward left Dunham House. Charlotte had waved them off and then returned to her bed chamber; she was still mulling over the information obtained the previous evening. Her thoughts were disturbed when she was sent a message she had a visitor. She hurried to the morning room, wondering who would visit, as she knew very few people in the area.

Elizabeth greeted her as she entered and introduced her to Mr O'Hara. He was a pleasant looking young man, who stood and gave a low bow at Charlotte's entrance. He smiled in welcome to Charlotte and explained he had lately been out of the area and had only just returned to hear about her accident.

"I took the opportunity of riding over immediately to see for myself that you are well," he said, fixing her with a wide smile.

Charlotte smiled at the visitor; she had a definite feeling she had met him before. "I am well, thank you, as you can see. The scar will be easily hidden under my curls," she said.

"You were very lucky," Mr O'Hara murmured, a sympathetic expression on his face.

179

"I have been very well looked after," Charlotte responded. "You will have to forgive me, Mr O'Hara; I know we met previously, but my memory has not returned fully. I'm afraid I cannot remember our previous acquaintance."

Mr O'Hara flushed slightly. "It is of no matter; we were excellent dance partners and, I am sure in the future, we will have the opportunity to be so once more."

Charlotte frowned at Mr. O'Hara's flush. She seemed distracted for a few moments as she tried to recall her previous meetings with him. Mr O'Hara chatted about his recent visit to London, and the ladies responded politely.

They were interrupted by the entrance of Lord Halkyn. He looked at Mr O'Hara with mild interest before bowing to the ladies and taking a seat near the window. His entrance stilled the conversation for a few moments, but then Mr O'Hara continued.

"Is Lord Dunham at home this morning?" he asked Elizabeth.

"He is; would you like me to ask him to join us?" Elizabeth responded.

"Ah, no," Mr O'Hara replied, again flushing. "I would like to have a private word with him, if it is possible."

"I'm sure it is. Would you like to follow me?" Elizabeth rose and led the way out of the room with Mr O'Hara close on her heels.

"Is that one of your conquests?" Stephen asked mockingly when they were alone in the room.

"You tell me," Charlotte responded tartly.

"He looks like he would moon over you," came the scornful reply.

"He obviously has good taste then," Charlotte responded, making Stephen laugh loudly.

Elizabeth returned to the room and raised her eyebrows at Stephen. "You sound happy," she said.

"I shall stop it immediately," Stephen responded a little coolly. He still had not completely forgiven her for her lack of faith in him.

Elizabeth and Charlotte made small talk, expecting Mr O'Hara to rejoin them when he had finished speaking to Lord Dunham. Both were surprised when fifteen minutes later Lord Dunham entered the room alone.

"Has Mr O'Hara left us?" Elizabeth asked her husband.

"Yes, he thought he would leave it to me to pass on his message," Michael said, sitting opposite Charlotte.

"All of a sudden this morning has become interesting," Stephen responded, managing to still sound bored, but he did sit a little forward on his seat.

Michael flicked a look at Stephen but ignored his comment. "Charlotte, you will not remember, but Mr O'Hara asked for your hand in marriage before the accident happened."

Charlotte flushed, but the three occupants were more distracted by the sound of Stephen sucking in a deep breath. He did not say anything, so Charlotte turned back to Michael. "Did he?" she asked hesitantly. She was terrified of the thought she might have accepted him and now be tied to an engagement.

"Yes, he did. He has asked today if he could renew his addresses to you, asking for my blessing for him to speak to you about the subject again," Michael said, aware of Stephen in the background clenching his fists.

"So, I hadn't agreed to anything?" Charlotte asked, almost sagging with relief.

"No, you, er, had actually decided against the match the last time we spoke about it," Michael said, smiling at Charlotte. "Do you not remember?"

Charlotte looked at Michael and then suddenly smiled. "I kissed him," she said simply.

"You did what?!" Stephen roared from the window seat.

Charlotte, Michael and Elizabeth all jumped simultaneously at the sound of Stephen's words. Charlotte flushed a deep red; Elizabeth looked stunned at Charlotte, and Michael tried to suppress a smirk.

"I-I kissed him," Charlotte repeated, more hesitantly this time. Stephen looked angrier than she had ever seen him before.

"I heard you the first time," Stephen ground out through visibly gritted teeth. "I was just wondering why you would do that and why you would admit it to a room full of people?"

"I just remembered," Charlotte tried to explain. "It just came out; I suppose it was the relief about remembering something."

"What else is there to remember?" Stephen snarled.

"Halkyn," Michael said, a warning note in his voice. He was not going to allow his young guest be bullied under his roof, even if the motivation was nothing more sinister than jealousy.

"Do you not think it is an important question?" Stephen asked with a snarl. "I should follow him and rip him to shreds, taking advantage of an innocent."

"I used him, not the other way round," Charlotte responded honestly.

Stephen looked as if he were fit to burst, but before he could say anything else, Elizabeth intervened. She had seen what appeared to be a flash of pain cross Stephen's features at Charlotte's words. "Charlotte, you are with friends, but you must be careful what you say. You cannot mean what your words suggest."

"Lord Dunham understood at the time," Charlotte said, appealing to Michael for help.

Michael did not know whether to laugh or groan at Charlotte's words. Halkyn looked ready to jump on him and pummel him into the ground, while Elizabeth looked so indignant at being kept in the dark over something like this, he knew he would suffer later. If he had the choice, he would take the pummelling from Halkyn; Elizabeth was far more frightening to him.

He sighed, "I did, and I still do, but I don't think it is appropriate to talk about it now, do you?"

Charlotte flushed and glanced at Stephen. "No, probably not," she admitted, looking down at her hands. "I'm sorry; I got carried away with the excitement of remembering a clear sequence of memories."

"It appears it wasn't the only time you got carried away if your memory serves you correctly," Stephen said, standing and walking to the door. "I wish you happy." He did not give anyone else a chance to respond, storming through the doorway and up the stairs. The room seemed to go still, as everyone heard the thud of his footsteps on the stairs.

"Thank goodness for sturdy craftsmanship," Elizabeth said lightly, referring to the strength of her staircase. "Now, I take it the kiss had in some indirect way something to do with Stephen?" She asked Charlotte.

"Yes," Charlotte said, blushing furiously. "It nearly got me into trouble then, and it looks like it's nearly happened again. I remember I had listened to everyone telling me Stephen was no good for me, and so when Mr O'Hara tried to kiss me, I kissed him back," she explained to Elizabeth.

"And what happened then?" Elizabeth asked.

"I pulled away when I realised it wasn't really enjoyable. Mr O'Hara wasn't very happy at my admission that I was trying to force myself to like him!" Charlotte admitted with a grimace as the memory became clearer.

Elizabeth laughed. "I can't imagine why! Oh, Charlotte, you could have got into so much trouble!"

"I know, especially as Lord Dunham and Mr Dawson discovered us alone together," Charlotte admitted. "Lord Dunham was very understanding."

"Oh, he was, was he?" Elizabeth said, giving her husband a clear indication she would not be so understanding for being kept out of such an incident. "I would not have been quite so pleasant to Mr O'Hara had I known he was going around kissing my guests."

"Hardly a serial offender," Michael said drily. "You can be assured I put him fully in the picture about my opinion of his behaviour. It does appear though he stills has a high regard for you, Charlotte, and would like to pay his addresses again. He assures me he would act in the correct manner this time."

"He seems a very pleasant young man," Charlotte started, trying to put her feelings into words without giving everything away to her hosts. "I'm afraid, although I have little to offer any man in the form of dowry, I could not accept his proposal. I am not attracted to him in any way, and I can't see that changing."

"Do you not wish to give it more time because of what has happened? You may feel differently if you spend more time in his company?" Elizabeth asked gently.

"No," Charlotte responded firmly. "There is no reason to try and force something when I know it would be futile."

"It is how you felt prior to your accident, so I am not surprised at your answer," Michael responded. "I said I would send a note to him advising him of your response. I feel I have heard all I need to be able to send out a clear message."

"Thank you," Charlotte responded meekly, full of relief.

Chapter 24

Stephen had never experienced jealousy before and struggled with the rage it caused within him. She had kissed another man. Not only had she kissed another man, she had kissed him after they had shared kisses: the memory of which haunted his dreams but obviously not hers. He wanted to despise her; instead the feelings he was experiencing just made him want her even more.

She had kissed another man after Stephen had offered for her. He could not even gloat that she would never receive another proposal; the damn fop had offered for her not once but twice. As he walked to the stables he ground his teeth. If he ever saw the man again, he would make him realise what the consequences were to anyone trying to steal his woman.

His woman. She was and would always be his as far as he was concerned. She had turned to him when she needed help. Stephen swung up onto his horse, but by the time he had reached the edge of the stable yard he was turning his dark mood in on himself. He had rejected Charlotte; he had made it obvious he had not taken the thought of a marriage with her seriously. It was no wonder she had rejected him.

By the time he reached the outer parkland he could no longer blame Mr O'Hara for proposing marriage. In fact, his proposal showed good taste; Charlotte was beautiful and charming. It was little wonder she had received a marriage proposal serious enough to be asked twice. He dug his heels in the horse's flank and set off across country. He needed to let off steam. He had to rid his mind's eye of the picture of Charlotte with someone else.

*

Charlotte escaped the house, her cheeks still warm with the embarrassment of confessing her feelings to her hosts. She was sure they must think her an immature miss, something at the moment, she could not really dispute.

It seemed ironic the man she wanted was anything but amenable, but the man she was not interested in had taken the trouble to seek her out and had asked to pay his addresses to her. She shook herself mentally; Stephen had been amenable when they spent the afternoon in the billiard room. He had been amusing, relaxed and charming. Something he had not been after Mr O'Hara's visit. She sighed as she strode out across the grounds; a walk and deep thought was required.

Stephen saw the figure long before he reached her. Her pelisse billowed out behind her as she walked briskly across the country. He had noticed how she always chose earthy colours: greens, creams, browns, yellows. They suited her colouring; even now, her hair contrasting against the browns of her jacket and bonnet. He smiled to himself; she was too beautiful to be constrained to such limited society, but he was glad she was. He could not cope with one rival; he would never cope with a ballroom full.

He knew exactly the moment she recognised him; her face blushed in the way he found charming. He groaned to himself; when had he started describing something as charming? He was beginning to realise, where Miss Charlotte Webster was concerned, any endearment was not misplaced. For the first time in his life, he began to wonder if he was becoming a besotted fool.

Stephen drew his horse to a stop near Charlotte and dismounted.

"Good afternoon, Miss Webster," he said bowing.

"Good afternoon," Charlotte said, curtseying, but looking at Stephen warily; he had never referred to her by her family name so formally before.

"Are you taking a general walk, or are you seeking something in particular?" Stephen asked, falling into step beside her, letting the reins of his horse hang loosely in his hand.

"Just a general walk," Charlotte responded, looking at him with trepidation. His demeanour was pleasant, but his body was still stiff, and she had the impression he was ready to spring into action: to do what, she was less sure of.

"In that case, may I join you?" Stephen asked, not really giving Charlotte the chance to refuse as he walked alongside her.

"Of course," Charlotte replied quietly. She watched the wind blow through hair peeking from under the brim of his top hat. She flushed slightly; she suddenly had the thought she had touched that hair before.

"Anything wrong, Miss Webster?" Stephen asked, picking up every change in expression Charlotte ever made.

"N-no," Charlotte stammered, flushing deeper.

"Perhaps you undertook this walk to remember more of Mr O'Hara's kisses?" Stephen said, unable to resist the urge to goad her.

"Perhaps," Charlotte responded primly. She was not about to respond to a man who was so obviously being unpleasant.

Stephen grabbed her arm and swung her around to face him. "Were you?" He demanded.

"That question has nothing to do with you," Charlotte fired back.

"It has everything to do with me!" Stephen snapped.

Charlotte had had enough of his behaviour. She felt the memories of what he had been to her, the way he had protected her, the way she felt about him, but she was not going to let him continue playing this game of one moment being nice to her, the next being an ogre.

"It has absolutely nothing to do with you or anyone else. I am sick to death of everyone having the advantage over me and presuming because of past behaviour they know exactly what I am thinking or remembering!" Charlotte snapped in return.

Stephen's eyes flashed at her; Charlotte was not convinced she was seeing anger there: there seemed to be something else. She took a breath and glared at him.

"You are so confident now your Mr O'Hara has returned to offer his hand," Stephen sneered. "I'll wager Elizabeth is planning the wedding as we speak."

"Why do you dislike Elizabeth so much?" Charlotte asked, ignoring the first part of Stephen's words. "I thought you were friends."

"So did I before she interfered with my life," Stephen snorted. "It has convinced me even more you can never trust anyone in this life."

"That is a very sad way of looking at things," Charlotte responded, no longer angry at him. His words very often made her want to comfort him and show him the world was not the horrible place he thought it was.

"It's the safest way," Stephen retorted. "Even you let people down, Charlotte."

"Do I?" Charlotte asked, genuinely puzzled. "How did I do that?"

"You acted as if you cared and then as soon as someone else came along, you forgot what had happened and left destruction behind you," Stephen said ambiguously.

Charlotte put her hands on her hips and glared at Stephen. "You are wrong."

"Tell me how," Stephen said mockingly.

"I will when I remember," Charlotte responded, turning away in frustration. She knew she had a connection with Stephen, but she still could not remember.

Stephen laughed behind her. The sound was bitter and made Charlotte flinch: not that she was afraid he was going to hurt her, but the sound affected her. She did not like knowing Stephen was not happy, and he certainly was not happy with her at the moment. While she was in the state of not being able to remember fully, he would always have the advantage. Charlotte took a few steps before she was stopped by Stephen's voice.

"Why are you walking away from me, Charlotte?" he demanded.

Charlotte turned and sighed before answering, "I cannot give you what you want Stephen," she said sadly. "I can't remember specifics; I know the memories are there, but for some reason I can't remember them. You are going to taunt me and taunt me, but I can't change the situation."

"But you remembered O'Hara," Stephen said, half way between petulance and anger.

"I remembered one moment; I don't remember anything else about him. He says we danced, but I have no recollection of it," Charlotte replied truthfully.

"It must have been some moment," Stephen retorted with a sneer. "I have been far easier to forget obviously."

Charlotte's heart ached to remember, to give Stephen some of the comfort she sought herself. She knew he had meant so much to her he still attracted her beyond her experience of how to deal with such strong feelings. She decided that, although it might be mortifying, she would be truthful with him.

"You are wrong," she started, her usual frown developing in the way that was the indication she was trying to remember. "With you it has been different. I have felt....I felt safe with you; protected, even though I could not remember what had gone on in the past."

"Safe and protected are not the words of a grand passion," Stephen said with derision.

Charlotte flushed but remained strong in her conviction it was important to have this conversation. "Is that what we shared?"

Stephen looked at the girl before him and almost slumped with sadness. "No, we didn't, Charlotte. I asked you to marry me but, because I couldn't offer you love, you refused me."

Charlotte's eyes widened in surprise. "And yet you have cared for me more than anyone else in my life has."

"With your history that wouldn't be hard," Stephen said with his usual self-derision.

"Thank you," Charlotte said.

"What for?" Stephen asked, this time his turn to frown.

"For caring as much as you did and making me feel secure. I know you responded when you could just have easily walked away. Thank you," Charlotte responded gently.

"You are welcome," Stephen bowed slightly and remounted his horse. "Good day, Miss Webster," he bowed and rode away, leaving Charlotte to stare after him in despair.

Chapter 25

Events at Dunham House developed that forced Charlotte and Stephen to concentrate on something else. Elizabeth went into labour before her expected date. Michael was reduced to a nervous expectant father as he walked up and down the dining room, while his wife, Miss Fairfield and the midwife tended Elizabeth upstairs.

Charlotte and Stephen joined Michael in the dining room. It was not the ideal place for many hours of inactivity, but it was the place Michael wanted to be: at the foot of the stairs in case he was needed.

Stephen tried to talk to Michael and used every subject he could think of to get a response from Michael, to make him think of anything apart from his wife in pain upstairs. Sometimes he was more responsive than others. Very often he would glance at the ceiling as if wishing he could see through the plasterwork into the room above.

Charlotte felt a little unwelcome. She had no experience of childbirth; the school where she had spent the last few years did not give lessons on what to do with nervous fathers. She poured tea and offered cakes and fancies, also trying to distract Michael. Her own stomach was in knots. Elizabeth had been a very good friend, and the labour was long. Charlotte knew how many women died in childbirth and prayed silently for the safe delivery of her friend and baby.

Eventually Miss Fairfield entered the room and indicated that Lord Dunham should follow her. She smiled at the remaining pair. "Mother and baby are well," she informed them quietly before leading the way to the bed chamber.

Both sagged with relief and were silent for a few moments. "I wonder whether it's a girl or boy." Charlotte mused aloud.

"It won't matter; it will be spoiled by both parents," Stephen said, half joking, half mocking.

Charlotte laughed with the thought, "I hope it is. I can't think of better parents to be born to."

Stephen stood as if impatient with the conversation. "They are good people."

Charlotte stood also, keen to be out of the room now the worry was over. "Yes, they are very fortunate. Although Elizabeth told me she never expected to be so happy when she was Lord Dunham's ward."

"Yes, he was a fool and could not see what was under his nose. He even tried to encourage me, although he quickly realised he'd made a mistake," Stephen said.

"You still proposed to her," Charlotte said, trying not to feel jealous and failing. It made no sense; she had been told Elizabeth had turned Stephen's proposal down, so she had no right to feel jealous about a proposal he had made to someone else before meeting her.

"I ultimately need a wife; Elizabeth was one of the few women I could bare to be around for more than a few hours. It made perfect sense at the time," Stephen responded with a shrug.

Charlotte shuddered, "That sounds so cold."

"I was being practical," Stephen defended himself. He should not let her affect him, but her condemnation angered him, probably because it reminded him of her rejection. "I suppose you are waiting for someone like Dunham to come along and sweep you off your feet?" The words choked him, but he forced them out.

"I'm not interested in a title or riches but someone who would care for me as Lord Dunham cares for Elizabeth; that would be something to aim for," Charlotte said.

"You should aim for riches; your looks alone will attract the best if you have a Season in London, as Dunham's sister is so keen to offer you," Stephen said, testing Charlotte with his words.

Charlotte laughed, "Now who is being silly and romantic? I have no dowry, a scarred face and an incomplete memory. Suitors with titles and riches will run for the hills; they will not want their lines of inheritance to be tarnished by someone so unsuitable. I am not sturdy enough stock to provide them with their future generation," Charlotte responded realistically.

Whether it was the thought of a handful of young Charlottes running through his house or whether it was the innate response he seemed to have to make everything right whenever she seemed vulnerable, Stephen did not know. What he did know was he covered the space between them in two easy strides and placed his hands on her shoulders.

"They would be mad to take any of those into account. You are perfect and should have a title!" he muttered as he pulled her towards him.

Charlotte did not resist what Stephen was doing, but she did not encourage him either. She was too frightened to make any movement in case he pulled away. His touch had stirred something almost painful within her; she needed to feel closer to him.

Stephen pulled her into his arms and held her close. He should let her go; anyone could walk in, and Dunham would not accept excuses this time. He had been angry enough when discovering them at the arrival of Charlotte's uncle. He had just responded by instinct; he had not wanted her to feel anything other than she was perfect and worthy of any title in the land. She would make a fine bride. He squeezed harder at the thought of her with someone else.

Charlotte wriggled at the pressure. "Stephen?" she said quietly.

"I'm sorry; I was just carried away with my thoughts, that's all," he responded, releasing her a little but not quite fully.

"Are you doing what I do, concentrating on memories that are just out of reach and hoping something will jolt your memory?" Charlotte asked teasingly.

Stephen looked down into her laughing eyes, the green seemed to shimmer. She was beautiful and even more so this close. He bent to lower his lips to hers. "Will this jolt your memory?" he asked before taking her mouth with his.

Charlotte had not realised how much she wanted his lips until the moment they touched hers. She did feel a jolt, straight through the middle of her body. She leaned into him and wrapped her arms around his neck. She was home.

Stephen moaned at her movement and pulled her closer. All thoughts of the dangers of them being disturbed gone. He wrapped her into an embrace that secured her body fully against his own. He wanted her to feel the reaction she caused in him.

Charlotte gripped the hair she remembered touching and pulled Stephen to her. She did not want the kiss to stop. It was as good as the first time, but this time without the fear and uncertainty. She pulled back in shock.

Stephen groaned and rested his head on her forehead. "Why have we stopped?" he asked, the hoarse tone in his voice showing how much the kiss meant to him.

"We've done this before!"Charlotte gasped.

Stephen paused before speaking, "What do you remember?"

Charlotte flushed, "I remember it was as good as this; only before, there was fear and something else."

"Every time?" Stephen asked, unable to stop himself.

Charlotte smiled, "There was more than once?"

"Oh, yes," Stephen said with feeling. "I think we should continue until you remember more." He stopped anymore conversation by pushing her against the dining room table and kissing her as she had never been kissed before.

Charlotte could not have thought another coherent thought with the attack on her mouth that she fully welcomed. She pushed against

194

Stephen as much as he pushed against her. His tongue explored hers as if he had never explored anyone else, and his moans almost drove her to forget all of her previous memories, not just a few weeks.

Eventually Stephen pulled away and placed his hands on the table behind Charlotte. "We have to stop!" he said, but he was gasping for control.

Charlotte still had her arms around him and with a feeling of being almost wanton, she nibbled along his jawline and bit his ear lobe. "Why?" she whispered.

Stephen gripped the edge of the table. Never before had he come close to some severely lurid behaviour in a dining room. He fought for control while smiling at Charlotte's attempts to encourage him to start kissing her again. He returned the kisses, he could not have refused her anything at that moment, but eventually he gained enough control to move away from her.

"Tiger, you will be the death of me. If Dunham finds us like this, he is likely to call me out!" Stephen said gently, trying to fix his cravat.

Charlotte looked mortified at his words. "Oh, my goodness! I'm sorry; I should have stopped you."

Stephen smiled at her; her pupils were dilated, her lips bruised and her skin flushed: she had never looked so beautiful. He leant over and quickly kissed her. "No, you shouldn't have, and now that you have remembered we have done that before, I am going to take as much opportunity as I can to repeat the process. I think it will help with your memory."

Charlotte laughed and did not disagree with the proposal. The thought of kissing Stephen again set her heart racing. After a few minutes Miss Fairfield re-entered the room. If she saw anything amiss, she did not give any indication of it.

"Miss Webster, Lord Dunham has left Elizabeth to write a letter to his sister and Elizabeth was wondering if you would like to spend a few moments with her before she has a rest?" Miss Fairfield said.

"Oh, yes, please!" Charlotte said happily.

Miss Fairfield smiled at the enthusiasm and once more led the way out of the room. Stephen was left to try to get the last vestiges of lust under control.

*

Charlotte entered Elizabeth's bed chamber slowly. The room was darkened, and it took a moment or two for her eyes to adjust to the dim light.

Elizabeth was sitting up in her bed her cheeks flushed from the exertion she had just been through. Her hair was still damp at the edges and clung to her cheeks and forehead. She was looking down at the bundle in her arms but greeted Charlotte warmly.

"Charlotte, come and meet the new member of our family," she said, her eyes glowing with pride.

"Are you well?" Charlotte whispered as she approached the bed. She had no prior experience of babies or birth and felt a little unsure of what to do.

"I am very well now," Elizabeth said with feeling. "There were points when I didn't think it would ever end, but now that she is here, I don't mind so much."

"She? You have a baby girl? How lovely!" Charlotte had reached the bed and was gazing down at the bundle of blankets and baby in Elizabeth's arms. She could see the redness of the baby's skin and a tuft of black hair.

"Yes, I have had to apologise to Michael for not producing an heir," Elizabeth said with a smile.

"Oh, is he very disappointed?" Charlotte asked, a little worried that Lord Dunham would be disappointed when Elizabeth was so obviously happy.

Elizabeth laughed, "He's not disappointed at all! He is the besotted uncle of three nieces and now the besotted father of a beautiful girl. There is still lots of time for an heir to join our family."

"What have you named her?" Charlotte asked, feeling sure a father like Lord Dunham would ensure his daughter behaved herself as she grew. Charlotte found him intimidating, and she was not related to him, so the bundle had immediate sympathy from Charlotte.

"Catherine Margaret Violet Birchall," Elizabeth said softly, more to her daughter than Charlotte. "We have named her after each of our mothers and Violet of course. This little bundle has a lot to live up to, being named after three wonderful women."

"She is lovely; and so small," Charlotte said in awe of the little baby. She felt a pang of something, whether longing, or hope she was not sure, but she wanted her own little bundles with the blonde hair and blue eyes of their father.

It felt almost as if Elizabeth read Charlotte's mind because she turned to Charlotte and, with her free hand, reached out and squeezed her friend's hand. "I have sometimes acted without thinking things through fully, but please believe me I have only ever had your best interests at heart."

"I know," Charlotte said, flushing a little. "I didn't mean the harsh things I accused you of." She remembered with shame accusing Elizabeth of being jealous of Stephen's feelings.

"I deserved them," Elizabeth said with a grimace. "I have always been headstrong, maybe because I have had to be, but luckily I married a man who is more considered than I ever could be."

"What do you mean?" Charlotte asked.

"I should have kept my counsel about Stephen's views on marriage," Elizabeth said honestly.

"I'm glad I knew; it obviously helped me to make my decision in refusing his proposal," Charlotte insisted.

"That's the problem. My words influenced you, and I think Michael was right. Stephen has changed since he met you; he has done things he would have avoided at all costs prior to meeting you. You don't realise it, but you have brought out the best in him. I am truly sorry I have caused you both to be unhappy when I only ever wanted what was best for the both of you," Elizabeth said.

Charlotte squeezed Elizabeth's hand. "I could never marry for convenience and, if that is what he was offering me, I could not have accepted his proposal, whether you had voiced your concerns or not," she reassured.

"I want us to be friends," Elizabeth said.

"We are and always shall be," Charlotte said softly, but she moved away from the bed. She realised how tired Elizabeth looked and said her goodbyes before leaving the room.

As she returned to her own bed chamber she mulled over Elizabeth's words; so her friend believed Stephen had changed because of the dealings he had had with *her*. The thought pleased her, although she did wish she could remember everything since, if she could, it would make life a little easier.

Chapter 26

Stephen found his bruised pride could be soothed when he received kisses from Charlotte. Over the two weeks Elizabeth was confined to her room because of the birth of Catherine, he was able to take full advantage of the change in circumstances. He was alone with Charlotte far more than he should have been; not only that, he kissed her far more than he should have done.

He took her on a walk and kissed her senseless in the rose garden. He took her for a ride and kissed her breath away by the fishing lake. He played billiards with her and made her legs weak by kissing her against the billiard table. In fact in every room that was free of servants, Stephen indulged in his desire to kiss Charlotte, fully, passionately and almost indecently. He barely kept a rein on his desire, but he did manage to stop himself from taking the next step. She was worth more than an illicit coupling.

Charlotte was a willing participant. It was strange to think she was behaving in the most wanton way she had ever done, yet she was happier than she had ever been. Every moment she spent with Stephen was a moment to treasure. He made her laugh, made her insides squirm with pleasure and made her feel as if life were perfect.

The reality of it was that life was not perfect. He had never mentioned anything about marrying her or renewing his addresses, but she was sure he must love her. He had never uttered the words, but his actions, the way his eyes lit up when hers met his, the way he sought her out, surely those were signs of love?

One afternoon Charlotte sat in the drawing room, trying to concentrate on her needlework while being read snippets of the gossip columns by Stephen. Where ever she was, he was not far away; in some respects she thought they must look like an old married couple, but she would not change a thing.

Michael entered the room and interrupted Stephen's flow of trivia. "This letter has just arrived for you, Halkyn," he said, handing Stephen the letter.

"Oh?" Stephen asked, laying the periodical down. "I'm not expecting anything."

He opened the letter and from the moment he started to read, his demeanour changed. He frowned and hunched forward, taking careful note of every word contained in the letter. When he finished, he crushed the letter in his grip and banged his fist on the arm of the chair.

"A problem?" Michael asked.

"There wouldn't be if this country wasn't run on the system of advancement because of who you know," Stephen said with annoyance.

"What's happened?" Michael persisted.

Stephen shrugged, "The letter is from Peters; it seems that Kersal has friends in high places after all. He should be swinging for what he's been doing, but there is an appeal being submitted by the Duke of Lingston, which means he will win. Who ever heard of someone hanging when a Duke steps in to vouch for one?"

"Surely Peters has enough solid evidence to support the case? I'm surprised Kersal has such a high-level supporter; he is only a Baron and, as far as I was aware, did not have any great friends." Michael guessed correctly the Bow Street Officer was efficient; he had seen him in action long enough to recognise real skill.

"Peters will have done his job, but obviously Kersal has something on Lingston that guarantees his support. Perhaps he is one of the men with unusual tastes. Laura seemed to suggest a lot of our contemporaries have needs that would disgust most of the population," Stephen said.

Charlotte gasped, immediately drawing the attention of both men. "I'm sorry, Charlotte; Halkyn should not have been so graphic in your company," Michael apologised, cursing himself for not stopping the conversation sooner. He had forgotten Charlotte was in the room she had been so quiet throughout the exchange.

"I-It's not that," Charlotte stammered. "I remember! I remember everything!"

"What do you remember?" Stephen demanded.

"Everything," Charlotte said, and then her needlework fell to the floor as her hands flew to her cheeks in horror. "Oh, my good God, what did I do?"

"Charlotte...." Stephen started, immediately wanting to protect her from suffering any kind of distress, but he was interrupted by Charlotte.

She looked at him in horror. "I remember everything!" she said. "I acted like a hussy; oh, my God, I am so sorry."

"You did not act like a hussy; you did the only thing available for you to do," Stephen said quickly. He noticed Michael watching with interest, but he had to ignore him; he would answer his questions later. "You had to get out of there for your own safety; the alternative doesn't bear thinking about!" he insisted.

Charlotte covered her eyes. "Everything that happened with Christopher; oh, my goodness how could I have been so foolish? I am nothing better than a common doxy." She stood and looked at Stephen, meeting his gaze with eyes that were filled with a mixture of shame and remorse. "I am truly ashamed and sorry for what I have done and for involving you. You acted like a gentleman while I behaved appallingly. Please excuse me." She left the room, closing the door firmly behind her.

"Halkyn? What on earth was all that about?" Michael asked.

"It looks as if I have just been taken for a fool!" Stephen responded, not sure whether to be angry or amused someone had fooled him so completely.

"You had better explain," Michael responded.

Stephen told him of the way Charlotte had gained his attention. "I didn't tell you at the start because there was no need. She was

201

embarrassed enough at having to tell you the rest of it without adding to it that she had dragged me into a room."

"I can understand why you both wouldn't make that common knowledge, but why does that make you a fool?" Michael asked, referring back to Halkyn's comment.

"Who did she mention? The footman that persuaded her to elope, and the comments she made were about what she had done with him. She obviously didn't tell me the whole truth when we met. It sounds as if she went further than words and kisses with him, and yet here I am thinking she was an innocent!" Stephen said bitterly.

"I'm not convinced she meant it like that," Michael defended his young guest. "She doesn't seem the sort to let someone compromise her. I'm more inclined to believe the story she told us at the start; she's just shocked at remembering. Don't forget it was a difficult experience for her; I think you should find her and talk to her."

"I think I need a drink first!" Stephen said sullenly. The reality was that he did not really want to know if she had been compromised by the footman because it would destroy him. How could he look at her knowing she had been with another when all he wanted was for her to be with him? He was being selfish; he acknowledged that, but he wanted Charlotte, and he reacted badly at the thought of her with someone else.

Michael was right though; Stephen needed to talk to her and find out the truth once and for all. Although he cursed his foolishness, he also wanted to make sure she was not too upset at remembering. After all this time it must be difficult to be suddenly faced with memories, especially as they were not pleasant ones. He took some moments to drink a brandy and collect himself. He needed to be able to speak to her calmly, or he would never find out anything.

Michael left the room, making some excuse. He thought it best to leave Stephen to speak to Charlotte alone. It was going to be a difficult conversation for them both, and they did not need his interference.

Stephen pulled the bell and asked the footman to send a message to Miss Webster to join him. He waited, trying to remain calm when his insides were churning. He started to pace the room but was interrupted when the footman returned to say that Miss Webster had left the house over half an hour ago.

The news did not bode well for Stephen's temper, and he strode out to the rose garden. It was Charlotte's favourite place; at least they could still be private. Stephen had not wanted to have the conversation he needed to have in a place that reminded him so much of the kisses they had shared, but it looked as if he did not have a choice. As he walked, he suppressed a smile, there were few places in Dunham House that would not remind him of their kisses; there was hardly a room where they had not indulged.

Charlotte was not to be found in the rose garden. Stephen continued looking for her along the pathways but, after an hour, it was apparent she was not in the immediate parkland. He returned to the house, suppressing the unease he was beginning to feel.

Miss Fairfield's assistance was sought when Stephen arrived back at the house. She had not seen Charlotte but went in search of her. She returned a little time later, her frown betraying the result of her search.

"I'm afraid, My Lord, that Charlotte is not in the house. The footman who saw her leave said she did not carry anything with her apart from her reticule, but she did appear to be upset and in a hurry."

"Damn it!" Stephen muttered, before apologising for his language to Miss Fairfield.

Miss Fairfield nodded her acceptance of the apology. "Is there anything else you would like me to do, My Lord?"

"Send someone to check if she has reached the village and tried to obtain a ticket for the stage," Stephen asked gruffly.

"Do you think she has left?" Miss Fairfield asked in surprise. This did not seem like Charlotte's normal behaviour, since even after the accident, she had appeared to be a steady young girl.

"I don't know; I really don't know," Stephen admitted, running a hand through his hair, part in frustration, part in worry. "Her memory returned suddenly, and it has caused her considerable distress; I don't know what she has done as a result of that."

"I see," Miss Fairfield said. "I shall have someone sent into the village immediately. We will find her, My Lord," she assured Stephen, before leaving the room.

Stephen sighed; yet again his feelings for Charlotte left him totally at a loss as to what to do. He had never felt so out of control in his life, and he hated not knowing what was going to happen from one moment to the next. His life had been so ordered previously. He looked at himself in the large mirror above the marble fireplace. His life had been ordered, it was true, but he had not been happy.

He groaned at his reflection. When had he suddenly wanted to be happy? Possibly from the moment Charlotte begged him for a kiss, begged him to help her and made him become a better human being in the process. His emotions had been in complete turmoil these last months, but he would not change a thing. The last two weeks had shown him what real happiness and contentment were. Yes, he had been intent on kissing Charlotte during every opportunity that arose, but he had felt something else. He had enjoyed laughing with her, talking to her, just being by her side for most of the day.

He rested his head on the cool marble fire place and laughed to himself. What a fool he was. He had ridiculed his friends for years and now he had just gone and done exactly the same: he had fallen in love. Completely and totally, just like any moon struck fool. He was in love with her, and now she had gone.

Worry surfaced again, and he stood straight. He needed to do something, and he probably needed Michael's assistance. He left the room and knocked on Michael's study.

"Come in," came the command.

Stephen opened the door and walked in, nodding to Charles as he approached the desk. "Charlotte is missing," he said simply.

"What do you mean missing?" Michael asked; he hoped it was not as a result of a fall out between the pair. He had left Stephen only two hours previously; he had presumed they had sorted out the upset over the recalled memories.

"When she left the room, she also left the house and hasn't been seen since. Your housekeeper is sending to the village to see if she is there or has tried to leave from there, but she is not in the grounds or the house," Stephen explained.

"Where can she have gone?" Michael asked. "Back to her uncle?"

"I doubt she has gone there without luggage or money, but who knows how badly upset she was? We need to find her before nightfall!" Stephen could not stop the worry from sounding in his voice.

"We will," Michael said firmly. "Charles, please have the house and grounds rechecked and check with Martha to see if she needs any help. I'm sure she has everything under control but just in case. The more help, the sooner we will find her."

"Yes, My Lord," Charles replied and left the room.

"If she has left the house, she's on foot; she won't have got very far," Michael said consolingly.

"She was so upset; I hope she doesn't do something stupid," Stephen responded.

Two hours later it seemed Charlotte had disappeared. There was no sign of her, and Stephen was setting out to search for her himself. She had not reached the village, as far as anyone could tell, so the likelihood was that she had fallen and was injured somewhere on the parkland. No matter how much Michael assured him if she was on the parkland, she would have been found, Stephen was determined to look for her himself.

Their argument about the necessity of this was interrupted by the arrival of Elizabeth. Michael jumped up when his wife entered the room. "Elizabeth! What on earth are you doing out of your rooms?" the concerned husband asked.

"I am come to see what has happened to Charlotte. I could hear that something was wrong and forced Martha to tell me. Has she not been found yet?" Elizabeth asked, sitting down and facing both men.

"No, I'm going to look for her; I was just about to leave," Stephen said.

"Running about the countryside will not achieve anything," Elizabeth responded.

"That's what I've been trying to tell him," Michael added in frustration.

Stephen looked fit to burst, "Well at least I will be doing *something!*" he snapped.

"You are a pair of fools!" Elizabeth said, annoyed with them both. "She could have been found hours ago if only you would have come straight to me."

"Why? Where is she?" Stephen demanded, for once ignoring the criticism of himself.

"There is only one other place she would have gone if she was upset. I'm surprised neither of you thought of it; she will be at the Hurst's farm," Elizabeth said. She was worried about her friend but could not help being slightly smug about the expressions that greeted her at her words.

"That's miles away!" Stephen said, dismissing the suggestion. "She was on foot."

"Yes, and how long was it before you realised she was missing?" Elizabeth asked.

"Probably about two hours," Stephen admitted.

"And in that two hours, do you not think she would have come across some form of transport, whether farm cart or curricle, that would have taken up a young lady and helped her along her way?" Elizabeth asked, shaking her head.

"I need my horse," Stephen muttered and left the room.

"You have our wish of good luck on your quest," Elizabeth said to the retreating figure, even though her words would not be heard. "I think Stephen finally realises what Charlotte means to him," she smiled at her husband.

"I hope so; I've left them alone enough over these last few weeks," Michael responded with a gleam in his eye. "I've never worked as much in my study before. I will be in despair if he didn't take the opportunity to use the time productively."

"Michael!" Elizabeth exclaimed, before bursting into laughter.

Chapter 27

Stephen rode without thinking. His driving force was that Charlotte was upset, and he needed to make her feel better. He had barely stopped to receive directions to the farm before setting off. He had kept away from the farm during Charlotte's stay there, but there was no possibility he could keep away now if she was there.

His horse covered the ground in impressive time, and there was still a small amount of light when he dismounted outside the farm. The two dogs barked their greeting until Mrs Hurst came out of the house.

"Can I help you sir?" Her tone was pleasant, but she seemed to be looking at Stephen with particular interest.

"I hope so," Stephen responded. "Is Miss Webster here?"

"Who are you?"

"I'm Lord Halkyn, and I need to see Miss Webster!" Stephen responded. He subconsciously stood taller to try and intimidate his way in.

His actions did not seem to impress Mrs Hurst. She looked him up and down and then met his gaze, all signs of friendliness gone. It was apparent she was not easily bullied or intimidated. "Well, unfortunately for you, she doesn't want to see you, so I suggest you get back on your horse and leave her be."

Stephen had not anticipated being refused entry and could have growled with annoyance, but he kept his temper. "I can't do that," he responded.

"I won't have her more upset than she already is," Mrs Hurst said firmly.

"I don't wish to upset her; I want to do exactly the opposite," Stephen said. "Please ask her to see me for half an hour, and if she still feels as strongly after then, I will never bother her again."

Mrs Hurst seemed to consider for a moment before nodding her head slightly and returning to the farm house. Stephen was left kicking his heels in the farm yard for ten minutes until Mrs Hurst returned.

"She will see you in the parlour," she said, indicating he should follow her. She led the way through the kitchen as she had done with Charlotte's other visitors when she was recovering from the accident.

Stephen sat in a chair in the parlour, his large frame filling the space. Mrs Hurst nodded at him before opening the door wider and letting Charlotte enter the room.

"Now you heed what I said," she spoke to Charlotte. "I will be waiting in the kitchen; if you need me or want this to end, just call me."

"I will, thank you," Charlotte said quietly.

Stephen stood at Charlotte's entrance and almost reached out to her, but the haunted look on her face stopped him. He had been sure about finding her and explaining everything, making it all well, but the expression of real sadness in her eyes made him wonder if he had made a mistake. He hoped against hope he was not the cause of that sadness.

"Charlotte, everyone has been worried about you," he said gently, indicating she should be seated.

"I'm sorry to have caused so much trouble. It would seem that is all I do these days," Charlotte responded.

"This is not like you, Charlotte," Stephen said gently. "Where has my tiger gone?" He smiled at her in encouragement, but his words only made her look even more upset. Her expression tore at his insides, and he reached out and touched her hand. "Tell me what has caused you to be so upset, Charlotte. I don't understand how your memory returning could be such a bad thing."

Charlotte smiled slightly, but it did not reach her eyes. "Yes, I have been struggling to remember so much, haven't I? Yet I should have continued to avoid the memories since they are so horrible."

Stephen tried to ignore the knot of dread in his stomach Charlotte's words had caused. "Did Christopher force himself on you?" The muscle in his cheek started to twitch.

"Christopher? No!" Charlotte said quickly. "Why would you think that?"

The breath Stephen had been holding whooshed out of him. "It was just that your reaction about regaining the memories was so bad I thought something must have happened you hadn't previously told me. With you mentioning the footman by name, I presumed it was to do with him," Stephen said honestly.

"No, there was nothing more happened than I explained; you insisted I be honest from the start, and I thought I owed you that for the service you gave. It is more complicated; I can't really explain it," Charlotte said, frowning and biting her lip.

Stephen leaned across to her and held both her hands in his. "Charlotte, my dear, tell me. Tell me so I can put that smile on your face again and kiss you until your legs can no longer support you," he said, his voice going husky at the thought of having her in his arms, Mrs Hurst next door or not.

Charlotte sighed, "I had fooled myself into thinking I meant more to you than I do, and regaining the memories just proved you will never think of me as anything other than a foolish girl who deserves nothing better than being offered illicit kisses." The words had rushed out of Charlotte, and she did not look at Stephen when she finished.

Stephen paused before speaking; a few weeks ago he probably would not have disagreed with her viewpoint, but now things were different. He had finally come to realise what was important to him and to realise what he wanted in life. The problem was he needed Charlotte to believe him, so he had to tread carefully.

"I never thought of you as a foolish girl. All I wanted was to make sure you were safe and to kill Kersal," Stephen said quietly.

Charlotte smiled at his words. "I always felt safe with you. I wonder why that is? I knew of your reputation, but from the first moment, I felt protected."

"I think you have the unique ability of seeing the best in me," Stephen said seriously. "I have an apology to make; I am sorry for the way I proposed marriage to you. You never deserved that, and I should never have behaved in such a cold way."

"Just because I believe in love, doesn't mean to say that you have to," Charlotte said with a blush. "I think I would have had more to complain about if you had tried to woo Elizabeth and been cold towards me; at least you were consistent!"

Stephen cringed with regret, which made him speak sooner than he had intended. "Charlotte, you deserve so much more than me: you deserve the Mr O'Haras of the world who will cherish you and care for you in a way that is steady and honourable, but I need to know: is there any hope for me?"

Charlotte stared at him. "Any hope?" she asked in disbelief.

"Yes, I'm far from perfect as you well know, but I am offering myself to you. I can't promise never to upset you; I can't promise never to frustrate you half to death, but please reconsider, and this time accept my offer of marriage," Stephen responded with feeling.

Charlotte looked at him in shock. Once the memories had flooded back, she had been filled with horror at the thought of how she must appear. She had certainly aged in the few months since her foolish elopement. She would never be able to look back on it with anything but mortification that she had been so foolish and naive for falling for such an obvious ploy played out so well by Christopher.

The events in Baron Kersal's home and then her approach to Stephen made her shudder. If anyone outside her trusted acquaintance ever heard of it, she would be cast off as a fallen woman. Her thoughts had become confused, mixed and unclear. All she could think of was that she had been thinking Stephen's kisses were a sign of his love, when the reality was he must think she was a doxy. Only a loose woman would respond so eagerly to his kisses; she had never once refused his approaches.

Now to her complete astonishment, he had renewed his marriage proposal. She should say yes immediately; if she had any sense she would and hope to gain his love over time, but caution made her pause. If he were unfaithful to her it would kill her.

"Why do you want to marry me? Why would you offer again?" Charlotte asked.

Stephen sagged a little; this was difficult. He was an expert at deflecting focus away from talking in such a way, but he knew it was necessary to try and prove to her he was worth the risk. If she did not think he was worth taking that gamble, he did not think he would be able to go back to society and continue as he had previously. If *she* did not believe in him, he was sure no one else ever would.

"Because I don't want you to leave my life. I want to be the one who makes you smile; I want to be the one you seek out in a room full of people. I want to be the one you go to sleep with every night and wake up with every morning," he replied.

Charlotte blushed at the implications of his words and, although she would not believe it possible, her heart started to pound a little faster. "But you can't promise to be faithful," she said sadly. That was the fact of who he was and because of her behaviour, he might not think she would mind about him having mistresses.

Stephen stood and approached the fireplace, gripping the edge of the mantelpiece in frustration. "Will my foolish words never be forgotten?" he ground out. "If I had married Elizabeth, I would have been unfaithful."

Charlotte took a deep breath, her fear of him being unfaithful being openly acknowledged. She felt as if a little part of her insides were starting to crumble.

"Wait!" Stephen interrupted. "Before you condemn me, listen to what I have to say." Charlotte nodded in agreement, but Stephen did not miss how much she had paled.

"Elizabeth wanted to live on her estate in Yorkshire; I wanted more civilisation than that. She didn't really want a husband, just the protection a husband's name could give her. I don't condemn her for that; I've seen marriages occur for similar reasons time and time again. If we had married and lived separately I would have been unfaithful; I certainly would not have felt as if I was shackled to anyone seeing them only once or twice a year. If we had lived together, who knows? I might have fallen in love with her. I don't know, but I doubt it. I like her, but that is all."

"It would have been a marriage in name only wouldn't it?" Charlotte acknowledged.

"Yes, it would. Do you know I voiced my concerns to Dunham about being unfaithful if we married?" he asked, looking slightly embarrassed at his action.

"No," Charlotte responded quietly. "What did he say?"

"He said the fact that I was worried about hurting you meant I wouldn't be unfaithful in the first place," Stephen responded, the usual running of his hand through his hair betraying his uncertainty. "He could be right; I don't know, but I do know one thing: when I had to return to Kersal's home, the thought of being with anyone else other than you sickened me to my core."

"You returned?" Charlotte asked, shocked.

"Yes, Peters insisted he needed an introduction to be able to visit the place without me," Stephen said. "It was a bloody awful night. All I wanted to do was strangle the man, and I had to behave as if nothing had happened."

"As if nothing had happened?" Charlotte asked. She was really asking had he been with one of the girls, but she could not voice her question.

213

Stephen smiled, guessing what she meant and taking hope that she sounded jealous. "We managed to arrange it that we spoke to Laura. She gave Peters a lot of information, but I have never been as glad to leave a place in all my life. I don't know what I ever found to be entertaining there."

Charlotte smiled a little, "As much as it grieves me to think of you there, I am glad for my sake that you went back."

Stephen stood before her and took her hands in his, forcing her to her feet. "Does this mean you have feelings for me, Miss Webster?" he teased.

Charlotte flushed and tried to pull her hands away, but they were held in a firm grasp. "You know how I feel," she said defensively.

"Do I?" Stephen asked, feeling as if finally he was approaching the conclusion he wanted. "I know you like my kisses, but I have previously been told they do rank with the best of them."

Charlotte looked indignant and really tugged to try and free her hands, but Stephen still kept a tight hold. "I'm sure you have; please let me go!"

"Why? So you can run away from me again?" Stephen asked. "I will chase you to the ends of the earth Charlotte until you have given me an answer."

"I should say no," Charlotte said, not quite meeting his eyes. "What if I am not good enough for you? What if you get bored? What if you leave me for another?"

"Those are a lot of 'what ifs'," Stephen said. He let go of one of Charlotte's hands and tilted her chin until he forced her to meet his gaze. "I don't know what the future will hold Charlotte. I am not going to lie to you and say I will be the easiest husband to live with, but I know some things for certain: I have never had a boring moment since the day I met you. I haven't thought of anyone else since the day I met you. I can't face not having you in my life. I'm afraid Charlotte. Afraid you won't stay with me, afraid something will happen that will upset you or hurt you and I won't be able to stop it.

214

I'm afraid if you refuse me I will never love another person as long as I live." Stephen took a deep breath. "I have turned into the sort of besotted fool I used to ridicule, and I want to remain in this state until my dying day."

"You love me?" Charlotte asked, the words she had heard making her feel lightheaded and a little bit nervous at the same time.

"I think I've loved you from the moment you demanded a kiss from me," Stephen said with a rueful smile. "Just being the fool I am, it's taken me months to realise it. Will you have me Charlotte?"

"Yes," Charlotte responded, almost throwing herself into his arms. "I will have you with all your faults, grumpiness and stubbornness!"

"I knew you were my perfect wife; none of this romance rubbish from my tiger," Stephen said sweeping her into his arms and kissing her.

Charlotte returned his kiss but eventually pulled away, cupping her hand around Stephen's cheek. "I love you, my imperfect knight in a frock coat and breeches; I will do anything I can to make you happy, but I can't promise not to want some romance along the way."

Stephen groaned, "I knew there would be a downside to this marriage lark!" he responded lowering his head for another kiss, but swinging Charlotte around, completely in contradiction to his words.

Charlotte laughed and whispered, "Kiss me, sir."

"Always," came the husky response.

The End

About this book

After writing The Inconvenient Ward, I wanted to give Lord Halkyn the happy ending I thought he deserved. No one should be so cynical about love, and I am a great believer in there being someone special out there for all of us who will accept us for who we are, faults and all.

I also wanted to bring in a Bow Street Officer into one of my stories, and this naturally developed as the story progressed. I have read many Regency novels that always refer to Bow Street Officers as Bow Street Runners; it was a term commonly used during the time. The difficulty I had with the term was that the actual Officers themselves hated the term 'Runners'; they felt it demeaned the work they did and was a sign they were not taken seriously. So, I decided my Bow Street Officers would receive the respect that anyone in such a difficult job should have and, therefore, I have always used their official title. I have created characters, rather than using actual officers, but I hope in my own little way, I have given them some of the respect they deserve.

Best wishes, Audrey.

About the Author

Audrey Harrison has always wanted to write or live in the Regency period, but life, work and problems with time travel stopped her. Anyway, circumstances change and the dream began! (Well, maybe not the travel back to the Regency period, but I would not admit to that anyone, would I?)

The Complicated Earl and *The Reluctant Earl* have proved really popular and the modern take on a Regency novel, *A Very Modern Lord,* has also done really well on Amazon Kindle.

When writing *An Inconvenient Ward*, it was going to be a stand-alone book, but as the story progressed, so did the sub stories. There is now a trilogy to the series: *An Inconvenient Ward, An Inconvenient Wife* and *An Inconvenient Companion*. Each book can be read alone, but I hope readers enjoy finding out about the other characters in the stories.

If you enjoy the books, please would you take the time to write a review on Amazon? Reviews are vital for an author who is just starting out, although I admit to bad ones being crushing. Selfishly, I want readers to love my characters just as much as I do!

I can be contacted for any comments you may have, via my website

www.audreyharrison.co.uk

www.facebook.com/AudreyHarrisonAuthor

About the Proof Reader

Joan fell in love with words at about 8 months of age and has been using them and correcting them ever since. She's had a 20-year career in U.S. Army public affairs spent mostly writing: speeches for Army generals, safety publications and videos, and has had one awesome book published, (italics, I'm on my kindle and can't get there) *Every Day a New Adventure: Caregivers Look at Alzheimer's Disease*, a really riveting and compelling look at five patients, including her own mother. It is available through Publishamerica.com. She also edits books because she loves correcting other people's use of language. What's to say? She's good at it. She lives in a small town near Atlanta, Georgia in the American South with one long-haired cat to whom she is allergic and her grandson to whom she is not. If you need her, you may reach her at oh1kelley@gmail.com.

Thank you for your support and, for your enjoyment, please find Chapter One of *An Inconvenient Companion*.

Prologue

London, Spring 1816

Alfred Peters, one of the new Bow Street Officers, visited Baron Kersal's home in London for the third time that week. His colleague, Martin Corless, was following the Baron in his day-to-day life, but it had been Alfred's role to infiltrate the inner circle. Lord Halkyn, an aristocrat who disliked the way Baron Kersal was developing his business, had provided the means to access the house, and Alfred worked in his usual methodical way, liaising with Corless until they gathered enough evidence against Baron Kersal.

The Baron, in addition to running a house seven miles outside the city where a variety of pursuits not discussed in polite circles were held, had decided he needed more funds and had branched out further. He had begun arranging the kidnap and forced marriages of innocent young girls, which was when Lord Halkyn had become involved. One usually used to enjoying some of the pleasures that Baron Kersal offered, he had helped to rescue Miss Charlotte Webster, who had been kidnapped. Once Miss Webster was safe Lord Halkyn vowed, with the assistance of Bow Street, to bring the Baron to justice.

Alfred had been introduced as Lord Halkyn's cousin and had convinced the Baron and his friends he was a keen gambler. He had secured a lot of information through one of the girls, Laura, who had helped Charlotte. Laura disliked the new activity, particularly as the girls being targeted were young. Alfred, being the man he was, gave the informant enough money to ensure, when the time came, Laura would be able to get herself out of danger.

Everything was coming together as they hoped. He had not needed to visit the premises again, really, but something had drawn him to it one last time. Alfred had always acted professionally; he took his job very seriously, but Laura had haunted his dreams since the evening he met her. She had seemed a kindred spirit, older than her years, a little like himself, having seen more of life than any decent human being should have. He told her they would never see each other again and, although he had visited the premises numerous times, he always stayed away from the girls.

This night though, he could not concentrate. He knew exactly why he had visited the house, and the fight with his conscience only meant he did not focus fully on gambling and was running at a loss. He tossed his cards onto the table and, with a sigh, pushed his chair back; his lack of success was giving the Baron back some of the money he had won earlier in the week.

Baron Kersal approached the young man, always ready to persuade a gambler to try and win back his losses, usually resulting in further losses for the player and more profit for himself.

"Good evening, Mr Peters," the Baron said genially. "Giving up so easily?"

"Yes, I'm not in the mood tonight," Alfred responded, taking a pinch of snuff.

"Some other entertainment then?" The Baron offered, always ready to offer something that would cost his visitors.

Albert paused; this was the moment he should walk out the door and never look back. He took another pinch of snuff while fighting his demons. He snapped his snuffbox shut and placed it carefully in his pocket.

"If that girl is available who I saw on my first visit, I think I could be tempted," he said with a convincing leer.

"Who was that?" The Baron asked, pleased he would be receiving further money from the young man.

"Laura: she was worth the money my cousin and I paid; she was very obliging, no matter what we did," Albert said, trying not to look too keen about seeing Laura again.

The Baron frowned, "Laura does other jobs for me these days; what about one of our other girls? Some of the younger ones are more than willing to spend an evening with a handsome young man." The Baron was sweating.

Alfred, with his tall slim frame, dark hair and green eyes set in a pale complexion, could be described as ordinary but never handsome. Anyone taking the time to look into his eyes would see a haunted expression, the result of seeing hardship and facing danger too many times. Alfred struggled to maintain his pleasant expression; he really disliked the Baron and would be happy when his colleagues raided the establishment.

"Laura had specialities I enjoyed. I would be willing to pay extra for her, but if not...." He left the sentence hanging, sure of the Baron's reaction to money.

Not one to disappoint, the Baron replied immediately. "Laura will be with you in ten minutes. If you would like to follow me, we can agree on a price."

Alfred nodded and followed the portly, glistening man into his office, where he conducted most transactions. It was better to be away from the eyes of the other visitors, especially when dealing with men who had lost a fortune gambling. He might not look as if he were anything other than an overweight aristocrat with questionable tastes, but Alfred knew his type could prove to be the most dangerous. If they could not protect themselves physically, men like the Baron always made sure they surrounded themselves with loyal staff who could.

When the deal had been done, a member of staff took him to a bedroom.

As with the Baron's other bedrooms, the room was minimally furnished; excess furniture was a waste of money in the Baron's eyes. The décor was clean and tidy, which was a higher standard than some of the other places that existed for the same reasons, but it was not extravagant. Everything in the house was there for the purpose of separating money from visitors. The door was left open while there was no girl in attendance. Alfred poured himself a glass of wine, beginning to realise what he was about to do. He drank the wine back in one gulp and poured himself another.

"Does an evening with me cause you to turn to drink?" came a voice from the doorway.

Alfred turned to see Laura, leaning against the door frame, a smile on her face. Alfred smiled in return and indicated she should come into the room by offering her a glass of wine. "Hello, Laura," he said quietly.

He watched as she walked into the room, closing the door behind her and letting her shawl fall over the chair before accepting the glass of wine. She was not stunningly beautiful, but her auburn hair and dark green eyes drew him to her like a moth to flame. She had signs of wrinkles developing, a mark of the difficulties in her life; she must only be around four and twenty. Girls in her trade started young and were cast off before they got too old. Like him, Laura had aged prematurely, a consequence of the struggle of being born on the wrong side of polite society.

"You've been a regular visitor here recently; I was disappointed when our first encounter didn't tempt you back," she flirted, as she sipped her wine, looking at him over the edge of the glass.

"I'm here now," Alfred said, his face never changing expression, but his insides feeling lighter at the fact she had shown an interest in him by knowing he had been on the premises. No one else would have taken notice; he was not handsome enough or rich enough to be noticed by the girls who worked there.

"Yes, you are," Laura said, circling him provocatively. "And what do you have in mind for tonight? Is it going to be different than last time?"

She was asking him if he was going to talk to her, which was all they had done on that first meeting; well, except for the two kisses they had shared. "I always think different is best, don't you?" he responded.

Laura flushed slightly but maintained the banter. There were peep holes in every room, so they could be being watched. Neither of them could give anything away, or they would not get out of the house in one piece. "I am here to please you, Sir."

"You can start by getting undressed," Alfred said, refilling his glass. He should get her on the bed behind the covers, so she would not be seen by anyone choosing to watch the activities of the house rather than take part. He wanted to see her undress though, and he knew the eyes watching would not be too interested at this point; they preferred the activity further on.

"As you wish," Laura responded. She slowly undressed herself. All her clothing was made to be removed easily; too many fastenings could result in ripped clothing, and that cost money to repair. She had no corset on, again for ease, and was soon naked before Alfred.

"What about you, Sir?" she asked, trying to keep the anticipation and warmth from her voice. As much as she had haunted Alfred's dreams, he had haunted hers.

"All in good time," Alfred said, placing his glass on the small table and striding towards her. He grabbed her and kissed her as he had kissed her last time, as if it would be his last. Laura responded to him immediately, wrapping her arms about his neck and pulling him further into her.

Alfred did not stop kissing her as he lifted her from her feet and carried her over to the bed. He climbed on after her and closed the curtains around them. There would be nothing more for the peeping toms to look at that night.

*

Hours later, Laura was nestled in Alfred's arms, facing his chest. She had never nestled with any other client, it was always do what had to be done and, once finished, more than likely on to the next client. She forced her thoughts not to dwell on her job and snuggled further into the warmth surrounding her.

"What are you doing woman?" Alfred chuckled, but he kept his voice low, not risking any conversation being overheard.

"You said I would never see you again," Laura said quietly.

"I tried to stay away," Alfred said. "I'm putting you at risk being here."

"It's a risk I'm willing to take," Laura said, kissing the smattering of hair that curled on his chest.

Alfred paused from stroking her back, "Laura, I cannot offer you anything," he said. She would not have a happy time being linked to him.

"I have not asked for anything have I?" Laura replied, still quietly, but the indignation was clear in her voice.

"Sorry, I just don't want you to get hurt," Alfred replied, kissing her until she smiled.

"I don't want you to get hurt," Laura responded eventually, but not pulling away fully from his lips. He had hinted Bow Street Officers did not have a long life span, and she worried he would come to harm.

"I know; you told me that when we first met," Alfred said, remembering the words she had said to him.

"In another life, I would have taken care of you," Laura whispered the words, as if reading his thoughts.

"In another life, I would have let you," Alfred responded, as he had on that first day.

No other words were exchanged as they showed each other through actions how much the words meant to them both.

Deep in the night, Alfred finally stirred. "It is time I left; if I stay any longer questions will be asked."

"I know; I was just being selfish," Laura said, a lump developing in her insides she knew by instinct it would be hard to move. This time he would not return; she knew that without any words being said.

"Kersal said you didn't usually do this sort of thing anymore. He isn't mistreating you is he?" Alfred asked. Case or no case, if she were being hurt, he would sort the Baron out himself.

"No, he isn't," Laura said. "I'm looking after the girls here; apparently I'm getting too old to see the gentlemen."

"How old are you, you old hag?" Alfred asked teasingly.

"Four and twenty; does that shock you?" Laura responded with mock primness.

"As a man who is a whole year younger, no it doesn't shock me, although I may have to try a younger model in future, just to see the difference," Alfred said before having the wind knocked out of him by Laura poking him in his ribs. "Ooof, woman, you are vicious!" He laughed, still careful to keep his voice low.

Alfred became serious and held Laura tightly to him. "I do have to leave now, but promise me you will be careful," he said.

"I will," Laura said, blinking back tears that threatened to spring to her eyes at such concern. She mentally shook herself; there was no place for tears In her world: life was what it was. There was no point repining now. She climbed out of bed and quickly got dressed.

Alfred followed her from the bed and dressed himself. He approached Laura and gave her a hand full of coins. "Thank you, Laura," he said, kissing her roughly on her lips before walking out of the room without looking back.

Laura stayed still a few moments before leaving the room and returning to her own private bed chamber. Once there she sat on the edge of the bed and wrapped her arms around her middle. "God, if you exist and you are fair, you will let me keep this little part of him. The future is too bleak with no reminder of him in it."

Chapter 1

Somerset, Autumn 1816

"That blasted man!" Martha Fairfield, housekeeper and former companion to Lady Elizabeth Dunham muttered to herself as she walked through the hall of Dunham House. She was always so calm, so collected, except when she was faced with Mr Charles Anderton and his interfering ways.

Why could he not keep to his own role of Lord Dunham's man of business? she grumbled to herself as she stomped up the stairs. Martha Fairfield never stomped, and it proved just how annoyed she was that she threw caution to the wind and allowed the footmen to see how agitated she was.

He was always *there*, offering his so-called help, giving his unwanted advice on matters that should not, no, did not concern him. Whoever heard of a man of business helping to find a nanny? There were clear lines of responsibility in every household, and Charles Anderton consistently crossed them. Well, he did when it had anything to do with her responsibilities; he never seemed to interfere with the butler or the cook the way he did with her. His actions resulted in Martha coming to the conclusion he had no faith in her abilities, something she was reminded of time and time again.

Initially, when they had first met, she had presumed it was because he saw her as a Lady's companion and, to be fair, many in that role had little wit about them. She had come across women who held the role, who had virtually no education or conversation showing any level of intelligence or understanding. Being grouped with them, although a tad unfair, was not really a surprise, and she had not felt any great antagonism, although he had managed to irritate her regularly.

Now, though, Charles Anderton had known her for well over a year, and in that time there had been a lot of contact between the pair. At one time they were on an equal footing, desperate their master and mistress would overcome the hurdles they had faced and acknowledge the attraction that existed between them. It had given Martha and Charles a common cause they had both tried to work on in the background in helping their employers along the way.

That felt a long time ago now, though, Martha reflected as she closed the door on her bed chamber for a moment. She did not usually escape from her duties during the day, but something Charles said, had hit a nerve, and she needed to gather her thoughts before continuing on with her tasks.

All he had said was she had no experience with children and nannies, which was true, but she had taken it as a personal insult. For some reason his words had made her feel less of a woman— somewhat irrationally, she acknowledged to herself. She struggled with the feelings coursing through her body, as the implication of his words had stirred something deep within her. It was something she usually managed to suppress.

She sighed and sat at her window seat, picking up a cushion and holding it tight against her stomach. She tried to calm herself, looking out of the Jacobean building and over the garden. The view was of the garden that spread out on the side of the property. It was a beautiful view that she enjoyed being able to see each day, and she had enjoyed watching the changes in the seasons because the gardeners at Dunham House excelled themselves. Her shoulders slumped. She knew what her destiny was and had accepted it long ago. Why did Charles Anderton have to stir feelings that would haunt her long into the night?

*

Martha Fairfield had been born into a genteel family. There were no titles linked to the family name, but there was enough wealth to provide a comfortable lifestyle. Martha was the eldest girl in a family of five children. Her two older brothers had indulged their baby sister even after a younger brother and sister had been born. It was a happy but uneventful life.

Martha was brought up to expect to marry a gentleman, probably someone known to the family already. She would continue to live in the area of Cheshire where she had been born, bringing up her own family in familiar surroundings with friends and family. Only she was to find out life sometimes did not always follow what was expected of it.

Her father died suddenly of a seizure. He was still young, and it was a complete shock to everyone who knew him. That, for the Fairfield family was not to be the only shock they had to endure. Their father had not been as good with his finances as they had presumed. They had been living in blissful ignorance until his death was announced officially when the creditors called in what was owed them.

Martha's older brother Thomas had acted quickly and sold off some of the land to pay off the debt, as he was a proud young man and refused to leave the debts outstanding. The continued good name of the family was important to all of them, more so with the new financial difficulties. Thomas then had the difficult task of sitting his family down and explaining the consequence of paying off the creditors. It was a difficult conversation in which he told them that their property would no longer sustain the family.

Martha's mother had taken the news badly, partly still grieving for her husband and partly through shame of what had gone on without her knowledge. Her children tried to reassure her, but she had taken to her bed for the foreseeable future, giving Thomas the further difficulty of dealing with an invalid mother and the costs associated with that.

The second eldest, William had immediately informed the family he was signing up to join the navy. He had always wanted to but had been persuaded into following a career in the clergy. The potential of joining the navy and earning more money while following the career he wanted was too much of a pull. At the same time as having the career he wanted, he would have the ability to send some money to his family each month, so it was a decision he found easy to make.

The youngest boy was too young to work, so he would stay within the family home. Thomas decided he would look to have him apprenticed when he was old enough.

Martha realised through listening to the conversations, that she, herself, and her younger sister Susan would have to secure marriages and soon. Susan was too young, but she would need to be married almost as soon as she left the schoolroom, something that was not ideal in anyone's mind. In her own case, Martha had come out the previous year and, although she had not received an offer of marriage yet, there were one or two young men she thought might offer for her in time. Thomas spoke to his sister about her situation in private.

"I didn't want to have this conversation in front of the others," he explained as they sat together in what had been his father's study.

"What is it?" Martha asked gently, thinking her brother had aged over the last few months, and she felt sorry for what he had faced and the decisions he had had to make.

"Is there anyone who wishes to marry you now, Martha?" he asked gently.

"No, but I have had only one season; I don't consider myself on the shelf just yet," Martha teased.

"Neither do I," Thomas smiled at his sister, but the smile was tinged with sadness. "The problem is, Martha: we cannot afford another season for you."

Martha looked at her brother, and the serious expression on his face helped the words sink in. Not being able to afford another season meant she would not be out socialising, which meant she would not come into contact with any gentlemen. That lack of social interaction would guarantee there would be no marriage proposals forthcoming. There were enough young ladies looking to marry for the available gentlemen not to have to search for someone they had met the previous year. Especially if she would no longer be attending the parties and, therefore, would be out of their social circle. Thomas was effectively telling Martha he could not help her to marry, condemning her to spinsterhood.

"Susan?" Martha asked quietly.

"Not even a first season unless things change dramatically in the next four years," Thomas said sadly. "I'm sorry Martha; I would if I could but, even without the expense of a season, the land we have left isn't going to sustain us. I'm letting most of the staff go; William's going into the navy will help: one less mouth to feed, and I think I will be able to get Henry apprenticed next year, but I cannot afford the expense which the rounds of entertainments would cost."

"Of course, you can't," Martha said practically. She suppressed the feelings of sadness and bitterness at what she had lost. It was not Thomas's fault; he was doing the best he could in the circumstances. She could spend her time hating her father, but all that would achieve would be to embitter herself, since her feelings towards him could not affect him. She had to be practical and help her family. "If things are so bad, I need to help as well."

"You will need to take on some extra duties around the house; without staff there will be more work for us all to do," Thomas said.

"Thomas, I cannot be a burden on you for the rest of my days," Martha said with a firm set to her mouth. "A spinster sister is a drain on what are already limited resources, and you cannot have such a burden for the rest of my life. I will seek a position as a Lady's companion; I have not the ability to be a governess, but I can be a companion."

"No!" Thomas said. "The situation is not that bad!"

Martha reached over and squeezed her brother's hand. "You need help, so let me do as William is doing and send some of my money home. It won't be much, but you will have no expense from me, and I can feel I am helping. Maybe by the time Susan comes of age, things will be a little different."

"I am condemning you to a life of drudgery," Thomas said quietly, taking hold of his sister's hands.

"You are not!" Martha exclaimed. "We could all end in debtor's prison if we do not pull together as a family. I am happy to do this, Thomas; it is for the best."

Martha had pushed aside her feelings of what could have been and secured a position with a lady who lived twenty miles away from Martha's home. It meant Martha could travel home twice a year and see her family. The lady was old but not an unkind mistress, and Martha genuinely cared for her. Martha felt real sadness when three years later the lady died, and Martha lost her position.

She returned home temporarily. Her employer had left her a hundred pounds in her will, an unexpected windfall for Martha. She gave Thomas half the money and kept half for herself. She was practical enough to realise, at some point, she would need some money for her retirement and, although she could save little out of her wages what with sending money back home, a legacy such as this could not be squandered.

When looking for another position, Martha decided to look for a younger person. She had enjoyed her time with her employer, but she did not want to be constantly grieving over the loss of people who came to mean something to her. She had mourned her dead employer as much as she would have done if it had been a family member.

Thomas had by chance heard of a man in Lancashire looking for a companion for his young daughter. Martha visited the property and met the young Elizabeth Rufford and accepted the offer of an appointment.

When, ten years later, Elizabeth married her guardian, Lord Dunham, Martha resigned herself to the fact she would have to seek another post, but Elizabeth would hear none of it. The pair were more than employer and employee: more like a mixture of sister, companion and mother all rolled into one. Elizabeth had insisted Martha had to stay with her and, when an opening arose in Lord Dunham's household, Martha became the new Housekeeper. She had not wanted to take up Elizabeth's offer of being with her without a defined role.

Martha was happy in the main. She was sending money home regularly. Her promotion from companion to housekeeper meant she was able to continue to build a nest egg for herself, adding to the money she had already saved. She was content in her role except where Charles Anderton was involved. He was Lord Dunham's man of business and very efficient, but every time he tried to 'help'....Martha could not bear his interference.

His regular offers of assistance had the effect of making her feel insecure in her position. He never undermined her as such; it was just his manner that seemed to imply he doubted her abilities. There was just the one time he had been there when she needed him; Martha shook herself, but she would not let herself dwell on that incident. She had shown her vulnerability then, and it was not an event she wanted to dwell on for a number of reasons.

She stood and wiped her hands across her face. Not one for dwelling on things that were out of her control, she pulled herself together once more. It was time to learn not to take everything he said to heart; they would be working together for a long time to come. An image of another life flashed before her eyes too quickly for her to suppress it. She felt an ache in her heart before she pushed it away. She grumbled to herself about her stupidity and strode towards her bedroom door. There was work to be done, and she could afford no more of this maudlin mood.

Printed in Great Britain
by Amazon